D1228904

GLENN ROLFE

AUGUST'S EYES

This is a **FLAME TREE PRESS** book

FLAME TREE PRESS
6 Melbray Mews, London, SW6 3NS, UK
flametreepress.com

US sales, distribution and warehouse:
Simon & Schuster
simonandschuster.biz

UK distribution and warehouse:
Marston Book Services Ltd
marston.co.uk

Thanks to the Flame Tree Press team, including:
Taylor Bentley, Frances Bodiam, Federica Ciaravella, Don D'Auria,
Chris Herbert, Josie Karani, Molly Rosevear, Mike Spender,
Cat Taylor, Maria Tissot, Nick Wells, Gillian Whitaker.

The cover is created by Flame Tree Studio with
thanks to Nik Keevil and Shutterstock.com.
The font families used are Avenir and Bembo.

Flame Tree Press is an imprint of Flame Tree Publishing Ltd
flametreepublishing.com

A copy of the CIP data for this book is available from the British Library
and the Library of Congress.

HB ISBN: 978-1-78758-578-2
US PB ISBN: 978-1-78758-576-8
UK PB ISBN: 978-1-78758-577-5
ebook ISBN: 978-1-78758-579-9

Printed and bound in Great Britain by Clays Ltd, Elcograf S.p.A.

GLENN ROLFE

AUGUST'S EYES

FLAME TREE PRESS
London & New York

For all the Muderinos, the Class of '96, and anyone
in the Grave Dancer's Union.

PROLOGUE

Spears Corner never knew it had an uninvited guest in its midst that August afternoon. One that would make the skin crawl on every parent in town if they understood what kind of monster was roaming their streets. In a green Dodge van, it searched for the next boy to quench a thirst and an urge that never faded, never eased, never disappeared. The downtown area, a two-block stretch along Water Street, was full of adults and children alike enjoying a beautiful sunny day. Squeals of laughter bellowed from little ones chasing each other up the brick sidewalks. The group of teens standing in Nirvana and Liz Phair t-shirts on the corner flung curses at the monster as he passed by: "Look, it's Chester the Molester and his fuck van!" "Fuck off, creep!" "Suck it, asshole!" The van rolled along. Just down the street, an old Credence Clearwater Revival song was being murdered by a howling kid with a beat-up acoustic guitar on the steps of the Spears Corner Public Library. This one caused the monster to brake. Salivating, its sweaty hands clenching the steering wheel, a desperate heartbeat throbbing in its neck, it always liked the loners. They made the best company.

Police sirens blared to life behind the van. Startled, the monster let off the brake and pulled ahead. The two police cruisers, their lights flashing, sped by.

The moment had passed. The van moved along, driving out of the crowded downtown area, and up the hill toward quieter parts of the town.

★   ★   ★

"Crap, Johnny," the new kid, Ethan, said, "that was close."

Johnny Colby was still shaking. He'd barely avoided getting run down by the asshole in the red Ford Escort. He hated riding bikes through the Shop 'n' Save parking lot. He'd nearly been clipped a dozen times. Nobody seemed to watch where the hell they were going. This guy had come out of nowhere and actually made contact. Johnny had been quick enough to raise his foot up and had his sneaker on the guy's hood before being bumped from his bike and landing hard on the blacktop.

"I just need a minute," Johnny said.

The jerk in the car shouted, "Stay out of the goddamn way" before hurrying off.

Asshole.

Ethan, a tall, scrawny kid, leaned his BMX against the bench and joined Johnny. "That cut looks pretty bad, man. You want to run in and see if they have some Band-Aids? I have a couple bucks left."

"Don't worry about it," Johnny said. He pulled the red bandana off his head and wrapped it tightly around his bloodied knee. He felt fortunate to come away with this wound and the scrape on his shoulder, and not to have his skull cracked all over the pavement. "It'll stop bleeding. Let's just get the hell out of here."

It wasn't until a couple hours later, when they were up the hill near the Spears Corner Common, that Johnny noticed the ugly van he'd seen twice already parked up ahead. He'd also caught it cruising by the front of the sports card shop earlier, and before that while they were skipping rocks into Jefferson Stream near the trestles. He hadn't liked the look of it or the way the vehicle seemed to have moved twice as slow as the rest of the traffic. He'd grown up watching *20/20* with his mom every Friday night. The weekly program had filled him with its share of nightmares – everything from catching AIDS from a dirty needle used on him at the doctor's like Ryan White, to being savagely attacked by an unleashed pit bull, or forced into a Satanic cult by older kids who listened to old bands like Slayer or that new group, Marilyn Manson and the Spooky Kids – but it also gave him a heightened sense of stranger danger, and this ugly van had his warning alarms going haywire.

"Let's cross the road," he said.

Ethan didn't ask why, he just followed.

When they crossed again further up the street, Johnny looked back and saw the van was gone.

Good.

Bikes in the grass, armed with Pepsis they'd picked up from the 7-Eleven on the other side of the road, Johnny and Ethan sat in the gazebo at the heart of the Spears Corner Commons.

"You think I could spend the night at your place tonight?" Ethan said.

"Ah, I don't know. I'd have to talk to my mom." Johnny didn't really know Ethan Ripley that well. The kid had just come to Spears Corner Junior High at the end of sixth grade a couple months ago. He liked the kid well enough, but enough to have to hang out with him all night? He wasn't sure.

"That's okay," Ethan said, dropping his chin and staring at the plastic bottle cupped in his hands. "It's just that my mom kind of sucks."

"Yeah, they all do, sometimes," Johnny said, unsure whether this kid was going to start crying or spill some sad, sappy story on him.

"She's...I think she's worse than most."

Aw crap, Johnny thought. *He's gonna spill.*

"My mom...she drinks a lot. Like, she's drunk all the time, ya know?"

"Sorry, man," Johnny said. He sipped from his soda, hoping his 'sorry' was enough.

"And my dad," Ethan began. Tears leaked from both of his deep brown eyes. "He lives up near camp, and when I'm at his place, he hits me pretty good. Sometimes, I don't know if I can take it anymore. If I should run away, ya know? Or just...."

Johnny had never seen a kid his own age fall apart before his eyes, except maybe in a movie. He was sure Ethan was about to come completely undone. That his skin was going to unzip and flood the gazebo with every bit of hurt and pain he had inside.

"Oh, shit, man," Ethan said, standing up and wiping at his eyes. "I'm sorry. I don't know why I told you all that."

"Don't worry about it," Johnny said. "Life sucks, sometimes, right?"

Ethan, red eyed, the front of his Counting Crows t-shirt wet from his tears, nodded and gave a weak, weepy laugh.

Johnny wanted to change the subject. He pointed to Ethan's shirt. "You like them?"

"Counting Crows? Yeah, they're my favorite band." His gaze

dipped, his hand nervously scratching at his neck. "I hope you don't think that's too lame."

"They're okay," Johnny said. "'Mr. Jones,' right?"

"Yeah, but the whole tape is really special. I mean, it is to me. It's like every song on there speaks to me in some way. Have you ever had a tape like that?"

He thought about it. He really liked a lot of different bands and their albums. He couldn't really pick just one. "I don't know," Johnny said. "Sure, like, *Nevermind* or *Ten*, maybe."

"Yeah, those are really good ones," Ethan said. After a few seconds of silence, he added, "I can make you a copy if you want to check it out."

"Is that the name of the tape?" Johnny said, pointing to the words scrawled across Ethan's shirt.

"Yeah, *August and Everything After.*"

"Cool," Johnny said rising from the bench lining the inside of the gazebo. "Come on, you ever been out to the Pits?"

"What is it?"

Johnny led him down the steps to where their bikes lay. "It's a bunch of huge sand piles the city uses for all sorts of stuff. Tons of people go out there with four-wheelers and dirt bikes or just to go shoot shit for like target practice."

"Are we supposed to go there?" Ethan asked.

"I don't know, really. My buddy Paul and his dad always go out there and ride. I've been with them a bunch of times and I've never seen any cops. Come on."

By the time they reached the Pits off Brunswick Avenue, they'd both wished they'd brought some more soda.

"The sun sucks today," Ethan said as they rode in through the open gate.

"There's another store, New Mills Market, just down that way," Johnny said. "Let's get a few jumps in, and then we can use those last couple bucks of yours to get something."

"Okay," Ethan said. The kid was finally smiling.

Good, Johnny thought. He didn't think he could stand another waterworks display from the guy.

"Wait," Johnny said, looking at Ethan's funny hand. "Are you going to be able to land okay, I mean, with your hand and everything?"

"Yeah, it's not as useless as it looks," Ethan said. He clutched his bike grip to prove it.

"Cool."

Johnny was curious as to what happened to his hand, but never felt right to ask. Ethan would tell him if he felt like it.

Johnny took the first two jumps off a smaller dirt pile before Ethan gave it a try. The kid made his first jump like a pro, getting some serious air and sticking the landing better than Johnny ever had.

"Wow," Johnny said, cruising over next to him. "That was freaking awesome. You must have done this before."

"I used to ride dirt bikes with my Uncle Pete before we moved."

"Well, shit, man, you're gonna have to show me how you do it."

Ethan's gaze drifted over Johnny's shoulder. Johnny turned to see what he was looking at.

"What is it?" Johnny asked, and then he saw.

The green van. The same creepy Dodge junk box he'd seen earlier sat parked near one of the taller sand piles a little farther in the pits.

"Oh my God," Ethan said. "Let's go see if he's all right."

Johnny didn't know what the kid was talking about until he noticed the man down on his hands and knees toward the back tire of the van.

His stranger danger alarms blared again.

"Ethan, wait."

But Ethan was pedaling toward the van in a hurry.

Johnny stepped on his pedal but couldn't force himself to follow. His insides felt cold. Gooseflesh broke over his arms. They shouldn't go near that man or his damn van.

He sat frozen as he watched Ethan dump his BMX to the dirt and walk over to the man on the ground. He appeared to be helping the man to his feet when the man snatched him by the hair and slammed Ethan's head into the side of the van. The man clubbed Ethan until the boy collapsed to the ground.

That's when the creep stood and pointed at Johnny.

Oh no, oh God, no.

Johnny wet his pants. The man grabbed Ethan up from the dirt, carried him behind the van, opened the back door and piled him inside. Slamming the doors shut, the stranger turned toward Johnny, who hadn't been able to move. Johnny's entire body trembled. He was crying as the man started for him.

The awful man had closed half the distance by the time Johnny finally busted loose from his paralysis and turned his bike around.

He couldn't go for Brunswick Avenue. The man would go back to his van, catch him, and run him down. There was a path they used to use that went all the way to Talbot Hill, which would bring him over to Bruton Street. From there he could hurry down Church Street and over to the police station.

Johnny pedaled as fast as he could. It felt like the strange man was Carl Lewis, like he was going to break another Olympic record and run him down. Johnny was going to get stuffed in the back of that van.

As he left the sand and dirt behind, his bike tires eating up the grass of the path, he dared a quick glance over his shoulder.

The stranger was no longer behind him.

He didn't look back again. He pedaled to Talbot Hill. When he got there, he saw his English teacher, Mr. Janz. He asked if he could use his phone, but Johnny never made it to the police. Instead, he called his mom to come pick him up.

He never told anyone what happened to Ethan Ripley. He was too afraid he would get in trouble for not helping him. For not stopping that man.

After the police pulled Ethan's body from Litchfield Pond, Johnny cried himself to sleep.

PART ONE
IN YOUR DREAMS
CHAPTER ONE

"We all have ours picked out."

Johnny wondered what the kid with the one eye meant.

"That one's mine," One Eye said. He pointed into the fog.

"That one?" Johnny said.

"Sure. Johnny, which one do you want?"

Johnny still wondered what they were talking about.

"What makes you think he gets to pick one?" August, a tall kid with a clawed hand, asked. His hollow eyes matched the straight black hair that touched his funny shoulders. Johnny thought it looked like he was wearing shoulder pads made of baby skulls beneath his faded blue Superman t-shirt. Johnny didn't like that August's shoulders made him think of baby skulls, but he thought that was August's fault. Somehow. And those damn eyes. Just two black holes....

"Pick one of what out?" Johnny asked.

"A grave, stupid," August said.

"A grave?"

"Come on, Johnny," One Eye said. "Don't mind August, he's just sore because he can't play ball with us."

August's black holes seemed to smolder. The clawed hand clutched tightly to one of his baby skull shoulders twitched, and then opened and closed.

One Eye bolted for the fog. "Come on, Johnny, before August gets us."

Johnny turned to run and tripped over a sign that hadn't been there moments before. Mud and wet grass smeared into his eyebrow where his face hit the ground. The placard lay on its side in front of him.

"Graveyard Land?" he said, reading the sign aloud.

The fog swirled to life, creeping forward, surrounding him where he lay. The sign vanished within the thick mist. He could no longer see One Eye, but he could hear him calling from far away, "Jooohhhnnneeee...."

Johnny's chest tightened. His teeth chattered. The surrounding fog prickled every hair on his arms.

Where's August?

He wanted to get up and run or try to find One Eye. Instead, he pulled his knees up to his chest and hugged them. Curled in a fetal position, Johnny cried. He searched the swirling fog. Two black holes peered back.

★　　★　　★

"Holy shit." John Colby scrambled from beneath his sheets. He reached out for the lamp on his nightstand and knocked the stack of magazines he'd been thumbing through before bed to the floor.

"What?" Sarah mumbled beside him. "What are you doing?"

He found the lamp and poked at the switch. The darkness retreated.

"What? Nothing. Go back to sleep, Sarah."

"What time is it?" she asked. Her voice was muffled from the pillow she'd pulled over her face.

"Not time to get up. I'm gonna go grab some water. It's all right. Go back to sleep."

She was out before he lifted his ass off the bed. He walked down the hallway and went straight for the kitchen sink. He didn't bother with a glass; he just craned his head to the faucet and took it straight from the tap. His horizontal view through the open rectangular window above was one of beauty. A gorgeous, full moon; the mostly clear night offered the thinnest clouds to float past its pale face.

Rolling like fog.

The thought brought back a piece of the bizarre dream. He'd been having them a lot lately. Always in the cemetery with these two boys seemingly alone in the fog. John ceased slurping the water and instead let the cool flow pour over his numb lips. A howl off in the forest beyond raked a chill down his spine. He lifted his head, ran his hands through his short, mostly brown hair, though specks of gray had begun to appear sometime over the last year, and listened. The yipping howl came again. The moon's beauty was tarnished by the trace of a bad dream and the cry of the nocturnal.

John wiped his mouth with the back of his hand and headed back to bed.

★　　★　　★

Morning offered a cabaret of warm sunlight, the smell of fresh-cut grass rolling in through the open window on a warm summer breeze, and the sound of Sarah singing Katy Perry from the shower. John raised his arms and stretched. The extension of muscles and a wonderful mix of Saturday morning's easy peaceful feeling made for that rare moment: life in perfect balance.

Pat must have already finished mowing the lawn. John had to give it to the punk. Mohawk notwithstanding, Pat was a morning miracle worker.

"Hey, Morning Glory, what's the story?" Sarah said. She stepped to the bedside in her blue silk robe with the pink flowers on it that he'd gotten her for her birthday a few months back. "I opened the window as soon as Pat finished with the lawn, probably about twenty minutes ago. Thought you might like waking up to the smell of magic." She said this with the smile that made him fall in love with her. He loved that she referred to life's good stuff as magic. Fresh lemonade on a hot summer day, snow on Christmas, hitting the search button on the radio and the first station it lands on is playing 'Walking on Sunshine'– magic. He still couldn't believe she'd said yes nine years ago. He was grateful every day.

"I was wondering how I slept through the mower. Pat still wearing his punk rock uniform?"

"He had his Mohawk spiked to the sky, sleeveless jean jacket with all those patches, but..."

"What?" John asked.

"He was wearing bright green shorts. Pac Sun. I'd know 'em anywhere."

"No sex pants?"

"Sex pants?" she asked.

"Yeah, you know, the plaid pants with all the zippers and bondage straps and shit?"

When she looked at him like he was weird, he said, "A guy I worked with once called them that."

She leaned forward and kissed his forehead. "Get up and brush your fangs, I want to kiss you like I mean it." Her brown eyes sparkled, casting a spell all their own.

"Yep, I'm on it." He jumped out of bed and glided around the corner to the bathroom.

*   *   *

After they tangled up the sheets together, he followed her dancing booty down the hall to 'the best part of waking up'. John figured this morning could challenge Folgers for the rights to that title. Sarah grabbed them each a mug, while he snatched the French Vanilla creamer from the fridge. Caffeine in hand, John went to sit at the table.

"No," Sarah said. "I hear the porch calling."

Sitting on the steps, staring at the freshly mown front yard, John sipped his morning buzz and hummed an old nineties song. It could have been something by Dinosaur Jr., but just as likely Everclear.

"So, did you wake up freaking out again last night or did I just dream that?"

Sarah's inquiry put a permanent hold on his mystery tune and placed a set of cold hands on the shoulders of his perfect morning. "Yeah, I had another crazy dream."

"Was it the same one? With those kids?"

He'd told Sarah about August and One Eye, not their names, but their oddness. "Yeah, it was messed up."

"You want to talk about it?"

He wanted to forget them, but at least relaying the dreams aloud killed their creepiness with how foolish they sounded.

"Yeah, I was by a field with those two I told you about—"

"Were you still a kid?"

"Yeah. I think we were picking out graves."

Sarah's lack of laughter didn't help scratch the creeps.

"Weird," she said. She took a sip from her Hug a Lobster mug and said, "Was the field someplace you recognized?"

She was great at helping him work his way back through his dreams. She knew just what to ask to jog the details from the places where his awake mind liked to hide things. He couldn't remember if they were here in Spears Corner or maybe in some movie he'd seen. Something screamed at him from the hiding place, but he just couldn't grasp it – a name, something that sounded like a board game or an amusement park.

"I...I'm not sure, but it was really foggy. So, maybe it was Spears Corner. We have a lot of foggy nights with the damn streams and swamps crawling through the woods."

"Well, maybe something from your past is nagging at you."

"Yeah, maybe." John doubted it, but just sipped his coffee and stared off into space. He no longer noticed the fresh-cut lawn, the brilliant golden rays warming his bare legs, or the pretty thirty-something at his side. He could almost see the fog, the sign – those two black holes. Goose bumps broke out over his arms. He shivered in the sun.

CHAPTER TWO

John hated that Sarah worked second shift, especially on Saturdays. Since she switched last fall, it had all but killed their concert-going ventures — a sad but fairly successful way of holding on to a fragment of their youth. Pearl Jam, Brian Fallon, and even Royal Blood had offered them the energy, the slipstream of that essential electric current that held the last of those creeping gray hairs and budding crinkles at the corners of their eyes at bay. More magic in Sarah's eyes — and his, too. His back gave him enough fits some mornings. He liked to blame it on the old mattress they slept on, but Sarah liked to remind him of his age. Whatever it was, he'd do anything he could to get a leg up on growing old.

Netflix and Mr. Peepers, their orange tabby, kept John company for the evening. Sometime between episode nineteen and episode twenty-two of *Arrested Development* he'd passed out.

Startled awake by a noise outside, John popped up from the sofa. The bowl of half-devoured tortilla chips in his lap crashed to the floor and exploded in a splatter pattern of ceramic shards. He could see the farthest pieces shimmering by the open front door. Had he closed the door earlier? He couldn't remember.

"Shit." He'd have to clean this up before — he glanced at the digital time on the screen: 10:44. Sarah would be home in half an hour. The sound of labored breaths outside the screen door iced his veins along with his clean-up concerns. He hadn't noticed before — the motion sensor light on the front porch illuminated the yard.

John sidestepped the broken ceramic at his feet, determined not to let their crunch give him away. He pressed his chest up against the far wall and angled his head back to scan the lawn. Nothing. He inched closer to the door and took another look. Something swished off to the right. Hugging the wall, he looked around the door for anything he could use as a weapon. Sarah's purple umbrella stared back.

Great, I'll have to hope whoever's out there has an unnatural fear of Mary Poppins.

He'd have to work with what he had. August's black-hole eyes crossed his mind. A fine time for his shitty dreams to be creeping up on him. Shaking the macabre dream kid from his head, John held his breath and listened. The steady chirp of crickets and the hoot of the old owl that nested just beyond the tree line next to the house made their presence known. The swishing and the labored breaths closed in. To the right of the door, the porch groaned. John's heart was in his throat. Ready to jab the intruder – or the strange kid from his dreams – John stepped forward, grabbed the umbrella, and shoved the screen door open.

"Jesus Christ!" the intruder screeched.

"Shit!" John said.

Pat Harrison, dressed in black from his hipster sneakers to his knit cap, sat on his ass, his back against the porch railings. His hands shook as he held them up in front of his face.

"Goddamn it, Pat, what the hell are you doing out here?"

Pat grabbed the railing above his head and hoisted himself up. "I lost my wallet earlier. I thought I might have dropped it in your yard this morning."

"Well, shit, man, why are you dressed like a thief and shuffling around out here in the dark?"

"You know this is how I always dress, and I didn't want to bother you or Sarah if I didn't have to."

John sat down in Sarah's rocking chair next to the door and placed the umbrella across his knees. He waited for his heart rate to return to normal and snickered at himself for considering the impossible. Dreams don't walk out into the night.

"What's so funny?" Pat said. The kid stuck a cigarette between his thin lips and sparked it to life under his palm.

"Nothing, Pat. Just…nothing. So, did you find your wallet?"

Pat crooked his jaw to the right, exhaled a cloud of smoke, and stuck a thumb in the pocket of his black jeans. "No. I saw that your lights were on and I was still trying to decide if I should come find out if you or Sarah might have picked it up."

"It didn't occur to you to try that first?"

"Fuck, man. I don't know what you guys are doing at this time of night behind closed doors. I didn't want to bother you unless I had to."

John wondered if Pat was referring to the screen door, or if the front door *had* been shut like he thought. He opened his mouth to ask as much, but "Got another one of those?" came out instead.

"After all this time, I didn't know you smoked. I never see any butts in the yard."

That line struck John as funny. He snickered again and said, "Only late at night behind closed doors."

Pat handed him a Camel and lit it for him. John took a drag, feeling the smoke hit his lungs for the first time in months. He liked smoking. He would have fit in well in the old days when cigarettes were cool and were just as welcomed in restaurants as they were in bars. He quit for Sarah after her aunt passed from emphysema.

"So, any chance you guys found it?" Pat asked.

"Sorry, Pat, honestly I haven't been beyond the porch all day. Sarah didn't say anything before she went to work."

"Shit."

"You're welcome to come back in the morning and hunt for it. Hell, I'll even help you."

"Cool. Thanks, Mr. C."

"Quit it with that *Mr. C* shit. You're making me feel like a teacher or some old church prick. After all this time, I told you just to call me John."

"All right…Johnny."

Irrational and downright foolish as it was hearing that name come from Pat's lips, John shivered.

"How's your mother doing? I haven't seen her in a while," John asked.

"She's killing it. You'd be so proud of her. I know I am."

"Does she know about this?" John asked holding up the cigarette.

"No," Pat said, removing his cap, the Mohawk beneath springing to life as he hung his head. The crazy hair wasn't even bent. John wondered what the hell the kid used to keep it so stiff. Hair Viagra?

"Don't let me find out you're doing anything else or I'll have to beat the snot out of your little punk ass."

"Of course not, man," Pat said. "This is my only vice. Well, that and making sure your lawn looks immaculate."

"Ha, well, you don't tell Sarah and I won't say anything to your mom. Deal?"

"Deal." Pat came over and shook his hand. "Well, I guess I'll be back in the morning."

"You need a lift home?"

"Nah, my bike's by the driveway." Pat put his smoke out on the bottom of his sneaker and tossed the butt to the lawn. He jumped over the porch steps – his rubber soles produced a *sla-slap* sound as he hit the paved driveway – and yelled back, "I'll pick that butt up in the morning, too. Good night, Johnny."

"I said you could call me John," he yelled back. Pat waved a hand and grabbed his bike from the small dip at the end of the yard. His reflectors shined in the porch light; two glimmering eyes spun away into the night.

Sarah's Subaru Outback zoomed in next to his car. John rose, his deadly umbrella in hand and highlighted in the Subaru's headlamps. She cut the engine and killed the lights. She stepped from the car and shook her head as John opened and twirled the umbrella.

"What are you doing?" she asked.

"Way-tin' for yew, m'lady." John's cockney accent was less Dick Van Dyke, and more Johnny Rotten.

"Was that Pat that I just passed?"

"Yeah." He closed the umbrella and held it at his side like a cane. "He thought he might have lost his wallet this morning mowing the lawn."

Sarah stepped up to him. He gazed into her eyes. They were both five foot eight, which made a lot of things line up well. There was an untouchable grace in her eyes as the sliver of moonlight landed just right across her face. It was mesmerizing, dangerous and sexy all in one. He kissed her full lips and pulled her into the shadows of the porch.

"You know what I'd like to do?" he said.

"I could make a couple guesses."

"Hold this for me," he said, handing her the umbrella.

She laughed as he swept her up off her feet and held her like he had on their wedding night. Her bag hit the porch with a thud.

"What the hell do you have in there, a brick?" he said.

"Oh dear, you know it's just *all* that money I make."

"Oh yes, your millions from the drugstore. Now, let's away with you."

Sarah laughed. John reached his foot out and wiggled it between the screen door, proud that his balance didn't falter even for a second. Sarah grabbed the cheap wood frame and pulled the screen door open further so they could go through.

"Such a romantic gesture. Carrying your old ball and chain over the threshold after all these years."

John, with his back to the door, clutched her tightly as he stepped sideways, sliding down the length of the wall and skirting the trashed salsa bowl still on the floor.

"What are you doing?" she asked as he put her down.

"You got me." He nodded at the shattered ceramic shards spread across the floor. "Not quite the noble gentleman caller you thought."

She shook her head and looked him in the eyes, a smirk upon her face. "You carried me so I wouldn't walk on broken glass. And they say chivalry is dead. Pshaw."

"Sorry about the bowl."

"Shut up and kiss me, you fool."

Holding his wife in his arms, he kissed her with all the magic in his heart.

CHAPTER THREE

"What do you mean I can't have this one? This is the one I chose," One Eye said. He flopped down cross-legged in the knee-high, dew-covered grass and planted his fists into his sunken cheeks.

"You don't get to choose a grave, dummy." August stood against a wrought-iron fence, pulling leaves from the maple tree stretched over the posts. Johnny thought it was strange the way August would pull them free, suck them into his mouth and then spit them over the fence.

"It's just a game," One Eye said. "August doesn't play, because he's no fun."

"I don't think Johnny wants to play your game, either," August said. He stared at the dark leaf in his hand, twirled it like a flower (*or an umbrella – Chim Chim Cher-ee*). "How about it, Johnny?"

"How about what?" Johnny said.

"You gonna play One Eye's silly game and choose one?" August asked.

One Eye perked up at this. "Yeah, Johnny, go ahead pick one, man."

"I...I don't understand any of this." And he didn't. Nothing about this place made any sense. He turned to August. "Have you ever picked one?"

"August doesn't play. He thinks he's better than us, because he's got a special job—"

"Shut the hell up." August stepped from the fence. His mouth tightened, his claw hand opening and closing at his side. Johnny was certain if there had been more light than that provided by the moon above, he would have seen smoke stream from the lanky kid's black eye holes.

One Eye stumbled backwards. "It's true." He looked to Johnny. "August is his special pet—"

"I said *shut up!*" August rushed at One Eye and spat a wad of chewed-up leaves in his face. But once they hit One Eye's face, they weren't leaves. They were spiders. Half a dozen quarter–size arachnids walked circles around One Eye's face like kids at the mall. One Eye yelped like a girl as he swatted at the bugs.

"Gah, I hate spiders." One Eye stood and tried to stamp on the bugs crawling away for their lives. He stopped and stared at August's empty holes. "You're the one that brought this upon yourself." With that, One Eye turned and tromped away through the grass and weeds. "You comin', Johnny?" he yelled back over his shoulder.

Johnny looked at August. He'd moved back to his spot by the fence and his leaf-munching routine. Johnny watched the grin spread across August's face as he chewed. He puckered his lips and parted them like someone making a fish face. One dark spider crawled free and skittered up August's milky cheek. Johnny watched the eight-legged critter disappear into one of the strange boy's hollow eye sockets. He'd seen them but he didn't really think August's pits were *actually* hollow. There was something in them. Something dangerous.

"Go on, Johnny," August said. "Run along."

Johnny turned before August could play his leaf-to-a-spider trick again and fell. The hole in the ground seemed endless. He spun in free fall and looked up to see August standing at the top of the pit, watching his descent. He puckered up and blew Johnny one of his arachnid kisses.

★   ★   ★

"John, John, Wake up."

"Huh, no, no, no!"

"Dear, it's just a dream."

Sarah's voice brought him all the way back (and all the way up). He opened his eyes. The beauty of yesterday morning's gold and glory was poisoned by the sickly rainy day Charlie Lopresti had promised on last night's eleven o'clock newscast. Thunder boomed, startling him.

Sarah lay down next to him, snuggled up close to his ear, and stroked his chest in the calming manner only she could have. He closed his eyes and listened to the rain pouring down outside. A thousand drops of reality welcomed him. He was safe.

"You wanna talk about it?"

"No." He reached across and caressed her silky-smooth forearm as she continued with her enchanting massage. Something tickled his forehead and took a dive toward his eyes. He jerked free from Sarah's embrace and smacked the crawling pest.

He pulled his hand away, feeling like an idiot. Sweat. He'd freaked out over a bead of sweat rolling down his forehead.

"Come on," Sarah said. She climbed out from the sheets, moved around to his side of the bed, and took his hand.

"Where?"

"You, me, nice hot shower."

He let her drag him off the mattress.

In his peripheral vision, he saw something tiny and dark disappear beneath his pillow. He pulled his hand free and snatched the pillow from the bed.

Nothing.

"John, what are you doing?"

He shook the pillow, knowing something would come free. Nothing did.

"Fuck," he said.

"Come on."

"I thought I saw a spider."

He let Sarah haul him away.

They're coming to take me away ha-ha.

He would have laughed at this thought, but he wasn't sure if 'they' were the boys in white coats or the kids picking out graves.

CHAPTER FOUR

With John at work, and her having the day off, Sarah managed to get in her daily yoga with her favorite YouTube yoga instructor, Adrienne. After that she picked up a few groceries for the week and made a trip to the bookstore all before ten a.m. She could have gotten lost in Barnes & Noble and stayed there forever. Instead, she made a list of books to hunt down at the Spears Corner Public Library, which she would hit up after lunch.

Books were what saved her as a teenager. When her dad bugged out and could no longer put up with her mother back in her crazy days, Sarah all but retreated into herself. She discovered the works of Stephen King and Anne Rice and would disappear for hours in the attic. She loved sitting up there and reading herself out of her real life. Books were less complicated. And when they were complicated, they always worked themselves out. She didn't have as much faith in real life. She loved her mom, but the woman definitely had an undiagnosed touch of some serious bipolar shit going on. And on her mother's worst days, Sarah would grab her books and hide away in the dark, comforting words and worlds of one of her favorite writers. She spent months dreaming of New Orleans and falling under the spell of both the city and the creatures. There were nights of visiting Castle Rock and Derry. She thought it was neat that they lived so close to King's stomping grounds. Bangor was a two-hour drive. They'd gone there once with her Grandmother Bernice, who lived in Ellsworth. Sarah waited until her mother had fallen asleep on one medication or another and taken her old Focus to King's house. She had the selfie to prove it. It was one of her prized pics, even if it was a little dark. Back then, cell phones didn't have built-in flashes or night modes like they do now. She vowed to go back one day, but even after moving to Spears Corner, less than ninety minutes from the place, she hadn't returned. Life just seemed too busy.

The same thing happened with her hopes of one day becoming a writer herself. She'd gone to college at USM in Gorham for a year when she met John and fell head over heels. He asked her to move in with him and she did. Sarah took the first job she could find and dropped out of college with every good intention of going back.

She was still young enough and had plenty of time to pursue a degree, but she only ever wanted to be like her heroes. She'd never even written more than one short story. The already long miles between her and Rice or King seemed beyond infinite.

Still, there were moments like this morning when she allowed herself the small pleasures of the bookstore or the library. Today, she'd ventured over to the how-to section for writers. She found King's *On Writing* and about a dozen books on how to start and finish your first manuscript or how to publish your first book. She'd browsed the section before, but it was different this time. It was as if they'd called to her. She took pictures of the ones that sounded the best and would look for them at the library later.

Unfortunately, it was the section a couple shelves down that had punched her in the gut – the pregnancy books. Books on baby names, and what to expect, and even books on the best yoga to do while with child. Thinking of it now made her sick to her stomach.

She walked to the kitchen and poured a glass of Merlot. Morning or not, wine always leveled out the hurt. Besides, it was her day off.

She and John had tried so hard to get pregnant. They even went to doctors and had a million tests run. According to medicine, they should have been able to conceive, yet they never could. She'd been pregnant once and had a miscarriage. She was only fifteen at the time and it was from the first time she'd ever had sex. The guy's name was Roger Dansby, and she never heard from the asshole again. She'd lost the baby eight weeks after finding out. She'd never told John about that. While they were going through their tests, she'd confided in her doctor, but he assured her that the miscarriage had no bearing on her current condition.

She finished her wine and considered a second glass, but since she genuinely did feel better, she passed and fetched her car keys from the counter instead. She'd go to the library and get lost in the old scents of dust and yellowed-paged tomes that held gateways to a million dreams.

There was a story inside her. She knew it. She just didn't know if she'd ever be able to write it. Maybe today she would find the courage to try.

By the time she got home, her arms full of books and her head full of ideas, it was nearly time for John to get out of work. She'd read nearly half of King's writing memoir in the James Spears Room at the library. She'd only meant to read a chapter or two but got lost in his tales of the writer's toolbox. When she was younger, the library back home served the same purpose as her attic in the dog days of summer when she'd melt just thinking about going up to her reading nook. Through the summer months, Sarah took her refuge in the library. They didn't have air-conditioning but there were fans throughout that kept it cool enough to be comfortable.

Today took her back to those days.

Besides the King book, she also grabbed a new one from Stephen Graham Jones and one from a new author who had just won a Bram Stoker Award, Gwendolyn Kiste. The book was called *The Rust Maidens* and the cover alone had drawn her in. She always left with an armful of books, and though she rarely managed to find the time to read them all, she liked to have options. The only thing she picked up that didn't really fit in was a book about dreams. It caught her eye as she was on her way to the desk to check out. *Dreams and Nightmares: Our Reality's Creations*. John had been having bad dreams a lot lately. She had talked him into seeing her old therapist, Dr. Soctomah, but it couldn't hurt for her to do a little research of her own. Books were knowledge, and thus, power. John would never read it, but maybe she'd earn herself some brownie points if she unlocked the mysteries for him and helped to bring his strange dreams to an end.

There was a reward she had in mind.

She wasn't prepared to admit it to herself yet, let alone whisper it to John. Despite the great depression each failure brought on, Sarah knew she hadn't closed the book on either of her own dreams.

CHAPTER FIVE

I need your time sheet in by 3 PM. This is the second week in a row and third time this month that I've had to email you about getting your work done on time. If it's not in by 3, I'll have to write you up.
Alison Dumars

★　★　★

John slammed his fist down on his desk.

"Is everything all right?" Kaitlyn asked. Kaitlyn Skehan was the hot brunette who transferred to Kennebec Community Comfort last fall. She'd been very sweet from day one and seemed to be one of his only competent colleagues since the big turnover the company faced two years back. She knew how to do her job and she actually gave a shit about her families, not just the paycheck.

Alison Dumars's ascension to boss disrupted an otherwise smooth-running establishment. And the evil bitch was desperate to keep her mismanagement hidden from her bosses. The numbers didn't lie, but if Alison was good at one thing, it was placing blame.

"Is Alison up your ass again?" Kaitlyn asked.

He ran a hand through his hair, sat back in his chair, and sighed. "At least this time it's not total bullshit. I've been sleeping like crap and falling behind with my damn time sheets."

"Well," Kaitlyn said, "I wasn't going to say anything, but you have looked a bit ragged lately."

"Oh yeah?"

"No, not really, you're still hot," Kaitlyn said, rolling her chair over beside his.

Kaitlyn was the kind of attractive that made men, even happily married men, nervous. She had long dark curls, deep brown eyes, and a smile that held the hint of the devil. It didn't help that she didn't even try to hide the fact that she was into him. John was fine until moments like this when she got close to him. He started sweating instantly. She knew he was married and didn't care. Most of the time she was pretty busy with her own caseload. Unlike some of the employees who had come and gone over the years, Kaitlyn worked her ass off.

"Don't you have vacation time?" she asked. "Maybe you should take some time to yourself. Get away from here."

"Yeah, maybe that's not such a bad idea. Thing is, having the caseload I do, she'd never let me go. Not anytime soon, at least."

"Well," Kaitlyn said, placing her hand over his, "I could help you out."

"You already have plenty of work on your plate." He eased his hand free.

"What if I got Brandon to help, too?" she said.

"What, the new guy?"

"He's been here almost a year, and he knows what he's doing."

"Didn't you guys go on a date?"

"Yeah," she said. "But I'm really into older guys."

"Yeah, yeah," he said, feeling his cheeks warm again. "Well, I know a couple of 'Nam vets at the hospital that might be willing to take you out sometime. Do you want me to give them your number?"

"Fuck you," she said, grinning as she rolled back to her desk.

"Listen, you might be right. I've earned a vacation."

"Good for you."

He closed his eyes and saw August and One Eye standing over an open grave.

"Fuck," he said, jumping up from his seat.

"Yeah, maybe you could take that lucky wife of yours to the Bahamas. Get away from this place and recharge."

Kaitlyn was right. He had at least three weeks of vacation time. He and Sarah could go anywhere they wanted – if Alison approved it.

"I'm gonna get a coffee. You want one?"

Kaitlyn held up her Jack and Sally coffee mug. "All set, but cheers."

He nodded and went out the door. He'd get some caffeine and bust ass getting Alison her damn time sheet. Then he'd ask for the time off.

Standing in the breakroom after setting a fresh pot to brew, John gazed out the window. The decommissioned railroad tracks sat behind the property between the office building and the Hanson Union River. The water glistened in the sun. It was mesmerizing. Maple trees along the backside of the building swayed over the wrought-iron fence.

A shape sidled up next to one of the metal posts.

It hadn't dawned on John that there was normally no fence of any kind between the tracks and the river, just rocks and brush.

The tall, lanky shape waved.

The coffee maker began to beep in time with each pass of his hand, a metronome lulling him into delirium.

"August?"

"John?" The shrill voice of his boss broke him from his daydream. When he looked out toward the train tracks again, the fence and the shape waving to him were gone. The river sparkled beyond.

"I trust you received my email," Alison said, standing in the doorway. Her needling, beady eyes seemed to simmer with wickedness.

He thought of August's hollow sockets.

"John," she barked again.

"Yeah, yeah, I'm working on my time sheet right now."

"Hmm, you sure could have fooled me. It looks like you're staring out the window daydreaming about recess."

For fuck's sake, cut me some goddamn slack.

"I don't care what you're doing," she said. "Just get it to me by three. I mean it."

She turned and left the room.

As John looked out the window, he could swear he heard a voice whisper: *"Johhhhhhnnneeeee...."*

CHAPTER SIX

That night, after going out for dinner at Margaritas Mexican Restaurant and having three drinks too many, Sarah made her way to bed early. John considered following her but wanted a smoke first.

He stepped off the porch and pulled the pack of cigarettes he'd bought on his way to work yesterday from his occasional hiding spot beneath the bottom step. Shaking one out, he eyed the shadowy area by the trees where he thought he'd seen movement the other night when he was out here with Pat.

Nothing shifted. It was just pure quiet contentment. He took a long drag and thought about what Kaitlyn had said today at work. *Take a vacation.* He'd toss the idea out to Sarah in the morning if she wasn't too hungover. If he did it, it would certainly be more of a staycation, like Tom Hanks' character in *The 'Burbs*. John didn't have an urge to travel anywhere. He just needed some rest, and a break from being prodded by Alison.

He'd gotten his time sheet in at the last possible second, bringing it to Alison's office and dropping it on her desk rather than taking any chances with the office email. She'd rolled her eyes and effectively let him know that he was still on her shit list until told otherwise. He thanked her and wished her a good night.

The thought had occurred to him that she might deny his request for vacation time, but he'd made up his mind that he was taking the time off or leaving the company. She could have it one way or the other. He was pretty sure she wouldn't let him quit; he still had a significant caseload, one that Kaitlyn offered to help shoulder if he needed it, and he was the longest tenured caseworker in the office next to Alison herself. She'd be up shit's creek if he quit.

That thought brought a smile to his face.

He stamped the butt out, picked it up, and walked back up the driveway to place it in the can under the porch. Reaching into the dark space, he felt light feet scurry across the back of his hand.

John gasped and jerked his hand out. A spider fell to the dirt and hurried from the moonlight.

Johnneeee.... Johnnneeee....

The whisper from earlier echoed in his head (or could he hear it now?).

A branch snapped somewhere behind him.

Scanning the bushes where he and Sarah had buried Buster, his old gray and white Tabby, last year, John swore he saw something. The harder he looked, the more his eyes seemed to lose focus. Amorphous shadows shifted like clouds, looking like one thing one second before changing to another the next. The outline of a face, eyes...then a branch, a pointy hat, an animal....

He closed his eyes.

It's all bullshit, he told himself. *There's nothing there.*

John clenched his teeth at the sound of scuffling feet.

Open your eyes. There's nobody out here but you—

"Johnny!"

The voice was like someone shouting a whisper from a dream.

He cried out, spinning, and throwing his arm back to swat whoever it was away.

Coming up with nothing but air, John clenched his fists and waited for the voice to come again.

"Who's there?" he asked.

Another twig snapped near the bushes.

"Pat? Is that you?"

He didn't know why the kid would be out here now, but he called to him anyway.

John crept around Sarah's Subaru and over to his Saturn sitting next to it. He opened the driver's side door, snatched up the knife he kept tucked under the front seat and shut the door as quietly as he could.

He flicked the four-inch blade out and started toward the edge of the yard.

"Listen," he said, "I have a knife." The words sounded stupid and weak as soon as they fell past his lips. "I don't want to call the cops. Just show yourself and no one has to—"

A pale face smiled from the darkness.

"Who...who...."

He stumbled backward, the knife trembling in his hand.

And just like that, the face was gone.

John no longer wanted to see what was out there. He closed the blade and hurried back inside, glancing back once before closing the door.

Nothing stirred.

★   ★   ★

He watched out the living room window until well after midnight, when exhaustion and inebriation finally overtook him. He poured the last few ounces of tequila from the bottle into his glass and swallowed it down.

It was all in my head, he said to himself, laughing.

He turned out the dim lamp across the room and made his way to bed.

CHAPTER SEVEN

August watched the light go out before making his way back to Graveyard Land. Passing through the gates, he felt their eyes upon him. They didn't understand why he could leave, and they could not. It was not his place to tell them.

"What did you see out there?" One Eye asked.

The scrawny little loudmouth sidled up next to August as he strolled past the graves and toward the fog that always surrounded his favorite tree.

The massive oak sat alone above the front cemetery. A memory always just out of reach had drawn him to this spot for as long as he could remember being here. Not that any of them recalled how long they'd been here or when they first arrived.

"Well?"

August would have rolled his eyes if he had any. Instead, he gave One Eye a shove.

"Leave me alone. I don't want to hear your annoying voice tonight."

The kid's silence spoke volumes. August spied him with his head bowed, shoulders slumped. One Eye was sensitive. While they were all on the meek side, One Eye seemed even more so than the others, at least when he wasn't talking nonstop.

August sighed and said, "It's not for us." They stopped at the base of the little hill. He gazed at the eyes peeking out from the gravestones. "It's not for any of us. Not anymore."

The little farmhouse, an innocent-enough-looking silhouette, stood out through the fog. The house rested at the edge of the cemetery. The evil within always keeping watch over them.

"Let me rest," he said to One Eye, placing a hand on the boy's shoulder. "Being away makes me tired. Besides," he said, nodding toward the farmhouse, "we don't want him checking on us, do we?"

One Eye shook his head.

"Go on," August said.

As the boy shuffled away into the fog, August faced the farmhouse a minute longer.

Something was going to happen soon.

Something bad.

Part of him wondered if he could stop it. If he refused to go along....

No, he told himself. There was no refusing here.

The fog rolled over the gravestones, little heads bobbed in and out, disappearing into the haze.

He sighed and made his way to the base of his tree.

He lay there and imagined what it would be like to still be among the living.

Then he remembered his last moments of that life...and wished he'd left it in the dark corners of his mind.

His body shivered with the tainted memory.

As he lay beneath the tree, he thought that here in Graveyard Land it seemed like time was standing still.

He wondered if it would ever let him go.

CHAPTER EIGHT

Sitting in the small waiting room of the psychiatrist's office, John wondered what could possibly come of this. Sarah had suggested he try a therapist and it irritated the shit out of him, at least at first. He wasn't crazy. He wasn't depressed. He was just sleeping like shit because his boss was an asshole and because of some weird dreams. After getting into an argument with Sarah and offending her about the type of people who go to therapy, he surrendered.

Sarah had come to Dr. Soctomah a few years ago after the last time they tried getting pregnant.

Thinking of what he'd said to her earlier, he felt like a complete dick all over again.

"John?" A tall, older gentleman with tan skin, dressed in Levi's, a Pink Floyd t-shirt and a plaid scarf, held out his hand.

John rose and shook it.

"Rik Soctomah. Come on in."

John stepped past him and into a cozy room with two couches, a desk piled with books, and numerous shelves filled with just as many ancient-looking artifacts. He knew shit about art and antiques, but the masks and statues were cool. There was also a little case filled with arrowheads and decorative bowls. It looked like something out of the Indiana Jones movies.

Maybe he has the Ark of the Covenant in here somewhere.

"Are these the real deal or replicas?" John asked, gesturing at the masks.

Dr. Soctomah closed the door and stood next to him.

"Mostly replicas. Are you into Native American art?"

"No, no, I just…it looks great." John looked around, placing his hands in the pockets of his jeans.

"Well, take a seat." Dr. Soctomah motioned toward the couches.

John hesitated to look from the cushy brown sofa to the brown leather one on the right.

"Whichever one you like is fine," Dr. Soctomah said. He walked past him and picked up a clipboard from his desk.

John went with the comfy brown sofa. As soon as his ass hit the seat, he knew he'd chosen correctly.

"So," the doctor said, as he sat across from him on the other couch. "Let's first touch on what's brought you here. Then, if you feel comfortable, we'll dive into your life history and get this thing going. Sound good?"

Hell no.

John nodded.

After a few seconds of silence, John guessed it was time to talk.

"Well, I'm here because…well, I'm…."

"It's okay, John," Dr. Soctomah said. "There's no judgment here. What's going on?"

He took a deep breath. "I'm having a lot of trouble getting good sleep. And…it's…well, it's probably nothing." He leaned forward and scratched his temple. He waited a second for the doctor to cut in. When he didn't, John continued. "I've been having these strange dreams."

The doctor scribbled something on his notebook and looked back up when he was done.

"I think the dreams, well, they're really more like…I don't know, they're not quite nightmares, but they are dark…bizarre."

"Are they related?"

"Yeah, actually."

"Recurring people, places, anything like that?"

"Yes."

John worked his hands together. His palms were sweating.

The doctor scribbled a few more notes.

"In the dreams, I'm a kid, eleven, maybe twelve, and we're always in a graveyard. Like a whole community of graveyards and there's… there's these two kids I always find myself there with. I don't know who they are, but they're always there."

"And in the dreams," Dr. Soctomah said, scratching more notes, "what are you and these two kids doing?"

"It's almost as if they're my friends, I guess. They always seem nice enough…well, August is…*different*."

Dr. Soctomah stopped writing. His gaze met John's. "August? You remember their names?"

"Ah, yeah, well, there's August and the other one, a short scrawny kid's name is…. One Eye. August called him by another name, a real name once, I think, but I don't remember it."

"Is there anything specific you guys do in these dreams that makes you uncomfortable?"

"Besides the fact that we're always in a cemetery and that one kid has one eye and the other has none and can spit spiders out of his mouth, you mean?" John wiped his hand over his chin and sat back.

"Okay, okay," Dr. Soctomah said. "It sounds like there's something your subconscious mind is trying to…sort through. It's affecting your sleep, which is affecting your health, your stress levels, and your focus. I think I can help you."

John sighed. "You don't think I'm losing my shit?"

"Not at all," he said.

Over the next forty minutes, John surprised himself as he opened up to the man as if he'd been burning to speak to someone his entire life, confessing his shortcomings, his fears but also the things that gave him hope.

"Time's up. You're a free man."

"Wow," John shuddered a breath. "I didn't expect to talk so much."

Dr. Soctomah smiled. "Sometimes, John, we just need someone to talk to."

John gave a nervous laugh as he stood.

"I want you to come back next week. We'll go over your life starting at your earliest memories and working as far as we can each session."

John smiled.

"Thanks, Dr. Soctomah," he said, as he stepped to the door.

"Next week, same time?"

"Well, I wanted to talk to you about that. I'm actually on a… vacation. Is there any way we can meet again this week?"

"Oh," the doctor said. "Ah, I'd have to look at my appointment book, but I bet we could figure something out."

"Yeah, I mean, I wasn't sure what to expect here, no offense."

Dr. Soctomah waved him off, smiling.

"I'll call you," the doc said. "It'll probably be later this afternoon. Does that work?"

"Yeah," John said. "Please, and thank you."

"Okay, John, well two things," Dr. Soctomah said as they stood at the door.

"First off, these dreams really interest me. I think we definitely have something there to work through. I want you to pick up a notebook and write down your dreams when you wake up. It's going to be your dream journal."

"Okay," John said.

"Secondly, have you ever thought about taking up running?"

"Every now and then," John said. "I used to run track."

"Running can be very therapeutic in itself. If I had to prescribe you anything today, that'd be it. Give it a shot. Try a run or two, nothing too long, maybe just an easy jog around the block, and see how you feel."

"Yeah, I'll do that."

John passed a young woman sitting in the waiting room with short blonde hair, dressed in a baggy sweatshirt and jeans, gnawing at her fingernails.

"Georgia," Dr. Soctomah said.

The woman got up and followed the doctor into the room.

⋆   ⋆   ⋆

To be honest, John felt better telling someone else about his dreams. Sarah had listened to him, but it was nice to have an unbiased third party to speak with about it.

Today was the start of his two-week vacation.

Alison hadn't been too excited by his request, but she didn't have much choice. He enjoyed watching her squirm for once when he said he wanted to use all his vacation time and he wanted to start this Monday. She exclaimed there was no way to get coverage that fast, but he told her he already had it covered – Kaitlyn and Brandon, the new but totally capable guy who just moved here from Providence, had agreed to take on his caseload. Alison acquiesced and here he was sitting outdoors at the Tap Room on a gorgeous summer afternoon drinking a cold beer and enjoying a haddock sandwich as he tried to figure out what to do next.

John was finishing his pint of Shipyard Summer Ale when a green van caught his eye.

An overwhelming sense of déjà vu tightened his flesh as his hands trembled. He stood and tried to get a look at the driver. When the figure behind the wheel turned to him, he saw the impossible.

August?

The pint glass slipped from his hands, shattering on the concrete patio.

The van slowed; a whisper prickled his skin.

Johhhhnnnnneeeee....

"Sir," the waitress said. "Are you okay?"

He looked down at the broken glass and heard tires squeal as the van sped away. It was like the world was in slow motion.

Turning left, he saw his fellow patrons were staring at him.

He gave an awkward smile, feeling like a dumbass as he crouched down to clean up his mess.

"Oh, don't worry about that," the waitress said. "Let me."

He paid his bill and made his way to his car.

With a cigarette in his mouth, his unease receding, he let his gaze wander down Water Street past the post office, and the consignment shop that now took up residency where Pop's Collectable Sports Cards used to be. He'd lived here in Spears Corner his entire life. He once dreamed of getting out, moving to Seattle with his guitar and trying to join the ranks of Pearl Jam and Soundgarden – the closest he ever got was a major case of stage fright at their eighth grade talent show that saw him make it halfway through the first song before he fled and embarrassed himself in front of Julie Heath. The next year, his parents divorced and went their separate ways, moving to opposite ends of the state. He refused to leave his friends and ended up moving in with his brother, Scott. Scott being nineteen and John only fifteen at the time, it wasn't the most ideal situation – food was scarce and so was his brother, who worked fifty hours a week at the Carlton Woolen Mill and disappeared on weekends to get blasted with their cousin Derek. It was a lonely six months before he walked in on his brother having sex with a girl on the couch. After that, Scott's good grace ran out and

John wound up staying with his best friend Ryan's family. He stayed with them until he decided to drop out of school, at which point Ryan's parents' good grace ran out, and they told him he'd have to move out. He got a job as a dishwasher at a local diner and at almost seventeen, got his own apartment (taking over his brother's place as Scott moved in with his new girlfriend two towns over), had his own light bill and bought his own groceries.

There was no sense of freedom or accomplishment, only failure, abandonment, and the constant struggle of trying to survive.

John watched as two boys on BMX bikes rolled by.

He found himself scanning the vehicles along the street searching for something out of a nightmare he couldn't quite remember.

CHAPTER NINE

"John," Sarah said. She placed her hands on his shoulders and whispered in his ear.

Normally, he found this to be an extreme turn-on but not tonight.

"What is it?" he asked.

"I've been thinking. And I wondered if…if you ever thought of trying again."

Oh God, not this. Not now.

His mind was all over the place as it was; the last thing he needed was the pressure or the hurt that came with them trying for a baby.

"Listen," she said, sliding next to him on the bed. She placed a hand on his thigh and looked into his eyes. John bowed his head. Sarah reached under his chin and gently brought his gaze back to meet hers. He felt like garbage for his brief irritation.

"I'm sorry," he said.

"Don't be."

"No, I just get so…."

Her eyes should have matched his hurt and his hopelessness, yet there they were, beaming like they knew something he didn't.

"It sucks watching you…go through all that heartache," he said. "I just don't know if I'm ready to witness that again."

"Believe me," Sarah said, "I know what's at stake. I just feel like… like it could be different this time."

And there she goes. This was how it went each time they got on the same page and decided together that kids just weren't in their cards. They agreed to enjoy each other and live their lives however they chose, not being tied to a school or busy with getting the kids to sports or dance. But then, that nagging need she had somewhere inside would make her forget all the frustration, all the grief and the disappointment.

"I know," she said. "It isn't easy for either of us. I know what I'm asking you to do. What I'm asking you to chance."

"I thought we agreed it was just the way it was supposed to be. You and me and that's it."

"I just feel like we can do it. We can *will* it to happen."

"Sarah," he started.

"Please, John, one more time, for me."

His sigh said it all. And he instantly wanted to take it back.

Her hand slipped from his thigh – a wave withdrawing from the shore.

"Sarah," he tried.

Her lips pressed tight, a slight quiver to her chin. Her eyes looked anywhere but toward his.

He reached for her, but she held a palm out to him and walked to the bathroom. She closed the door and shut him out.

"For fuck's sake," he muttered. He rose and left the room, taking his pillow with him.

What had she thought he was going to say, *'Yah! Let's fuck and try for disappointment. I can't wait to see you cry. I can't wait to have to jerk off for the rest of the year because sex reminds you of our failure. Yippee fucking yah!*

He stopped in the darkness of the living room.

He was an asshole.

She was probably crying alone back there, and he was out here stomping around like a selfish prick.

There were cool couples out there, like his friend Kris and his wife Betty, who had purposefully chosen not to have kids because the world was going to hell. Sarah's cousin Virginia and her husband were doing the same thing. They just didn't want to deal with kiddos and the unnecessary challenges they presented. Capable couples who were happy to abstain from the societal norm.

Try as they might to be content without a family, John and Sarah would never be like their friends. He knew it. They *had* wanted kids. The dream of having a couple of mini-mes laughing and running around, playing with toys, and waking them up in the night was something they talked about soon after they began dating.

He wanted to forget it, to let it go, but Sarah clearly had not.

Deflated, sitting on the sofa in the dark with his face in his hands, John couldn't hold back the tears.

*   *   *

At some point, he had downed a couple beers and passed out on the couch. That night, his dreams kept to themselves as if the boys from Graveyard Land had sensed his pain and given him a reprieve.

John slept long and deep with teardrops in his eyes.

CHAPTER TEN

Sarah lay there alone in the dark, screaming at the world for the hand she was dealt. She hated herself as much as she hated John right now. He was right. Trying for a baby was asking for regret. It was chasing devastation. Masochistic and sick. Did she really think it would happen this time? That they could *make* it happen? Unanswered prayers were worth a pile of shit.

No matter how much she tried to convince herself having children wasn't in the cards, to give up, to move on, to live a life of freedom with John, she sensed something big for them in the future. They were a great couple, but they were destined to be an even better family.

The worst part was that she couldn't forgive him. Even though she understood what he was saying, how he was feeling about not only himself but her, she couldn't quiet the hurt or the rage.

She kicked the shit out of herself for bringing it back up.

Tears stained her pillow as Sarah eventually cried herself to sleep.

*　　*　　*

She slept undisturbed until the sunlight bled through the blinds and cast the room in its annoying brightness. Rousing from a dream she couldn't remember, Sarah sat up, rubbing the eye boogers away. She could feel the heavy bags beneath her eyes, two puckering leeches pulling her life force away like a couple of energy vampires.

Checking the alarm clock, she saw it was eight seventeen.

She rose begrudgingly from the warmth of her bed, shambled out of the room and down the hall to find the house empty. John's fuzzy, blue blanket was scrunched up at the end of the sofa beside his pillow. A couple beer cans sat on the coffee table next to her stack of library books, and his dirty socks lay on the floor. He'd gotten up and gone out already.

Good.

Normally, their alternating schedules, him on days, her on nights, bothered her, but sometimes it was necessary. She was grateful for his absence this morning. He was on vacation, so she didn't know where he'd gone, but she needed a little time to wallow in this pain and think about last night. She hoped wherever he was he was feeling like shit.

What did he have to do? Have sex with her? That was it.

She knew that wasn't fair, but her selfishness was so damn loud right now.

She wanted a baby. She wanted to try.

Tears threatened her exhausted eyes, and she tried to keep them from bursting free.

Shaking her head, Sarah went to the fridge and focused on anything else. Eggs, breakfast, the most important meal of the day. Protein. Energy. Yoga.

As she exhaled sharply in the refrigerator light, she felt slightly better.

"Namaste." She breathed the Sanskrit word, bowing to the bigger picture.

She refused to let her emotions wreak havoc on the rest of her day.

She asked Alexa to play Taylor Swift as she whipped up some breakfast. Hauntingly beautiful piano accompanied the singer's melodies. The combination trickled like a fresh spring stream. A line about a girl having a marvelous time ruining things made Sarah smile bitterly.

★   ★   ★

After a walk down the block, followed by a twenty-minute yoga session, Sarah felt much better. A little self-care was all it took to reset things. She sat down, feet tucked beneath her bum on the couch with a cup of Tension Tamer tea, and opened Stephen King's book on becoming a writer. She only had about thirty pages left when her gaze left the words on the page and landed upon the dream book. She dropped the King title to her lap and leaned forward to snatch the non-fiction book from the coffee table where she'd left it in hopes it might attract John's attention.

She tucked her bookmark in the paperback and swapped books.

Skimming through the first few chapters, she found a section on guilt:

Dreams where you're concerned you may be found out suggest you should feel guilty. The hidden aspects of your true nature and not being true to yourself in your life can manifest into wickedness that could have you waking up with feelings of guilt or shame.

On another page she read:

Dreams have a way of reminding you about acts you should or already do feel guilty about, acting as a reminder of errors you've committed against friends or loved ones, or even strangers in your life.

John had mentioned feeling like his past was there in – what had he called it – Graveyard Land? It gave her the goosies just thinking of such a place. She'd had a friend named Veronica in junior high. Veronica's little sister was crushed to death in a freak accident with Veronica right there watching her. She often spoke of the bad dreams she had most nights afterward. Sarah had visited her sister's grave with her a few times and always felt her skin prickle at the cemetery. Veronica said it was her sister's ghost standing with them. At some point, Veronica moved away. Sarah heard from a mutual friend years later that Veronica's best friend, Tyrese, was brutally beaten on her way home from Veronica's house one night for being transgender in the wrong part of town. She wondered what kind of dreams that gave the grown woman now.

John had said he couldn't think of any specific triggering incidents in his past, but the human brain is very good at protecting us. The natural automatic response to compartmentalize things was a feat of self-preservation. Knowing how her husband had grown up, his happy childhood sent spiraling as he entered his teenage years, his formative years, how he'd all but been abandoned by his parents and left to fend for himself against all those trying and confusing times at fifteen, it broke her heart. There was no telling what his mind had set aside in his daily struggle to navigate the ever-changing world around him.

She thought of him waking in terror. What was it he feared in those dreams? Something about a boy and spiders? John had mentioned something about eyes. Weird eyes? No eyes? She couldn't remember, but they'd wondered if it was the dream's way of telling him he'd seen something or maybe there was something he couldn't see.

She flipped through the book and was somewhat surprised to find a whole section on seeing people without eyes or not having any yourself.

Seeing people without eyes symbolizes a need to protect a relationship.

Further down the page she read on:

Dreaming of others without eyes indicates a refusal to recognize a problem. It can also indicate that you are hiding something.

It was the spiders though…. He'd woken up convinced that spiders were under his pillow. She scanned the book and was dumbfounded by what she found:

Spiders can symbolize women and female power. The spider is often thought to represent motherhood and motherly figures.

Well, fucking shit, she thought.

They'd always been so in tune as a couple. Had he sensed she was going to put trying for a baby on the table again? The mysteries of the human mind never ceased to amaze her.

Then she remembered the notebook.

John had purchased a notebook yesterday. When she asked him about it, he told her Dr. Soctomah had suggested it.

Setting the dream book aside, Sarah stood.

John wasn't back yet but could come through the door any moment. She didn't know how private the diary or whatever it was would be. Maybe he wouldn't give a shit if she looked at it. Maybe he would.

She took one last glance out the front window to make sure he wasn't home yet, and then sought out the notebook.

It wasn't hard to find. John left it sitting on the nightstand next to his side of the bed. He'd slept on the couch last night, so there was probably nothing in it yet, but she looked anyway.

Inside the cover he had written *Dream Journal.* That wasn't surprising, but what did slip a tendril of unease through her was the sketch beneath it. A figure with strange bony shoulders, a gnarled left hand and scratched, blacked-out eyes. The figure stood among some crudely drawn gravestones.

This was one of the children he kept seeing in the dreams…his name…. John had said it at some point she was sure, but she couldn't recall it now.

She looked to the first page and found it.

August and One Eye are there waiting for me every night in Graveyard Land.

One Eye wants me to play games. Not sure why or what it means. He said August couldn't play or wouldn't play. Something about him being special or having something special... I can't remember. This made August mad and he scared One Eye away. He twirls leaves at the fence and stuffs them in his mouth. He turns them into spiders. I guess August scares me, too.

Graveyard Land scares me. There are lots of other kids there. All of them are boys like me, One Eye and August. But the others never come near us, and they never speak. I don't know why not.

The graves go on forever it seems.

I guess it all scares me.

★ ★ ★

That was all he had so far, but it was enough to give her the creeps. Gazing at the ugly sketch of August, she shuddered and closed the cover. She set it on John's nightstand and jumped back.

A black spider the size of a quarter scurried over the dream journal and out of sight behind the nightstand.

Sarah hurried out of the room and back to her fictional horror stories.

She was suddenly feeling less upset with John and couldn't wait for him to get home. She didn't want to be alone.

PART TWO:
WALKING INTO SPIDERWEBS
CHAPTER ELEVEN

Pat awoke to his baby sister, Ada, jumping on his bed.

"Get up, Paddy," her tiny cartoon voice demanded.

His eyes still closed, his face planted in his pillow, he moaned, "Ada, go watch Doc McStuffins or something. Paddy needs to sleep."

She fell silent. Her wiggly movements ceased. Sleep called to him, trying to pull him down where the good heavy stuff waited in the pitch black. He knew better. Turning his head, he opened one eye and spied her sitting there at the edge of his bed, her little arms across her chest, bottom lip puffed all the way out, eyes aimed at the floor.

"All right," he said, slugging his way out from beneath his weighted blanket. "Come on, pipsqueak."

"Yah!" She clapped her chubby little hands and did some sort of run-in-place hopping happy dance before grabbing at the pile of books on his floor.

"What's this?" she asked, her little eyebrows knitting together. She reached down and lifted the paperback.

It was a book called *The Anatomy of Evil*. The cover was a sort of x-ray of a face from the eyes down and was way too creepy for his little sister to be looking at.

She dropped it and picked up the next one. "Yuck, Paddy. I don't like clowns."

"Neither do I, Ada," he said, taking the book about John Wayne Gacy out of her tiny hands.

"Why you got those?"

"Ms. Davis from the library gave them to me. I have to take them back. Those are some icky covers, huh?"

She nodded, still mesmerized by the true crime books.

"Go on and get," he said. "Make sure Doc is helping everyone. I just have to go pee before I come watch it with you. Okay?"

He had to scoop the books up and put them on the other side of his bed before her smile returned.

"Race ya!" she said, and scampered out of the room as fast as her little feet could carry her.

His mom stepped into the doorway as he pulled on a shirt from the floor.

"Sorry," she said. "I was just starting another load of laundry. I told her to leave you alone."

He stepped next to her and kissed her cheek. "No worries, Ma. There'll be plenty of time to sleep when I'm dead. Besides, she did the pouty lip."

"Oh no, she didn't."

"Yep. She's a step ahead of us."

"Takes after her big brother," she said. "And just like Ada loses half her toys..." She produced his wallet from her back pocket. "Found this in the laundry."

"Shit, thanks, Ma. I thought I lost it at John's." He tossed the wallet to his bed. "If you really feel bad about Ada waking me up you can make me some bacon and coffee. I mean, if you *really* love me."

She slapped his shoulder as he started down the hall.

"Yeah, yeah," she said. "Keep it up and you'll be the one making *me* breakfast."

"Paddy, come on," Ada said. "Doc's gonna save another stuffy."

"Coming, Ada," he said, turning to his mom. "I like my coffee with lots of cream and my bacon extra crispy."

"All right," his mom said, "but I expect you to prove your landscaping skills later. Every lawn in the neighborhood looks immaculate, yet you let ours grow wild and free."

"Paddy!"

"Her Highness beckons," he said. "I'll take my breakfast in the television chamber, please."

His mom threw a rolled-up pair of socks at him as he stumbled into the living room to find Ada mesmerized by the Disney magic come to life on their TV.

★　　★　　★

An hour later, Pat rolled down Aikman Street on his bike, heading for J & S Oil to fill the five-gallon gas tank for the lawn mower. His mother's not-so-subtle jabs about their lawn growing wild had got his attention. Riding alone, he got to thinking. If he expected the town to see past his Mohawk and take his burgeoning landscaping business seriously, he needed to treat his own yard like a showroom. He'd mentioned the idea to John of making his neighborhood lawn-mowing business into an actual legit gig. He expected John to tease him, but instead John encouraged him to go for it. Pat would be sixteen in a few months, but he'd realized a couple things this year – he liked making money and he liked being his own boss. He'd worked at Wendy's for two weeks in March and that was enough. He understood pretty quickly the bullshit fast food workers had to put up with from customers and management alike. When his mom said he needed to make his own money if he wanted to buy things, he started shoveling driveways after the last snowstorms of the season and then went straight into mowing lawns after that. This past week, he'd taken on so many jobs around Spears Corner that he'd had to hire a buddy, Danny Rich, to meet the demand for services. Danny was his first employee. And it wasn't stopping there. Pat had already started saving for a snowplow. Hell, he'd planned on buying something cool for his first car – an old Rambler or Maverick if he could score a good deal, but with the idea of growing his business, he switched gears and instead bought a working 1988 Ford F-150 off old man Keisling out on Devil's Creek Lane.

Pat had been driving since he was thirteen. One of his mom's cooler but equally fucked up and incapable of making good decisions boyfriends, Neal, taught him on the dirt roads of the trailer park. It wasn't long after that that Neal, who'd lost his own license for DUI, had Pat running him to the store so he could get beer and score junk. With all that early experience Pat had no doubt he'd get his license on the first try.

He rolled into the parking lot, set his bike on the side of the store next to the stack of milk crates, and went inside to pay ahead for his gas. He gave the cashier eight bucks and ran back out to fill the red plastic can.

He was finishing up when a green van slowed on the street in front of him. He more felt rather than saw the person behind the wheel watching him. It gave him the heebee jeebees. He placed the gas nozzle back on its handle. He turned around, squinting to try and see the person behind the wheel of the creepy van more clearly, but the vehicle squealed its tires and hurried down the road.

On the way home, he found himself looking over his shoulder, expecting to see the green van again at any moment lurking after him. He'd never been an anxious person. Not after all he'd been through in his life so far. Living with a drug-addicted mom could have completely ruined him, but somehow, Pat managed to not only take care of himself, but also take care of his mom and Ada. Cooking, cleaning, making sure Mom didn't choke on her own vomit when she passed out on the bathroom floor. Making sure Ada was fed and changed and was paid attention to. It had been a hard couple years before John Colby came into their lives, but Pat did things as best he could. He'd avoided getting him and Ada taken away from his mom twice by the skin of his teeth before John was assigned as their caseworker.

John turned out to be a godsend. He came into their situation and instantly recognized and acknowledged Pat's work and applauded him for what he'd survived rather than treating him like a child. John worked Pat into the plan to help his mother. It wasn't easy, but John eventually got Pat's mom to open her eyes to all her son was doing to keep them functioning and moving forward in the face of such incredible adversity. Far from your average thirteen-year-old at the time, Pat would have done it all if he were old enough to get a job.

And once John convinced Pat's mother to get clean, she said she knew she'd never go back to that way of living. True to her word, she found the light and bathed in its grace. She ditched all the Neals in her life and started a new job last winter, landing at the Maine Department of Health and Human Services helping other families in need.

Pat was smiling, thinking how proud of his mom he was, when the green van zoomed past him before its rear brake lights blinked into existence. The vehicle stopped two houses down from the entrance to the trailer park. The van sat there idling in the middle of the road, waiting.

Pat coasted to a stop and watched from the sidewalk.

It felt like the world had stopped.

In those beats between his lungs fighting for air against the inside of his chest and the sleet-like sensation dragging his backbone like a lake filled with human remains, Pat saw every nightmare he'd ever read about in the true crime books that fascinated him so much pass before his eyes as he clutched his hand grips.

When the van pulled away, Pat stood caught somewhere between hyperventilating and throwing up.

CHAPTER TWELVE

That night, Pat dreamt of the green van he'd seen and the shadowy figure behind the wheel. He couldn't remember what happened in the dreams but knew it had been cold, so cold that frost formed on his eyelashes and something far worse waited just out of sight.

★   ★   ★

The alarm clock buzzed like a swarm of hornets, irritating Pat from the depths of sleep and delivering him into a new day.

"Shit," he muttered. It was only five in the morning. The day waits for no man. If he was going to take on the world, he needed to rise and shine before everyone else. Grabbing his headphones, he hit up Spotify and started his morning playlist.

The riff to the Eagles' 'Life in the Fast Lane' offered hope and gave him enough get up and go to make it to his bowl of Cap'n Crunch. He knew it wasn't cool for a punk rocker to listen to seventies bands not called Ramones, Sex Pistols, or his personal favorite, the Clash, but hell if he didn't love Don Henley's voice. Joe Walsh's riff gave way to the Clash's 'London Calling', Bad Religion's 'Los Angeles is Burning', and The Interrupters' 'Take Back the Power'. By the time he was at the Kendricks' house on Mayflower Street, he felt ready to conquer the world.

Most of his elderly clients wanted their work done early, and he wouldn't disappoint.

He finished two lawns by the time Danny rolled up in his dad's old Chevy.

"Dude," Danny said. "It's fucking hot as sweaty balls out here."

A poet.

"Yep," Pat said. "I hope you brought your water bottle. You have Mr. Chang and Ellen Hargrove's place."

"Ms. Hargrove?" Danny said, his eyes bulging from their sockets.

Ms. Hargrove was the MILF of Spears Corner, recently divorced, and totally strutting her stuff for anyone who passed into her orbit. Pat had prepared for Danny's complaints about the crazy August heat and knew he could motivate his sole employee with their lovely former sixth-grade teacher with the nicest tits in town.

"Dude, I freaking love you." Danny jumped from the truck and hugged Pat.

"Okay, okay," Pat said. "Just do a good job and maybe she'll offer you some lemonade."

"Fuck, if she's tanning or swimming, I will give you anything."

"Just do a good job and be cool."

"Yeah," Danny said. "Of course."

*　　*　　*

Three hours later, they met up downtown at Gerrard's Pizza.

Pat saw the sly grin Danny was wearing and knew something happened. "Spill," he said.

Danny sat back in the booth and gazed out the window trying on his best James Dean. "She tanned in her leopard print bikini," he said.

"So? I've seen that. I mean it's spectacular, but so what?"

"She asked me to help her."

Shit.

Pat edged forward. "Help her?"

He was suddenly jealous of Danny's growing grin.

"Sunblock."

Pat's mouth went dry. "What?"

"She asked me to put sunblock on her back," Danny said. "Top off."

"Fuck you."

"I swear to God, man," Danny said. "Swear to God."

Pat leaned back and bit his lip. "Man, as if."

"Yeah, I'm just fucking with you," Danny said. "I saw her in the bikini for like two seconds and then she disappeared into the house. I mean she looked great and it gave me plenty of fuel to keep my motor runnin' while cutting her grass, but I didn't rub her in any way."

By the end of the day, sunburnt and exhausted, he and Danny

decided next summer would call for another helper or two. After Pat paid Danny his take of today's earnings, they parted ways. Danny had offered Pat a ride, but he declined. He liked the way the wind felt against his sweat-covered skin after a hard day's work as he rode his bike home.

The last job had been out near Crescent Cemetery, one of the twelve graveyards in Spears Corner. A thought occurred to Pat as he cruised by and smelled the freshly cut grass.

Twelve graveyards.

One small town.

A lot of graveyards.

A lot of jobs.

Unless each cemetery had its own caretaker, he might have stumbled upon a jackpot. He made a mental note to check with the town office tomorrow. Danny was heading out of town with his brother and their cousins, so there would be no chance for crosstown jobs, not without Danny's truck. Pat would make the most of it and look into the graveyard business.

A soft voice caused him to brake.

"Hello?" he said.

Gazing into Crescent Cemetery, he could have sworn the place had been smaller. Looking at it now, he saw a path he'd never noticed before leading to another one beyond the last grave. He scanned the other pathways and the graves between them for a car or signs of anyone at all.

After setting his bike in the little gulley between the graveyard and the road, Pat walked to the first of the three pathways. Something about the trail at the back center of the place called to him much louder than any imagined voice.

At the start of the little path at the back of the cemetery, there was a slight dip, surrounded on either side by foot-high rusted fences. He walked from the front cemetery and entered the shaded trail. The trees held hands above him, creating cover like some sort of amusement park tunnel. As it opened to a larger, and judging by the poor condition of the gravestones, much older section of the cemetery, Pat felt uneasy.

Dead center stood a huge tree, two of its branches broken and bent, hanging over a number of graves and covering more from view.

As weird as it was that he'd never noticed any of this before, Pat's growing sense of commerce and opportunity began to sound in his head. Surely someone was in charge of cleaning up such a mess, and whoever it was wasn't doing a very good job. A smile barely had time to trace his lips before a strange boy stepped out from behind the tall stone monument off to Pat's right.

Something looked off about the guy's dark eyes peering at him, almost as if he had on some small black goggles or weird European sunglasses.

A vision of Johnny Depp's Willy Wonka came to mind.

"Hey, hello?" Pat called.

Whoever it was stayed mostly out of sight. Only the top of his face peeked out over the monument.

The boy did not respond.

"I'm just...." What *was* he doing? Wandering?

The temperature dropped.

"I'll leave you alone. Sorry."

Pat hurried back the way toward the trail, suddenly nervous that whoever was out here might follow.

"Tell him..." a voice whispered.

Pat stopped dead in his tracks halfway back to the front cemetery.

He felt the hairs prickle on the back of his neck and the oddly cooler air grip his insides and threaten to never let him go.

"I'm sorry?" he asked, not daring to glance back.

"Tell him that August says hello."

The voice sounded like it was nearly on top of him. He spun on his heels and saw – no one.

Movement on the ground just behind him caused him to jump.

Tons of black spiders the size of fifty-cent pieces scurried from the path and toward the woods surrounding the place.

Pat hated the little eight-legged freaks. Ever since Seth Rowe told him they made babies in your hair or climbed into your mouth when you slept, Pat had never been anything but a complete and utter fraidy cat around spiders.

He nearly fell as he stumbled away from them.

He ran to his bike.

All the way home, he swatted at his neck, back and shoulders. It was only the wind, but his mind refused to allow him to commit to that truth.

Tell him August says hello.

CHAPTER THIRTEEN

December 1991

Llewellyn Caswell waited for his moments. Patience was one of his strong suits and why not? He would do anything to nab his boys. Even if it meant not being back home for his elderly mother. He would make it back to Maine someday. He remembered a Creedence song about someday and how it never comes.

Right now, Henry Bixby was saying his goodbyes to his group of trouble-making friends. Llewellyn had watched them throw chunks of ice at numerous vehicles passing by. He'd worried that they'd spotted him across the road once, but it was just the big ugly kid in the red, white and blue jacket pretending to talk tough to someone.

Llewellyn had walked these streets near this time of night for weeks watching the boys gather down the road and around the corner from Chinook Park. Every time they broke up to head home for curfew, Henry walked alone down Belmont Street, while the others made their way back through the park together. Oh, how many times he'd wanted to overtake Henry on his way home. But Llewellyn was patient. He hadn't been caught in the fifteen years he'd been taking them. That takes discipline and wherewithal.

"See ya guys tomorrow," Henry said, placing his hands in his jacket pockets. The puffy brown coat looked too big for the boy. It practically swallowed him whole. Between the huge jacket and the eye patch that covered one of the lenses of Henry's thick glasses, Llewellyn wanted to scoop him up and carry him away.

The group barked farewells in return; the big ugly one mentioned something about his pecker and Henry's mother. Llewellyn was half tempted to cross the street now and smash the large loser's teeth in and shove his own cock in the kid's bleeding mouth. No one fucked with one of his boys. Not after he'd imprinted upon them.

He liked that term. *Imprinted*. It's what animals did. He'd seen a lion cub imprint on a human on one of those programs on the Discovery Channel. It was astounding. They recognized the human as their mother. An instant bond.

While it wasn't quite the same for Llewellyn and his boys, it assured him that no matter the circumstances, they would all be together in some spiritual capacity forever.

He pressed down the stiffness in the front of his pants, licking his lips before pursuing his golden goose.

Zooming ahead, Llewellyn rounded the corner of Lucy Lane and Belmont Street. He pulled to the curb, threw on his hazards and stepped from the car.

When the boy walked around the corner, Llewellyn's heart quickened. Snowflakes descended from the clouds above, coming down like a thousand arachnids in a ballet of cold, hypnotic dust, littering the earth in a gathering threat.

Henry stopped in his tracks.

"Oh, hey," Llewellyn said. "Can you help me?"

After a moment's hesitation, the boy approached with a hopeful look upon his face.

A feeling akin to one you got in your stomach when you hit the big drop on a roller coaster trundled through Llewellyn's body.

"What's wrong?" Henry asked. He stopped in the middle of the empty street, not an inch closer.

"I'm not from around here and I seem to be having some engine troubles. Would you happen to know where I could find the closest pay phone?"

Henry scanned the road left and right, his teeth suddenly gnawing at his lips.

Llewellyn saw the nervousness rising in the boy. Like animals, human beings could sense danger.

"Well, uh…" he said. He glanced over his shoulder from the direction he'd just come from. "I think I just passed one…back there—"

Llewellyn made his move.

"Walk over to the car and get in the passenger seat or I'll blow your fucking head off right here and be gone before the cops can show up to tell your parents you're dead."

Henry stared at the gun in Llewellyn's hand.

His chin quivered.

"I'm going to count to one and then pull the fucking trigger."

Henry hurried around the car as Llewellyn guided him to the passenger side and opened the door for him. The kid took one last glance around, hoping to spot a witness, someone to save him, but there was no one.

Llewellyn got behind the wheel, set the gun in his lap and flicked off the hazards.

"We're going to go back to my place for a little while and hang out. When we're finished, I'll drop you off at home. Understood?"

"Please..." Henry whined.

"Understood?" Llewellyn repeated, menace seething into his voice.

"Please, I don't want to go with you...."

"Don't make me kill you, Henry."

"How...how do you know my name?"

Llewellyn gazed at him, lust pounding through his veins.

"I know the names of *all* my special boys."

He started the car and pulled away into the snowy night.

★　　★　　★

The papers reported that the missing child, Henry Wilfred Bixby, was last seen by his friends leaving Chinook Park Sunday evening. His parents pleaded to the nation on the *Today Show* for the person who took their Henry to bring him home. It was his thirteenth birthday, and Christmas was only three weeks away.

Henry Bixby never came home.

CHAPTER FOURTEEN

1993

"Shut that fuckin' shit off," Llewellyn heard the ghost of Steve Norton shout from the other side of the door.

Steve Norton wasn't even here; he was just a phantom walking the hallways. No one could tell Llewellyn Caswell what to do anymore. Norton, his mother's demon fiancé, was dead two months after he first hit Llewellyn with the wrench. His mom thought Steve had just walked out on them and never come back. Llewellyn knew better.

He was drunk and mean, Llewellyn remembered....

Norton had swept Llewellyn's mother, Loretta, off her feet and the two were engaged within a matter of weeks. She had no idea what kind of monster she'd let into their lives. Steve Norton was a mechanic and an active member in the Ku Klux Klan. He was only in Llewellyn's world for a moment in time, but he'd certainly left an impression. Within weeks of moving in with them, Norton began dishing out the hurt, both physical and mental. The belt one night, a wrench the next, a "you fat little fucker" here and a "you a faggot, boy" there, the son of a bitch revealed his true depravity soon after. One night, while his mother slept, Norton, drunk and horny, burst into Llewellyn's bedroom and raped him.

Two nights later, with his mom helping out at the church's bean supper, Llewellyn found an inebriated Norton passed out in front of *Three's Company* and smashed the claw end of a hammer into the top of the man's head.

Llewellyn tossed a blanket from the recliner to the floor and shoved the dead man on top of it to keep as much blood away from the sofa as he could. After wrapping a garbage bag around the man's ruined head, he rolled the body onto his plastic sled and hauled him out the back door. It took every ounce of strength he possessed, but Llewellyn managed to pull the sled into the woods and back to Litchfield Pond at the edge of their property. He loaded the man's clothes with rocks and rolled him into the murky water.

The mysterious disappearance of Steve Norton hung over him and his mother for years, but with no body and no evidence, the police eventually cleared Loretta and her overweight son of any wrongdoing.

The results were a mixed bag as Loretta, her reputation sullied by the local sewing circle, squirreled herself away in the farmhouse and never dated again. Her heartache was enough of a burden for Llewellyn to witness. He didn't want to tell her how wrong she was to miss the man.

The memory of caving in the back of that monster's head carried with it an excitement that Llewellyn sought out time and time again.

His boys brought him to that place. And when they were finished, despite what he told them about going home, he made them vanish from the earth just like Steve Norton.

*   *   *

Now at his home in Wisconsin, stewing in a drunken haze, he ignored the phantoms of his past and turned his attention to the fly in his web.

"Please, I won't tell anyone."

The boy sat in total darkness of Llewellyn's living room closet, bound at the wrists and ankles, naked and scared.

"Please, mister, just don't kill me."

Llewellyn groaned in agitation. Begging was not something he rewarded. It only fed his rage.

He stood, walked to the stereo and turned the AC/DC album up until the walls threatened to crumble. He poured a tumbler of Knob Creek and drank down its fiery promise.

Opening the closet door, he smirked down into the glistening eyes of the youth. The devil he kept within whispered suggestions and Llewellyn took up each one.

The boy's screams – a choir of sadistic glee and carnal wonderments – went on well after midnight. At some point, he gave up and died. Into the dirt crawlspace the broken body would go, coated in boiling lye and wrapped in a plastic sheet until Llewellyn could find a good time to bury whatever remained with the others.

In the morning, he stood in the window gazing out at his front yard and thought of all the others buried out there in his Graveyard Land.

A thought skittered from the darkness. Someday, it would all be over. He'd be caught or he'd be dead. Either way, it didn't seem fair. If only there were a way he could make his Graveyard Land last forever. He'd do anything to stay with his boys.

That was the day Llewellyn decided to challenge the impossible.

CHAPTER FIFTEEN

"Welcome back, John," Dr. Soctomah said as he stepped aside and directed him into the cozy room.

John took his time looking over the native artifacts. "What tribe do you belong to?" he asked, staring at a map on the wall tracking the tribes of Maine.

"Excuse me?" Dr. Soctomah asked.

"Oh, sorry, I assumed you were—"

The man laughed, his smile matching the warmth of his brown eyes. "I'm just messing with you. I'm sorry, I really shouldn't as your therapist. Passamaquoddy. My sisters and mother live on the Pleasant Point Reservation up there, just a little north of Lubec." He pointed to the eastern part of Maine. "It's beautiful coastal country. Have you ever been up that way?"

"No," John said. "I think Bangor is as far north as I've ever been. Do you get to see them often?"

"A few times a year," he replied. "But come, have a seat."

John took the same sofa as the other day.

"Thanks for fitting me in again so soon," John said.

"I'm glad you wanted to be here. Some people I see once and never again. Glad to see that's not the case with you. Plus, I had a cancellation and voila!"

"Yeah, well, thanks. I appreciate it. And I'm still dreaming about strange kids, so…."

"Is that the dream journal?" Dr. Soctomah nodded at the notebook in John's hands.

"Ah, yeah. Did you want to see it?"

"That's not necessary. It's more for you to keep track of things as you remember them. Anything of interest over the last couple days?"

"Well, to tell you the truth, Sarah and I are having a different issue at the moment. It sort of makes this," he said, holding up the journal, "seem small."

"Do you want to talk about it?"

"She wants to try for a baby again."

"I see. And you?"

"I...." John hesitated. "I don't want to see her go through that again."

"When did this come up?"

"Just the other day."

Dr. Soctomah made some notes.

"What about you, John? Do you want to try again? Without worrying about Sarah's feelings. Is having children still a *want* for you?"

"I mean, I...I don't know. Part of me is finally comfortable. You know? But another part wouldn't mind, but...."

"Then, maybe you just need some time to think it over."

"I got mad when she brought it up. I mean, not right off, but I said some things I can't take back. And so did she." John hung his head and gazed at the cover of the notebook.

"Well," Dr. Soctomah said. "You guys have been down this road before. She's let you know what she wants, it's okay to react, but now, I want you to sit with it. Give it time. I'm sure she'll wait for you to weigh it out."

John nodded.

"How about running? Have you been out yet?"

John grinned. "I picked up some new shoes this morning. I was planning on going out this afternoon."

"Good. I really think you'll find it therapeutic. Now, I'd like to go over your history. Is that okay?"

"Sure," John said.

"Let's start from your earliest memory."

★   ★   ★

They covered his relatively happy childhood, up to his parents' divorce, and his decision to fend for himself. Dr. Soctomah checked his phone and stopped them momentarily. His next appointment had canceled. He offered John the chance to double up their session today.

John agreed, thinking it best to plow through this while his walls were down. They talked about his year and a half of couch surfing, before he took over his brother's apartment. That led to deciding to work instead of finishing school, and then to his father's death.

"That's time," Dr. Soctomah said.

John wiped the tears from his cheeks. He couldn't believe he'd cried, let alone twice. First while talking about his parents' divorce, and then again about his father's passing.

"That was, uh, heavier than I thought it would be," John said.

Dr. Soctomah squeezed his shoulder and said, "It is amazing what we're able to power through when we're focused on surviving the day."

"Yeah. We don't have to do that again, do we?"

"It shouldn't be so bad going forward."

"Thanks, Doc," John said, stepping to the door.

A photograph on the wall next to the door caught his eye.

"Is that Fairbanks Cemetery?"

"Yes," Dr. Soctomah said. "That's my great grandfather's tribe in 1846."

"The Passamaquoddy used to be in Spears Corner?"

"I'm afraid the history of this town is not a pretty one, especially for my people."

"Oh, I'm sorry."

"A story for another time, perhaps," Dr. Soctomah said.

"Well, I gotta run, Doc," John said. "Literally."

"Good. Make sure you hydrate. Tell Sarah I say hello, won't you?"

"Of course...if she talks to me tonight."

"Give her time. And give yourself a little, too." He winked.

CHAPTER SIXTEEN

John's first run reminded him why he'd quit. He made it just over a mile down Hinkley Road before a cramp bit into his side. He pulled up to give himself a break. A horn blared, causing him to nearly jump out of his new Nikes. Burt Marsden drove by in his Silverado, laughing and waving.

Burt was an old school nemesis. He smashed John's left knee in a Hall-Dale/Spears Corner rivalry football game back in '96, effectively ruining John's already ultra-mega slim chance of making his way out of this tiny small-minded town. Back then, John had been one of the fastest kids in school and after two years of track in junior high, Coach Hersom asked him to try out for the high school football team. With his parents on the fast track for divorce, his home life on the brink of destruction, John tried out and landed the starting tailback position. Freshman year, he ran like hell. Running with grit and guts and speed like he was desperate to get the fuck away from it all. He was projected to annihilate the state record for yards in a season when Marsden dropped a shoulder to the side of his right knee.

The knee still ached a little when it rained, but damn if it didn't feel good to run, almost like he was shaking off years of rust. Marsden now owned a beef market up the road. John forgave him years back, but the old grudge resurfaced for a few weeks every September when the NFL season started.

Dredging up his own potential from the past combined with Marsden's timely presence gave John the fuel he needed to press on. He wiped his mouth with the bottom of his Guns N' Roses t-shirt, took a deep breath and shoved off.

'Running with the Devil', the old Van Halen song, played on a loop from his phone serving as musical motivation. His Fitbit – a birthday gift from Sarah – tracked his miles, heartbeats per minute, and the time it took to make the distance between Jenkins Cemetery, which was the tiny graveyard two houses down from his place, and Fairbanks Cemetery over on Spears Corner Road.

It seemed insane to be out in this heat under the afternoon's white-hot threat, but it felt like his penance. After acting like such an ass to Sarah, he deserved a little suffering. Slowing to a snail's pace, John glanced down at his soaked t-shirt. It looked like he'd just stepped from the shower fully dressed. His bandana was doing a shitty job of preventing the moisture from stinging his eyes.

He gave up on the dream of running the whole trek and walked his ass to the entrance of Fairbanks Cemetery. Slowly catching his breath as he strolled along the pathways, he stopped the music coming from his cell phone. It seemed somehow sacrilegious or rude to disturb the dead. The sudden quiet derailed him.

The graveyard had easily quadrupled in size compared to what it had been in the photograph from Dr. Soctomah's office.

"The history of this town is not a pretty one."

He'd known the photo had been taken here because of the massive oak tree at its center. The thing still stood like a monument.

John had never noticed any native names on the headstones here.

His gaze landed upon several of those engraved on the markers. Jim Greeley. Date of death August 15th.... Preston Peacock, August 23rd.... Greta Hinkley, August 5th.... Finally, he saw a veteran that died in September.... For a few seconds, the coincidences were fucking with him.

He'd had dreams the other night of August and One Eye and the task of picking a grave.... It had to mean something. Either that or he truly was losing his mind. In which case, Doc Soctomah could hopefully prescribe him a remedy and at least make things easier on Sarah. She had given him the cold shoulder each night since their argument about trying for a baby. He wasn't budging and so far, neither was she. He tried to talk to her about the dream the other night and she straight up shut him down, telling him to save it for his next session.

Whether he deserved it or not, it stung.

He managed to jog most of the way home, a total of two miles, and was happy to find Pat waiting there on the porch.

"What's up?" John asked, taking a seat next to the water bottle he'd left under the shaded overhang.

"Jesus, Johnny," Pat said. "You're drenched, man. Why are you exercising in the middle of the day?"

"I'm a masochist. And I told you not to call me that." He gulped down a couple swallows of water, gasped his satisfaction and went back for more.

Pat said, "I was cruising around. Got my work done early today, and...."

His hesitation caught John's attention. "What is it?"

Pat was fidgeting, a nervous tic he had back when John first came to his family. Something was bothering him. John hoped to Christ his mom hadn't slipped up. It happens, but he just didn't want to see it happen to Trisha.

"Okay, okay," Pat said. He wasn't looking at John. Instead, his gaze bounced all over the place. "Okay and I'm, like, probably just being crazy, but...."

John stood. "Do you have any smokes?"

"Yeah, yeah," Pat said, reaching into his pocket.

"I'm out of smokes. Mind if I bum one of yours?"

"For real? Are you sure it ain't gonna finish you off?"

John knew his body would prefer he didn't, but it was more to help Pat relax. "I'll be fine."

Pat handed him one and lit it for him before lighting his own. After a few drags, John did indeed regret it, but Pat stopped fidgeting and met his gaze.

"I think someone's following me," he said.

"What? Like who?"

"I don't know," he said, after taking another drag. "I could swear I've seen this van around town recently. I've never seen it before this past week, and I don't know, maybe that's why it sticks out, but it feels like it's watching me when I see it. It stopped in front of me at the gas station the other day and then it passed me on my way home and just sat in the middle of the street out front of my trailer park."

Despite the heat, John's insides turned to sludge like a bowl of day-old ice cream left in the corner of a teenager's room. The curdled feeling was too much to keep from his face.

"Are *you* okay?" Pat asked.

The green van from the other day outside of the Tap Room. The shadowy figure behind the wheel....

"John?"

"Oh, yeah...you were right." He tossed the remains of the cigarette to the ground and stamped it out.

"Yeah," Pat said, putting his hands in the pockets of his black cargo shorts. "Well, like I was saying, it's probably me being paranoid or whatever but...I don't know."

"Have you gotten a look at the driver?" John asked.

"No, it seemed like I was at a bad angle both times, or it was too dark inside the van or something."

"Have you told your mom?"

"No," Pat said. "She doesn't need to be worrying about me riding all over town for work being chased by some boogeyman."

The term induced another sinking feeling in John's stomach.

"Do me a favor," John said. "If you see it again, try to get a look at the plate."

"Yeah," Pat muttered.

"I believe you, you know."

"I'm probably nuts."

John saw the van in his mind. He shook his head. "No, I think I've seen it, too."

He saw the glimmer of excitement in Pat's eyes.

"Really? Where? When?"

"A few days ago, downtown by the Tap Room."

"Weird."

"Yeah, but it's like I had this strange sense of déjà vu. There was something so familiar about it, but I can't figure it out."

"It is an old van," Pat said. "Maybe it belongs to someone in town, or someone that's come back to town?"

"Hmm," John said. "I don't know. Just be careful, all right?"

"Yeah, of course."

"Well," John said. "What are you doing now?"

"Nothing, really. You?"

"I'm on my staycation. I got in my run, now I was just gonna sit on my ass for the rest of the day and watch movies while Sarah's at work. You want to stick around for a bit?"

"What are you watching?"

"Have you ever seen *The 'Burbs* with Tom Hanks?"

"Is that the Forrest Gump guy?"

John put his hand on Pat's shoulder. "My friend, come on in. You are in for a treat."

★　　★　　★

Later that evening, John gave Pat a ride home. The kid had loved *The 'Burbs* and they followed it up with another eighties horror comedy classic, *The Night of the Creeps*. On the way over to Pat's house, they were both looking around, scanning the roads and sidewalks like a couple of paranoid fools. Pat took his bike out of the backseat and hurried to his house. John drove away, thinking back on the two of them watching the 80s flicks together. He felt like it was a bit of a father-son moment or at least a big-brother thing, introducing Pat to a couple of films he considered to be classics.

Father-son.

He shook the thought away. No way, he wasn't going back down that road. But how cool would it be to have…a son?

Damn you, Dr. Soctomah.

He remembered what he'd told the doc about his own father. Sure, his dad was there, but at the same time, he kind of never really was. Roy Colby worked fifty hours a week. From four thirty when he got home until seven p.m., he sat in his recliner in the corner of the trailer chain-smoking Marlboro Lights and drinking through a six pack of Schlitz. John would sit on the couch watching TV with him, everything from *M.A.S.H.* or *Coach* re-runs to *A Current Affair* or parts of *Entertainment Tonight*. On the weekends, it was auto racing, or Clint Eastwood movies. John stuck around for most of the films, but he couldn't stand watching cars zoom in circles. Rides to the store included his dad's coffee cup, which was always filled with beer, and his father crooning along to the oldies station. They never really talked, but just being with him in some sense was better than nothing.

When his mom left, and dad found a new girlfriend half an hour away, they drifted the rest of the way apart. It was bad enough when his mother gave up and left, but somehow, his dad getting dressed up and going out for the night crushed him more. Their TV time evaporated and eventually so did his dad.

Now that he was a grown man who dealt with broken families and sometimes got to glimpse what a loving, functioning unit looked like, even in the face of economic strain and healthcare hardships and all the normal things burdening families every day, a lot of whom also had to take care of kids with special needs, it finally occurred to John that good parents don't give up on their kids. Ever.

At barely sixteen, he'd been without either of his.

Shortly after John's football injury thanks to Marsden, John's father suffered a stroke. He died two days after Thanksgiving that same year. John would give anything to sit down, have a beer and watch an episode of *Coach* with him again.

He was surprised to find himself crying as he pulled into his driveway.

$$\star \quad \star \quad \star$$

That night, he mixed himself a stiff drink and called it an early evening. Emotional shit had a way of draining him twice as fast as anything else. He was already half asleep when Sarah came home, got into her pajamas, brushed her teeth, and lay beside him.

Neither budged.

Stubbornness was a fucking bitch.

He heard her sigh before he fell asleep.

CHAPTER SEVENTEEN

She'd be crazy if she didn't admit that John's stubbornness didn't piss her off. They'd both been run through medical tests. Biologically, they should be able to conceive a child, but it had yet to happen. Sarah always figured it had something to do with her losing her first and only pregnancy as a teen. Maybe God was punishing her for her premarital sex. That seemed a bit extreme and ridiculous, but religion, belief and faith were funny things. They seemed to find a way to exonerate men for such behavior and devour women for the same.

John slept like the dead at her side. Unable to quiet the thoughts shooting through her mind, Sarah got out of bed and went to the kitchen for a late-night glass of Merlot.

They hadn't seen much of each other in the last two days, purposely giving one another some much-needed space. Unlike their usual little fights, this one continued to loom over them. She had never conceded to giving up the hope of them having a family. She may have gone along with the idea for the sake of moving forward, but the desire simmered when it wasn't burning. Right now, it was a four-alarm emergency.

Sitting in the dim glow of the stove light they left on at night, Sarah tried to pick at the scab a little more. Why not? Her brain wouldn't shut off; she might as well force the issue. Why now? Why was the desire so intense?

What was making it so do-or-die *this* time?

It wasn't like John didn't have other shit he was dealing with, he did, but even so, she couldn't tamp this down.

So, what was it?

While John was pretty self-sufficient, their relationship was strong.

She'd known a girl when she worked at a cell phone store who got pregnant to trap her boyfriend. She confided in Sarah that she'd caught him texting other girls, and she figured having a baby would lock him down.

John hardly made comments about celebrities he found attractive. She never saw him ogling ladies even when they were half-naked at the beach. He was still human; there had been porn, but nothing that concerned her.

Maybe it was their opposite schedules. Some days they didn't really get to see each other except to say goodbye or good night.

She poured another glass and stared at her Chromebook.

The idea of writing was always exciting for her. Yet, she hadn't really tried, at least not in a while.

Write away the pain.

She'd found it cathartic when she was in high school.

She looked at the clock on the stove. It was just after midnight.

What could it hurt?

She gave herself a half hour just to see what happened.

Starting the computer, Sarah opened a new document and typed the first title that came to mind:

'Walking into Spider Webs'.

She knew it was a song from her teenage years, but it somehow felt appropriate, considering the tangled mess she and John seemed to be wrapped up in at the moment. A smile cracked her face in the blue light of the Chromebook's screen.

No one would see this, she reminded herself. King said something to that effect, something about writing with the door closed, right? She took a sip of her wine and began to type.

* * *

By the time she saved and closed the document, she was finishing her third glass of wine. The stove clock read nearly three in the morning. But something miraculous had happened. She'd written a story. And she felt...better. She was also having trouble keeping her eyes open.

When she carefully made her way back to bed, she saw John twitching under the covers, unable to stay still. This is what he did when he was having one of his bad dreams. Sarah considered waking him, but she would be useless in her current exhausted and buzzed state.

She was out as soon as her head hit the pillow.

*　　*　　*

"Johnny, you don't look so good," August said. He was standing by the overgrown oak tree between the front two graveyards.

Could you be sick in a dream? Or sad?

"I was looking for you," August said, still leaning against his tree.

"Yeah? What for?" Johnny asked.

"Yeah, August," One Eye chimed in. "What were you looking for Johnny for?"

August reached up to a branch and held his hand palm up for something there to crawl onto him. Johnny couldn't make out what it was from where he stood. One Eye stepped forward as the ever-present fog crept around their feet.

"Better you mind your own business, don't you think?" August replied. His tone was dark; his focus remained on the eight-legged creeps wandering across the palm of his good hand.

"Why don't you leave them spiders alone," One Eye said. "They give me the heebee jeebees."

"*Everything* gives *you* the heebee jeebees," August said.

He let the spider, a rather large black one, Johnny could see now, crawl across his palm and down his thin, bone-white arm.

"You never answered me, Johnny," August said.

"Did you say you were looking for me?" Johnny asked.

The spider crawled over August's baby-skull shoulders and up the side of his cheek before disappearing into his ear.

August didn't reply. A smile split his face as though an invisible blade had slit it open. A perfect black facsimile. It was…ghoulish.

"Come on, Johnny," One Eye said, tugging at Johnny's arm. "August has been acting weird lately. You're better off sticking with me."

They were walking toward the graves and the other boys when a question popped into Johnny's head.

He turned.

"Hey, August," he said. "*Where* were you looking for me?"

"I was in the woods, silly."

"The woods?"

"Outside your house," August said.

"But we live in a trailer park. There's no woods near us."

"Not that house, Johnny," he said, stepping forward.

"Come on, Johnny." One Eye tugged at his arm. "I told you he's being a weirdo."

Johnny pulled his arm free and started toward August.

"What house?" he asked.

"How about this?" August said. "How about next time, *you* look for *me*."

The way it seethed out of his mouth prickled Johnny's flesh. He turned around and looked for One Eye. The boy was gone. They were all gone. He was here alone with August and his wicked smile among the graves.

In the distance he heard a vehicle's engine rev to life.

Headlights peered through the swelling fog like two yellow eyes seeking him out.

When he looked back to August, he had vanished, as well.

The vehicle revved its engine.

Was that the van?

Before he could get a good look, it raced toward him.

Johnny ran, purposely crossing over graves in hopes that the vehicle wouldn't pursue him.

He was breathing heavy, his gums hurt, his legs felt like rubber. Suddenly, he was sweating through his t-shirt. His long bangs stuck to his forehead.

The graves never seemed to end.

He had stopped to catch his breath when the roar of an engine growled out of the darkness and bore down upon him.

Johnny raised his arms and screamed.

★　　★　　★

"John, wake up!"

He opened his eyes, raising his hands, startled.

Sarah looked more irritated than concerned.

"Have you talked to Dr. Soctomah about your dreams yet?"

"Yeah," he breathed.

"You're trembling," she said, some sympathy slipping into her voice.

He tried to steady his hands, but it took real effort.

Sarah sighed and sat down on the edge of the bed beside him.

"Well," she said, "it's probably not work related...the dreams, I mean." She couldn't meet his gaze. She looked toward the bedroom window. "Do you think it's me?"

He reached for her chin and turned her face toward him. "No, why would you think that?"

Her lips turned down at the corners of her mouth. "Because I asked you to try for a baby again."

He pulled her into his arms. The intimacy felt good.

"Of course not," he whispered. "Don't you ever think that."

He wasn't a hundred percent certain that the baby talk had nothing to do with his fucked-up dreams, but he didn't want her carrying his weight over it. Besides, the dreams had started up before she mentioned anything to him about trying again.

"Yeah, but you could have, I don't know, intuitively sensed it."

"Huh, you think?"

"I don't know," she said. "Let me show you something. Turn on your lamp."

He flicked on the bedside light and squinted at the sudden intrusion of brightness.

Sarah reached down to her stack of library books, pulled out the second from the top, and flopped it down between them on the bed.

John picked it up and read the title.

Dreams and Nightmares: Our Reality's Creations.

"When did you get this?" he asked.

"A few days ago," she said. "I've been jotting down notes. Here, let me see."

He handed it over and she flipped through, pulling out a white note card. "These are the ones I thought made some sense with what you've told me about your recurring dreams."

One by one, she handed the cards to him.

He read the note on guilt. *Reminders of acts you should or already feel guilt for. Errors you've committed against loved ones or friends.*

Her note titled 'others without eyes': *refusal to recognize problem/ indicate that you're hiding something.*

'spiders'

Symbolize women and female power/often represent motherhood/ motherly figures.

"So, this is you connecting the dots back to you," he said.

She nodded.

He considered the other notes. Dr. Soctomah seemed to agree something was buried in his subconscious, something that was probably shrouded in guilt.

"Well, like I said." John took her hand, brought it to his mouth and gave it a kiss. "This all started before and I'm pretty sure I don't have enough sense to intuit all your wants and needs."

She looked at the alarm clock.

"It's only four thirty. Do you want to catch some more sleep?"

He placed a hand on hers and kissed her cheek.

"John Colby, are you intuiting my wants, right now?"

"I hope so," he said, kissing her neck.

She pulled away, raised her t-shirt over her head and tossed it to the floor.

"Come here," she said.

★　★　★

In the morning, he walked her to the door, gave her a kiss, and reassured her one last time that she had no reason to feel guilty.

"I love you," he said.

"I love you, too."

He watched her get into her Subaru and back into the road. She waved and drove away.

John started to close the door when his gaze stuck on the shadows among the trees at the end of the driveway.

How about you look for me.

August's words from last night's dream sent a shiver through him like a ghost among the graves.

CHAPTER EIGHTEEN

John set out on his run shortly after Sarah left. He was up to three miles today. The knee hadn't acted up so far, but he didn't want to push it either. He wouldn't make it full speed all the way home, but if he walked for a bit, he might catch his breath enough to push it a good chunk of the way.

A car slowed next to him. "Hey, hot stuff."

Kaitlyn Skehan smiled at him behind her sunglasses. Dua Lipa blasted from her Toyota Camry. She began to sway behind the wheel. Sweat glistened over her breasts that were barely held in check by the halter top she was wearing.

"Good to see you out here in them sexy shorts," she said. "How's the vacation going?"

"It's definitely more of a staycation. It's been interesting." He left it at that. "How is work going?"

"Oh my God, Alison is so mad. She fucking hates you, but me and Brandon are killing it. She's got fuck all to complain about and its driving her up the wall."

"Awesome," he said.

Fingering the sunglasses down the bridge of her nose, her lips glistening with either gloss or sweat, she said, "You're going to owe me, you know."

"I know. I'm in your debt. Whatever you want."

"Careful, John. I might come calling one of these nights."

He backed away from the window. "Well, I mean, anything within limits."

She pouted. "Well, let's just see where the road leads us. You enjoy the rest of your vacation, and give me a call if you need anything."

He waved as she blew him a kiss and drove away.

John shook his head and continued toward the graveyard.

* * *

As he approached the entrance to Fairbanks Cemetery, he found himself half a world away. He didn't know if it was all this fighting with Sarah lately or just some sort of spell cast over him by his co-worker, but Kaitlyn was invading his thoughts. He'd seen her out of her work attire before, but not like just now.

Shaking his head again as he entered the cemetery, he decided not to beat himself up over nothing. Fantasizing about someone and actually following through on those fantasies were two different beasts. It was okay to admit that someone was attractive.

Halfway up the path, he began noticing the graves.

His gaze moved from headstone to headstone, falling upon the death dates again. August 1st. August 22nd....

John stopped and closed his eyes.

He breathed in the smell of freshly cut grass and the hay from Peacock's Horse Motel across the road. It was peaceful here.

"Have you picked one yet?"

One Eye's voice echoed in his head, disrupting the moment of contentment. When he opened his eyes, the name before him seemed familiar.

Ethan Ripley. Born September 9th 1982. Died August 16th 1994.

"In memory of my dearest boy."

Eileen Ripley, Ethan's mother, lay next to him. She died that same year.

Of course, Ethan Ripley. The new kid who'd shown up at school halfway through seventh grade. John felt bad for most new kids, so he befriended Ethan. The kid was gangly and strange, but they shared an affinity for baseball cards, rock bands, and riding bikes. As far as John could remember, Ethan didn't have any other friends in town.

"Help you with sumpin'?" A large, round man with a gray mustache and beady eyes moseyed up next to John. The man pulled a faded blue bandana from the back pocket of his dirty slacks and wiped the sweat from his brow. John got an eerie vibe from him; there was something off about his eyes. They were somehow too dark, too glazed, like he'd seen too many dead bodies and been mesmerized and somehow tainted by the macabre sights. It was a lot to ascertain from a simple look, but it struck John just the same.

"I was just out for a run."

"Huh," the man said, stuffing the rag back in his pocket and nodding toward the gravestones of the Ripleys. "Pity what happened there. You from town?"

"Ah, yeah. I grew up here, never managed to find my way out." John scratched his neck. "Can't seem to recall what happened to them. I think I knew Ethan, for a little while, I guess."

A smirk lifted the man's lips.

"That boy went missing. They found him in Litchfield Pond couple days later, just back yonder." He gestured out past the cemetery. "After that, his mum killed herself. Got drunk and just…well, I won't go into the gory details." The smirk rose again before he coughed and spat a glob of mucus on the pathway.

"Funny, I…I don't remember…any of that," John said.

"You was probably too young then. Kids got better things to remember than kidnappings and suicides."

Had Ethan been kidnapped?

John wanted to ask but wanted to get away from this man even more. He didn't like his eyes or that disturbing grin.

"Well, I'll be running along. Nice talking with you," John said. He started to head toward the road.

"Say, did you ever look for him?" the man asked.

John stopped.

"Excuse me?"

When he turned back the man was waddling off, heading across the graves. Beyond the back corner of the cemetery, through a copse of trees, John could see the corner of a weathered, white farmhouse. Most of the home was blocked out by the rusty, corrugated metal shed next to the trees. The man was heading in that direction.

Did he live there?

Maybe he was the caretaker.

Did you ever look for him?

Had he actually heard the man ask that or had he imagined it?

Not for the first time this month, John wondered if he might be heading to his own cozy white-walled room at the Riverside Mental Health Facility.

Ethan Ripley. Kidnapped and murdered. August 16th 1994. How the hell could he forget that?

He looked toward the farmhouse and saw the beady-eyed creep watching him from his yard.

Fuck this.

He turned and headed out the way he'd come in.

As his jog became a run, he felt a compulsion to put as much distance between himself and the graveyard as he could. Like if he ran hard enough and fast enough and far enough, he could escape the horrible feelings that seemed to be waiting for him just out of sight.

Could you run from nightmares?

Did you ever look for him?

Isn't that what August had said in his dream?

You look for me.

Did you ever look for him?

Whether it was coincidence or just his mind playing tricks on him, John felt out of step. There was something he was missing.

CHAPTER NINETEEN

1994 (1)

The summer his mother died, Llewellyn Caswell came home. The local police in Wisconsin had been demoted when the FBI was brought in. The heat was on. The feds declared that they were closing in on the person the newspapers and now national media were calling the Ghoul of Wisconsin, the man they suspected was abducting young boys all over the state, making them disappear into thin air. Llewellyn had never done the things he did for the notoriety. Did the sudden attention thrill him? Sure, a bit, but it wasn't his reason for chasing the dragon, if you will. His actions were all about his need, his compulsion, his driving force. Artists *needed* to create, to unleash, to give everything they had to their passion because there was no other choice. For Llewellyn, it was exactly that. There was no other way of life. *This* was everything.

When his mother fell ill earlier in the year, just as the local Wisconsin papers and news channels began unleashing their theories in a desperate attempt to flush him out, Llewellyn headed home.

It wasn't a cakewalk. There were unmarked cars constantly casing his neighborhood day and night. He had his suspicions that they might even have undercover cops watching him. He wasn't taking any chances. He left the house that July night at three thirty in the morning. Like a thief in the night, Llewellyn slipped out through the back door and slunk by the tall wood fence of one of his neighbors. A rented Mazda he'd purposely parked two streets over on Maple waited for him. From there, he drove to Lancin and caught a flight to LaGuardia, and then to Logan. A Greyhound bus carried him to Portland, Maine, where his cousin Alvin picked him up at the station on Saint John Street and brought him home.

Llewellyn hadn't seen Spears Corner since leaving nine years before. The forty-five-minute drive up Interstate 95 allowed him to reflect.

He was both free from the scrutiny and attention of the law dogs sniffing him out and yet crestfallen from being so far from his boys.

"Your mom gave me the house," Alvin said. "She hadn't seen you, hadn't heard from you and I—"

Llewellyn waved him off. He wouldn't have given the house to himself either. He was far from son of the year material.

"You stayed with her, took care of her," Llewellyn said. "Besides, I have no intentions of sticking around."

A Garth Brooks song came over the radio.

Llewellyn loved the country singer. He listened to the ruminations about a boy and his lover one summer long ago and let it sweep him away. He'd had many a romance in his days here. None of the girls had been what he'd call pretty, but he didn't really think of any woman as pretty. Still, the motions of a relationship had been engaging and kept his secret desires at bay, at least for a while.

Alvin spoke very little as he drove, and for that Llewellyn was grateful. His cousin was as loyal as family could get, but he wasn't close to being what you'd call a conversationalist.

When they were teenagers, they'd raised plenty of hell together. They got drunk, got high, and may have coerced a few younger friends into doing things they didn't want to do. They were free to experiment and when out of his mother's sight, that's just what they did. The thought now made Llewellyn have to shift in his seat.

They pulled off the exit, rolled down Route 126, and made a stop at Bower's Market.

"You want somethin'?" Alvin asked.

"Mom still got my old Dodge?"

"Yeah, but I mean somethin' here at the store?"

"We got any spirits at the house?"

"Mm hmm, bottle of Bacardi and nearly a whole fifth of Allen's."

Llewellyn couldn't stand rum, but the coffee brandy would suit him fine for the night. "I'm good."

"All right then."

As Alvin went into the store, Llewellyn watched his cousin's neck crane at the boy coming out. The kid was tall and rail thin. Bony shoulders slumped and head down. Llewellyn's gaze locked on to him and followed the kid and the sad-looking woman he accompanied to the station wagon at the pump.

He promised himself he'd behave while he was here, and he would, but a man had a right to dream.

Alvin came back out with a thirty rack of Coors Light.

"You're welcome to a few of these, but I get the most."

"Sure, sure," Llewellyn muttered.

"What is it?" Alvin asked.

"Nothing. Nothing at all. Let's get moving. I'm exhausted."

The old farmhouse was just a ways down the road. Llewellyn tried to relax and enjoy getting the chance to sit down and have a drink, but something kept tugging at the corner of his mind. A voice, a hunger that never seemed to let him be.

He pounded three brandies and then started in on Alvin's beer.

Drunk and unsteady, Alvin passed out on the sofa. Llewellyn walked outside and stood gazing up at the stars. The hot summer night clung to him like a second skin as he sweat the way he only ever did when he was digging in his yard. He let it trigger him, just as the sight of that thin boy had earlier. He stepped from the porch, walked around the house and saw it sitting there on the back lawn.

His old 1976 Dodge street van.

He knew that very moment, he was going to break his promise.

Loretta Caswell's funeral was quick and only attended by a few of his mother's remaining Yahtzee friends, his Aunt Ginny, and Llewellyn and Alvin. That was it. The reverend and the small group of attendees made their way out. Being that Alvin was the caretaker of the cemetery, it was he and Llewellyn who placed Loretta's casket in the ground. Llewellyn could barely recall her kindness, though he knew she had been loving and caring. He looked back fondly on trips to Old Orchard Breach, Funtown USA amusement park, Fort Knox and closer swimming holes like Whippoorwill and Damariscotta Lake. Of course, then the memories of Steven Norton came back and the darkness in Llewellyn's soul returned.

Llewellyn spat on the casket. Whether she was ever cognizant of Norton's abuse toward him or not, she was supposed to keep him safe. She had brought the bastard into their home. He had taken him out.

Alvin handed Llewellyn a shovel.

After shedding their formal coats, they rolled up their sleeves and began to bury Loretta Caswell.

Afterward, he wandered the cemetery, his fingers grazing the tombstones as he passed them. So many people feared these places. The land of the dead, a land of bones. There were no souls here, but... there were places where they – the dead – did congregate. Where they could assemble or return.

A smile lifted his features as Llewellyn walked through the trees and straight to the van parked halfway behind the corrugated shed. The sun was high in the sky and summer was in full swing. Downtown Spears Corner would be crawling with activity.

The engine turned over. He put it in Drive and listened to the four-speed engine purr, quiet as a mouse, then started toward the livelier part of the city.

His skin tightened. There was a tingling beneath his flesh, a promise of things to come. An urge, overwhelming and intoxicating, slithered around him. His hands clenched the steering wheel then eased up, before clutching it white-knuckled tight again. His breath quickened. He felt like he could explode in his pants at any second. Wiping his hand across his mouth, he realized he was salivating. God, the anticipation was almost too much. He was out of control. He was ready to give himself over to the one thing that made it all okay.

The ghoul stepped on the gas and moaned in pleasure as he neared the Spears Corner Common.

He would feed his need.

CHAPTER TWENTY

Pat set out to learn who oversaw the upkeep of the cemeteries in town. Since there wasn't an office at any of the graveyards, he decided the town hall would be his best bet at figuring out who to contact. If he were lucky, maybe they'd have someone there who was in charge of setting it up.

The town hall building was directly beside the Spears Corner police station. Since Spears Corner was not a big town, the buildings were just one story each, though he suspected they had basements. He walked into the front door of the town hall and saw a woman with big hair who looked like she was in one of the eighties flicks he'd just watched with John.

Deborah said the nameplate on the desk. He heard the song from the movie *Baby Driver* – he wasn't sure the name of the band – start playing in his head. If only she looked like Baby's Deborah. Instead, she was a plain-looking sort, nothing particularly pretty or unattractive about her. What did stand out were her bangs. They reached over her forehead like a clawed hand.

"Can I help?" she asked.

"Uh, yeah, I hope so," he said. "I was wondering if you might know who, uh, who is in charge of doing the landscaping and mowing for the graveyards in town, ma'am."

She smiled. "Oh, don't call me *ma'am*, it makes me feel old. It's just Deborah if you like." Her smile reached her eyes, and Pat thought it made her look prettier. "And may I ask *why* you'd like to know about the cemetery caretakers?"

"I'm hoping I can maybe see if you might have any openings for those jobs."

The corners of her lips fell slightly.

Oh great, now she thinks I'm some wannabe grave robber or sick creep.

"You want to *work* in the graveyards?" she asked.

"Well, I do landscaping and odd jobs around town, ma—Deborah," he said catching himself. "I was thinking there might be some money to be made there is all."

"Huh." She looked him over. "It's nice to hear a young man with ambition." The smile drifted back into place. "It's not something you see every day. Let me take a look at something."

She began typing.

John had told him the importance of first impressions. Pat thought he was doing okay. He'd kept his Mohawk tucked under a Red Sox ballcap and wore a plain white t-shirt with his cargo shorts. It wasn't a suit and tie, but it was as close as he got.

"Well," she said, "it looks like they're all contracted to two men. Two with a Mr. Edward Fuller and the rest with a Mr. Alvin Caswell."

"Thanks for looking," he said.

"Sure thing."

He was about to head for the door when he stopped and turned.

"Would you happen to know which of them covers Crescent Cemetery?"

"I can check for you," she said. After a few seconds, she said, "Alvin Caswell covers that one."

"Oh, okay. Thanks."

"Is there anything else I can do for you today?"

"No, you've been awesome, Deborah. I mean, you've been great."

"Good luck – what was your name?"

"Pat. Pat Harrison."

"Well, Pat. If you want to see about becoming an assistant of some sort, you could always talk that over with Mr. Fuller or Mr. Caswell. You never know, they might be glad to have a helper."

"That's a great idea. I think I'll do that."

"I wish you and your endeavor well," she said.

"Thanks."

★ ★ ★

He stepped out the door into the hotter-than-hell blacktop parking lot. He wondered if either of the caretakers would be willing to take him on as an apprentice. He thought of Alvin Caswell. That was a lot of graveyards for one person to handle. Maybe he'd be willing to let Pat help out.

Or maybe he'd start with the other guy, Edward Fuller. You never knew, maybe the guy had better things to do and just kept the job because he was used to it. Maybe he'd be glad to let someone do the small stuff.

★   ★   ★

At home, grateful his mom and Ada were out, Pat Googled Fuller's address and phone number on his cell. While he wanted to call and ask over the phone, John had told him things that were important in life were always better done face-to-face.

He set out on his bike to the address. It was about six miles away on the Hallowell-Litchfield Road. He didn't mind riding the distance. He passed Bower's Flea Market and Bower's Meat Market. He stopped at the latter to grab a bottle of water before pushing on to his destination.

The number 172 was painted in black on the dented white mailbox at the end of the driveway under the name of Fuller. An old, blue Chevy was parked on the clear part of the small lawn. The rest of the yard was a mix of clutter – a rusted Volkswagen Bug sat on cinder blocks next to a stack of pallets. Beside that a row of chipped and cracked clown statues led to a screened-in porch, where a man rocked back and forth.

"Hello?" Pat said.

The rocking chair stopped with a creak.

"Who's that?" the man barked out gruffly.

It didn't quite have the effect of a big dog, but it startled and unsettled Pat just the same.

"Hi," he managed. "Mr. Fuller?"

"Yes. What is it?"

"My name's Patrick Harrison. I was wondering if I could talk to you about the work you do for the city at the…the cemetery."

Silence settled in. Pat's nerves were on high alert.

"Well, come on over here where I can see who the hell I'm talking to."

Pat tamped down his nerves as best he could and started toward the porch, stopping just outside the tattered screen door.

"Huh?" the man muttered. He coughed until he hacked up something nasty and spat it out one of the few screenless windows near him. "What in the hell you want to know about the cemeteries for?"

"I...I'm trying to start my own business, a landscaping business, and being that our town has, you know, a bunch of graveyards, I thought there might be at least a couple I could do, sir."

"How old are you?" Fuller asked.

"Sixteen this fall, sir."

Fuller leaned back. "How'd ya know to come to me?"

"I went down to the city hall and asked who was in charge of taking care of them."

"And you come to me first, huh?"

Pat didn't know what to say, so he nodded.

Fuller grabbed the pack of cigarettes from the stand next to him, shook one free and lit it. He broke into another coughing fit after the first drag, but just gave Pat a yellowed smile.

"You know I only got two, right?"

"Yes, sir."

"Hmm." He took another drag and exhaled. "How do I know your business sense can be trusted? You know what goes into taking care of one cemetery?"

"Not really, no, but I'm a fast learner."

After looking Pat over another minute, Fuller said, "I can tell you're serious. No one comes knocking on my door. Least not anymore."

Pat's stomach knotted with anticipation.

"Tell you the truth," Fuller said, "I'm getting too old to be out there baking in the sun or freezing my ass off in the cold." He bent forward, rested his elbows on the bony knees poking from his dark green work pants, and squinted. "You come help me out tomorrow morning. Meet me at Babbs – you know where that one is?"

"Yes, sir," Pat said.

"Good. Meet me there, and if you're still interested, we'll see what we can figure out."

"Yeah, of course. That'd be great."

"You look a little funny, but so did I when I was your age. I had hair down to my asshole, and I was out smoking dope and fucking off all day. I sure as hell wasn't starting any business but trouble. Yeah, you meet me out front of Babbs at eight a.m. sharp. We'll go from there."

"Thank you, sir."

"Now get outta here and leave me be."

"Yeah, of course."

Pat walked away, trying not to pump his fist or act too giddy. It wasn't a straight deal but he had a chance to prove himself.

"Eight a.m.," Fuller barked. "Don't be late or you can just stay home."

"Yes, sir," he called back as he reached his bike at the mailbox. "Eight a.m., I'll be there."

When the old man didn't reply Pat got on his bike and rode away.

CHAPTER TWENTY-ONE

The next morning, Pat arrived at ten minutes of eight. The sun was up, but it was a day that held the promise of rain. It was warm and muggy, with a slate of dark clouds on the eastern horizon. He was bouncing on his Doc Martens, a Red Bull and a bowl of Cocoa Pebbles in his tank. He was anxious to prove his grit.

Fuller arrived twenty minutes later in his battered Chevy truck.

Pat said nothing about the man's tardiness.

He watched as Fuller climbed out of the vehicle, taking the lit cigarette out of his mouth long enough to spit a wad of phlegm to the road, before making his way past Pat.

"Well, ya showed up. That's a good start. Come on," he said, "follow me."

*   *   *

The morning cruised by as Pat listened to the limited words Fuller spoke and did everything asked of him. With the grass mowed, the browner patches of ground watered, and recently placed flowers tended to, Fuller called for their first break.

"You bring anything to eat?" the old man asked as he let down the tailgate of his truck.

Pat hadn't thought to pack anything. "No, I wasn't sure how long we'd be here."

"I figured as much." He walked to his passenger-side door and pulled out a paper bag and two bottles of water. After placing the bag on the tailgate, he pulled out two wrapped foot-long subs. "Stopped at the market and had the gals make up a couple ham Italians." He set one on one side of the tailgate, hoisted himself up on the other end and began to open his sandwich. "Well, I know you're hungry. You did most of the work and I heard your guts rumbling and grumbling like a regular ramblin' gamblin' man. Take a seat and eat, or you can go home and stay there."

Pat couldn't hold back the smile. He scooted his rump up on the gate and opened the Italian. The smell of onions and green peppers had him salivating before he took a bite.

They ate in silence. When they were both finished and the waters both drained, Fuller's cell phone rang.

He pulled the ancient black flip phone from the front pocket of his dirty work shirt and fell into a series of ah-yuhs and yeps and a-courses, before hanging up and putting the phone away.

"Well," he said, wiping his hands on his pants. "I was gonna have us do some tree trimmin', but it looks like we get to see what you're really made of. That was the town hall. We got us a hole to dig."

"Dig?"

"Yessah," he said. "You ain't wimpin' out on me already, are ya?"

"No, sir. It's just… don't you have a machine for that?"

Fuller nodded. "Ayuh, I do, I do. Maybe I just want to find out what you got."

The old man wanted to test him. Hell, if Pat wanted it bad enough, he was about to prove it.

"Well, in that case," Pat said. "I guess time's a wastin'."

Fuller nodded behind his yellow-toothed grin. "Couldn't have said it better myself."

After gathering a pick, two shovels, and then dragging a wheelbarrow from the bed of his truck, they set out to find a spot. According to Fuller, there were no other family members of the recently deceased buried here, so just marking a good plot would suffice. Near the back of the cemetery, Fuller placed down a faceless two-foot by one-foot grave marker and, using a can of white spray paint, marked out the dimensions of the grave.

The storm held off. It was nearly three-thirty in the afternoon by the time they had the hole half done. Fuller reached out a hand and helped Pat out. They set their shovels atop the wheelbarrow.

"You done good, son," Fuller said.

"Why'd we stop?"

"Hell, my back's killin' me. You showed me plenty."

"But shouldn't we finish it?"

"I'll get the backhoe for that."

"I was thinking while you were busting your ass in that hole. You show me what you can do, maintaining and keeping up with this one for a few weeks, and maybe I can take you on in an official capacity. Be some pay in it for ya, too. You good with that?"

"Yeah, yes, sir."

A soft wind had kicked up. Pat felt a couple raindrops hit his face.

"Looks like we finished up just in time. We're gonna need to hurry to get the tarp over this one and set up the yellow safety tape. Come on. We get that done and you're free to go."

★   ★   ★

Pat declined Fuller's offer of a ride home. It only rained hard for about ten minutes. After sweating his balls off in that hole, the rain felt glorious. He was nearly home when he spotted the green van. It was heading in his direction down Jackson Street. Pat didn't feel like dealing with this strange asshole's shit today, so he cut across a lawn with a faded Trump sign and pedaled his way to Gilbert Lane.

He turned his head to be sure he wasn't being pursued and saw the van idling before the Trumper's lawn. It sat down the grassy alley, watching him for twenty seconds before squealing away.

This is getting way too fucked up.

Pat hurried home, checking over his shoulder every few seconds.

When he got to his yard, he parked his bike out in back of his trailer and hurried through the mudroom door. His heart hammered in his chest so hard he thought he might have to sit down. He'd never had an anxiety attack and hoped this wasn't his introduction to them.

He considered calling John and asking if he'd seen the van recently, but Ada spotted him and shouted out "Paddy's home" before he had a chance.

CHAPTER TWENTY-TWO

John's mouth watered as soon as he stepped through the door, stricken by the intoxicating aroma of Sarah's habanero and garlic chicken wings. After his most interesting session with Dr. Soctomah and sweating from his most grueling run yet, he was hungry enough to eat a dead body.

Dripping from head to toe, he peeked his head into the kitchen and saw Sarah placing the delicious hot wings onto a large plate.

She saw him and smiled. "Hold on," she said. She went to the fridge and pulled out two Voodoo Ranger IPAs and set them next to the steaming plate on the island. "Join me for dinner?"

"I should probably shower first," he said.

"Come eat," she said, reaching for a wing. "You can shower after."

The food was nice, but the smile meant they'd passed their latest hurdle. Successful marriages are all about meeting your problems head-on and working through them together.

He stepped over to the kitchen sink, stuck his head under the faucet and guzzled water from the tap. He wiped his lips and used a kitchen towel to pat the sweat from his face, neck, and chest before taking up the stool across from her.

One bite in and he was moaning. "Dear, you have perfected the art of the hot wing."

They had nearly finished the plate of twenty wings when she downed the last of her beer and gazed at him.

"What?" he asked, swallowing the last bite. His tongue was on fire and his brain felt like it was melting inside his skull, but that was just the way he liked it. He couldn't think straight, but he did his best to give her the attention she was obviously seeking. "Come on, out with it."

"I wanted to say sorry for...for the way I've been acting the last couple days."

"It's okay, Sarah. I get it. And I thought we made up pretty well the other night." He stood. "I'm sorry, too."

She shook her head. "You have nothing to apologize for. I'm the one with the dumb idea."

She bit her bottom lip and dropped her chin.

John walked to her and wrapped his arms around her.

"I love you," he said.

"I...I still want to try."

The words swarmed and stung.

"Fuck, Sarah," he said. "I thought we were over this."

"Over *this*?" she said.

"Yes. I'm sorry, okay? I'm sorry I can't give you what you want. I can't...I can't give you a baby."

He glanced at her face and saw her crumble before him.

Clenching his jaw, he shut his mouth in order to stem the damage. He kissed the top of her head, and said, "I'm taking a shower."

As he walked out of the kitchen, he heard her start to cry.

John paused in the hall, too pissed to comfort her, before heading to the bathroom and slamming the door.

★   ★   ★

When he was out of the shower and dressed in shorts and a fresh t-shirt, John returned to the kitchen.

"Sarah?"

The dishes were where they'd left them after dinner.

He went to the living room. The TV was off.

"Sarah?" he called out to her again.

It was then that he saw the note taped to the front door.

★   ★   ★

John,

I'm sorry me wanting to try for a baby again is upsetting you. It's probably not fair to you, but this is something I need to do.

I'm going to my mother's for the night. I need some space and I think you do, too.

Please consider it again, for me.

Love you,

Sarah

John grabbed his car keys. The elation of being past this latest baby talk had effectively been stomped into the fucking ground. He needed a drink, something stiff enough to shut his brain down for the night, but he didn't want to be home, either.

CHAPTER TWENTY-THREE

"Asshole!" she cried. Taylor Momson wailed through her speakers about it being just tonight as Sarah cruised the back roads to her mother's house in Sabattus. John was a selfish prick. The sun lit the sky with a brilliance worthy of Heaven's envy when he cast his attention upon you, but too often if it didn't make him happy, it wasn't going to happen. The potential was something she saw in him from day one. He was so great with other people. She admired his success at work, what he'd done for families he worked with, especially what he'd accomplished with Pat, Ada, and Trisha Harrison. They were practically family now. But just once, she wanted to feel like his priority.

She knew his weakness. Expectations. Leave him alone and to his own devices and you could stand back and watch him shine, but try to push him toward his potential and he'd shut you out. She knew it was a defense mechanism; he'd survived on his own for so long starting when he was way too young to do so. She got it, but they'd been married for seven years now. At some point, he had to face his fears. Fear of expectations, fear of failure, fear of change.

Her mother's house came into view. Pulling into the driveway, she checked her face in the rearview mirror. Red, puffy eyes looked back.

"What happened?"

Her mom stood next to the car.

Sarah shook her head. "I just need a night away."

"Come on," her mom said. "I'll put on some tea."

"You got anything stronger?"

"Hmm. Yeah, I think I've got a little something in the fridge."

Inside, they sat at the kitchen table.

Since seeing a doctor and getting on medication to help with her bipolar symptoms, her mother had really turned her life around. It was incredible to see.

"Here you go," her mother said, sliding a sweaty tumbler in front of her. "I had some Margarita mix in the fridge. It's my summertime treat. Damn this humidity."

"Thanks, Mom," she said, cupping her hands around the cool, wet glass.

She explained the fights she and John had been having, the baby talk, and John's reasons for not wanting to try.

"He's got as much at stake as you," her mom said.

"What?"

"Oh, don't be like that, Sarah. He's right about one thing, you're not the only one who hurts when it doesn't happen."

Sarah simmered within. She didn't come to hear her mother take John's side.

"Do you know if he thinks about it still?"

"No, Mom." Sarah sipped her drink. "I just see him with Pat."

"The boy with the funny hair?"

She nodded. "He'd be such a great father."

Her mother reached over, placing her hand on Sarah's.

"If it's meant to be, it will be. You guys are young yet, you still have plenty of time."

"I know, but—"

"He knows how you feel. He knows what you want."

She was right, damn it.

They had two more drinks before Sarah asked if she could stay the night.

★　★　★

In her old bedroom, she sat upon the bed, the tequila hitting her hard. A poster of Eddie Vedder hung on one wall, Marilyn Manson on another. She was surprised her mother hadn't at least taken down the Manson one.

She leaned back against the pillows and turned on the TV atop the dresser. Chip and Joanna Gaines and their kiddos wandered across their farm, talking about chickens, God, and family. Right about now she'd pray to a chicken god if it got her and John a family.

She had known how John would react. That he'd probably get

upset, but she just wanted them to be a family so bad. She wanted a baby.

The tears slipped free.

Her timing was pretty shitty considering he was already stressed out because of his boss and dealing with his awful dreams. He'd only just started therapy.

And she tried to put this on his plate. Her mother was right. He knew how she felt, and that would have to be enough for now.

As she lay down, Sarah watched the Gaineses and hoped one day she and John might stand a chance at having something similar.

CHAPTER TWENTY-FOUR

John settled for a dark corner at The Tap Room. In all their years together, throughout the challenges they'd faced and conquered, never once had either one left for the night out of anger. Even through her nights of pain or irritation with him, or stupid budget night squabbles, they got over themselves and came back to the table to hash things out. Always. His biggest fight had been when he wanted to buy a 2015 Dodge Challenger. He came in with his own plan, having money for a down payment well underway in his savings account, but her stepsister Morgan's wedding in Ireland had been coming up and she had the trip all planned out. In the end, after a few drinks, he saw that his dream car wasn't exactly a priority. They had a great weekend at Morgan's wedding and there was no way he ever thought seeing Ireland would be as incredible as it had been. She was right.

Sarah was always right.

Well, not this time.

He sat in the corner stewing in his rage as one drink led to the next.

His mind was sloughing through the landmines he wanted to see explode into brilliant starlight behind his eyes, when someone slid in beside him.

"Hey, John," she said.

"Kaitlyn?"

"What are you doing out?" she asked.

Dropping his gaze to the empty glass spinning in his hands, he thought about telling her he just wanted a drink, but when he opened his mouth, his emotions spilled his guts.

"Sarah and I had a fight," he said with a sigh.

Reaching around the glass, she placed her hand on his.

"Are you all right?"

He turned his head and found her deep brown eyes taking him in.

His face was already flush from the alcohol, but he felt himself burn a few shades brighter under her gaze.

"A few more of these and I will be," he said, raising his glass.

They stared at one another.

His throat suddenly dry, he chugged down the beer.

He knew he should pay his tab and head the hell out now. The way Kaitlyn looked at him was dangerous, plus she looked amazing in her way-too-tight t-shirt and her curls framing her gorgeous face.

"What are you all dolled up for?" he asked.

She pouted out her bottom lip.

"I got stood up."

"I'm sorry," he said.

"So was I until I spotted you."

Their gazes locked a second too long.

"I have to go to the ladies' room. Do me a favor, order me a Jack and Coke?"

"Sure," he said.

She got up, dressed in a plaid skirt and tall boots.

He finished his drink as the waitress stopped.

"Get ya another?"

He should say no, get up, and go home.

But instead he ordered Kaitlyn's drink and another beer.

Just one drink, he told himself. *Don't be rude just because you can't handle hanging out with an attractive woman who isn't your wife. She's had a shitty night, too, plus you do owe her.*

Their drinks arrived just as she came back and squeezed in next to him.

"Thanks," she said. She brought the straw to her shiny lips and gazed at him as she sipped from it.

"I owed you, so I guess we're even."

"Oh, come on," she said, placing a hand on his forearm. "The drink's a nice start, but do you know how crazy some of your case families are? Do you?"

He laughed.

"Yeah," she said. "Maybe a couple more of these bad boys and we'll be close."

The little devil on his shoulder was tap dancing. By the time he finished his beer, he didn't see the harm in having a few more.

*　　*　　*

It was almost two hours and way too many drinks later when she got them an Uber.

John's brain felt like it was hanging upside down, swimming in booze. When the car began to move, he felt Kaitlyn's hand on his thigh.

He wasn't thinking clearly when she brushed against his crotch.

Voices battled to be heard inside his head as the car pulled up to a little one-story home and let them out before driving away.

John mumbled about walking home even though he didn't know what street they were on or which direction he would go.

"I need to sober you up. Come on," she said, hooking his arm in hers and walking him to the door. "I can't let you go home in this shape. You could get in big..." she leaned into his ear and whispered, "...trouble."

As soon as they were inside, she slammed him against the door, pressed herself against his chest, and kissed him, slipping her tongue into his mouth. Part of him was trying to think about directions and walking home drunk, the other part was a dumb teenager again and fell under her spell.

She pulled him beyond the entryway, past the living room and down the hall. Pushing him into her bedroom.

"This is a onetime offer, John," Kaitlyn whispered, her hand undoing his jeans. "I know you're married. I don't care what brought you here, but I've wanted to do this for so long."

"I know," he slurred. "but...."

"Shhh," she whispered in his ear, licking his earlobe before dropping down and pulling him free from his boxers. "I see part of you is happy to be here with me."

She put him in her mouth, and he felt too discombobulated to react.

As she went to work on him, he gave in and let go. All the stress of the past few weeks was suddenly gone.

*　　*　　*

When he woke up the next morning, the sun shining directly in his eyes, he was met with a splitting headache. It wasn't until he reached for his cell phone on his nightstand that he realized he was in the wrong fucking place.

Oh shit.

Kaitlyn lay naked beside him, her long brown curls spilled across the pillow.

Stupid shit. You stupid, dumb ass, drunk, fucking asshole.

He slid his feet to the floor and stuck his pounding head in his hands.

He'd never cheated on anyone before. Yet here he was, his clothes scattered at the bedside, shrouded in a wave of guilt and shame.

All because Sarah wanted to try for a baby.

The thought crushed him.

★   ★   ★

Kaitlyn apologized with a devil's grin, but whatever her part in the deed had been, he was the one who didn't go home when he should have the first, second, or third time. This one was on him.

He walked back downtown to fetch his car from The Tap Room, the angry morning sun burning hot as hell and working his hangover like Clubber Lang to a soul-broken Rocky Balboa in *Rocky III*. John had no idea what to do now.

He was contemplating whether to hide his mistake, though he was certain the guilt would eat him alive, or come clean and take his punishment, whatever Sarah deemed that to be, when he spotted the green Dodge van. It was parked on Water Street.

It was the last thing he wanted to deal with right now, but his feet were already carrying him toward the mystery machine.

This was the vehicle harassing Pat. John could take the oddness of seeing the van everywhere, but the thought of it doing the same thing to Pat, well, he wouldn't stand for it.

As he closed in, he could see there was no one in the front. He glanced around to see who was near him. He didn't want to look like some kind of a car thief, so he acted like he was giving it a look over. A Dodge fan admiring an antique.

An elderly couple passed him on his right; he nodded, and

continued with his appraisal of the vehicle. When he finally made his way around to the back, half expecting someone to jump out and clobber him like this truly was some kind of horror movie come to life, he saw the license plate.

MIBOYZ

Something clanged behind the back doors.

His heart raced as he stepped back and waited to see who or what was going to come out.

Everything around him – the disheveled man with nasty dreads and tattered clothing, the pigeons walking their mad two-step across the street pecking at scraps from a discarded bag of Lays, the cars in the distance rolling along with various tunes cranking out through rolled-down windows – seemed to suddenly slow and move like something out of *The Matrix*. His focus honed in on the dark windows of the back doors. He swallowed hard, John waited for the monster to show its face.

The sudden blare of a horn caused him to cry out.

"Get the hell out of the road, you stupid asshole," a man in an American flag bandana barked and shook his fist from a Ford F-150.

John hadn't realized he'd retreated so far.

Turning away from the truck and its spirited driver, he stepped on the sidewalk and tried to get a hold of himself.

He was getting in his own head.

His nerves were just beginning to settle when the person watching him from down the road beside the Magic Card and Gaming shop waved.

Tall, lanky limbs, bony shoulders, and a face he couldn't make out. He knew who he was looking at – August.

Im-fucking-possible.

A chill raked its icy claws down his spine.

Moving without thinking, John walked toward the dream kid.

August hurried down the street away from him.

John ran, headache and hangover be damned.

August glanced back once, his face still a warped slate John couldn't force into focus, then disappeared down the old stairwell next to the Christian bookstore.

John pushed on, his stomach now elbowing him.

He ignored the nausea and ran faster. He turned the corner and watched the shape disappear from the little stairwell.

"John." Beau Connors, owner of the bookstore and former Spears Corner gym teacher, stepped out the door and tried to engage him in one of his pointless conversations. Beau had given him the creeps since John was a teen. He assumed the guy was a pedophile even though he'd never heard anything of the sort anywhere else. Sometimes your instincts just kept you away from certain situations.

He chose not to acknowledge Beau as he hurried past him and down the stairs that led to the back parking lot.

When he ran out the opening, he had to shield his eyes from the blazing sun, squinting to see where August had fled.

He was gone.

He was never here, his mind scolded him.

Last night's booze finally caught up to him. His stomach flipped.

As he yucked his guts up mere feet from the little passageway, all of John's shame came crumbling down upon him.

Beau Connors was down the steps and at his side like a horny schoolboy with a chance at scoring with the first girl that showed any interest.

"Are you okay, John?"

He wished this guy would stop using his name like they were best fucking friends.

John waved him off.

"Rough night," he said. "But I'll survive."

"You should come by the church sometime…."

John was up and hurrying back up the steps before Beau could lay into him about Christ and all that jazz.

"Sorry, Mr. Connors," he said. "I gotta get back home."

His car was actually in the back parking lot just a little ways to The Tap Room, but he had to see if he could catch August going back to the van.

As he stumbled out onto Water Street, he saw that the van was gone.

"Fuck," he said.

He looked back and saw Beau coming up the steps.

That was enough to spur him forward. It would be quicker to go back down the tunnel, but he wanted nothing to do with Beau.

John walked his tired, confused, and shameful ass down the street the long way back to his car.

*   *   *

When he arrived home, he shuffled inside and fell face first onto the sofa. He let the mental and physical exhaustion take him away.

Unfortunately, it brought him back to his dreams and back to Graveyard Land.

CHAPTER TWENTY-FIVE

"Johnny," One Eye said. "You really shouldn't have done that."

Johnny stood behind a familiar white farmhouse. The window to the back door had a brick-sized hole in it.

"If August finds out, he's gonna...well, he's gonna pick your grave for you and put you in it sooner than later."

Johnny turned around and saw the fog holding the trees and gravestones in its loving embrace. Part of him knew somehow that he and One Eye were not in a safe place. This was out of bounds, being near this house. He gazed ahead at the hole in the window. And not only had he trespassed and broken the laws of Graveyard Land, he'd apparently launched a strike at the house. He didn't know why he thought of it as such, but the thought came as clear as day.

"We have to go," One Eye said, grasping Johnny's shoulder.

"Yeah," Johnny said. "Let's...let's get the hell out of here."

Johnny was about to run when movement in one of the other windows of the house stole his attention.

"Johnny, come on," One Eye whined.

"Wait."

He knew they should move now, before....

Before what?

Before *it* saw them.

The Ghoul.

The shadowy shape in the window grew. A hand grasped the ugly yellow curtain and began to pull it aside.

"Johnny!"

His heart was in his throat. Johnny's curiosity and naïve bravery faltered, collapsing into a pile of dying maggots. Johnny no longer wanted to see the monster of Graveyard Land.

"Run!" Johnny shouted.

The boys hurried through the small thicket of trees that separated the farmhouse from the rest of Graveyard Land and didn't look back.

When they reached the first set of graves, One Eye pulled Johnny down.

His head thumped against the ground. Stars spun to life and whizzed in and out of his vision before settling back where they belonged.

He groaned.

"Shhh," One Eye hushed him.

Squinting to get his knocked noggin back on track and see what One Eye was so upset about, Johnny had to clamp his hands over his mouth to keep a gasp from escaping.

August loomed like a shadow, a burning candle in his good hand. He was looking for them. Did he know it was Johnny and One Eye or was he tipped off by the Ghoul that someone was off the reservation, trespassing on the sacred grounds?

A million questions spun like tiny tornados in Johnny's head.

Was August the Ghoul's watchdog? His Renfield? Would he turn on them? How did he know they were out here? Was August one of them...or something else?

He wanted to bombard One Eye with his queries, but he didn't dare to breathe let alone speak.

After a few more seconds, August continued away from them, toward the farmhouse.

They watched until his dim light disappeared beyond the trees.

"That was way too close," One Eye said.

"Where's he going? Won't the Ghoul think he's the one that broke the window?"

One Eye dropped his chin and shook his head.

"What's the deal?" Johnny asked.

When One Eye's blue orb found him, Johnny saw the fear devour the kid's gaze.

"I can't...I can't say anything. I...."

"What is it?"

The boy shook his head and got to his feet.

"Maybe another time—" One Eye searched the trees for August. "Not here. Not now. We need to go." He looked at Johnny. "August isn't going to be happy. He's...."

"What?" Johnny asked. "What are you not telling me?"

But One Eye fled.

Johnny gazed back toward the farmhouse.

It was all something to do with the Ghoul and that farmhouse. Whatever the motivations and reasons here in Graveyard Land, the answers were in that house.

Johnny had begun to follow One Eye when a branch from one of the trees scraped across his neck.

A cool wetness seeped from the wound.

Dropping to his knees and reaching for his throat, Johnny saw the name on the grave in front of him.

Sarah...Sarah Colby.

Sarah?

He raised his hands and saw the inky blackness covering them. Steam rose into the cooling night air. The fog crept around him as he realized his palms were covered in blood. *His* blood.

Johnny stared at Sarah's name chiseled in stone here of all places in Graveyard Land and collapsed into the empty grave before him.

PART THREE
DISARM
CHAPTER TWENTY-SIX

Helping Fuller was a start, but Pat had bigger plans. On the notepad by his bed, the name and address of the other cemetery caretaker stared back at him – Alvin Caswell – the man who held the keys to the kingdom, so to speak. Surely, he wouldn't mind letting Pat take one, maybe two of the jobs. Fuller hadn't seemed too keen on Caswell, but as far as Pat knew in this life so far, there was no reward worth its weight without risk.

"Paddy, you wanna play Moana with me?" Ada asked, holding her Moana doll out to him.

"I can't right now, kiddo, I gotta get to work."

She pouted and made those all-too-powerful puppy dog eyes at him.

"Oh no, you don't," he said. "I should be done early today. How about when I get back?"

Ada put her head down. Her shoulders slumped as she hugged Moana, and muttered, "Okay."

"Listen, how about I bring you back a treat?"

She raised her gaze; a slight curl lifted the edge of her little mouth. "A candy bar?"

"Sure," he said. "You want a Nestle Crunch or peanut butter cups?"

"Both."

"Ha," he laughed. "We'll see. I'll definitely get you one of them. Then I'll be Maui and we'll get that heart of Te Fiti. Deal?"

She nodded, grinning from ear to ear.

He kissed the top of her head and passed his mom at the door.

"Where are you off to now?" she asked.

"I'm going out to see Mr. Caswell. He's in charge of a bunch of the cemeteries in town."

His mother crossed her arms. "*Alvin* Caswell?" she said.

"Yeah, why? Do you know him?"

"I don't *know* him, but...."

"But what?"

He didn't like the seriousness on her face.

"He's like the town's creep."

"So?" Pat said. "You can't judge people by the rumors you hear. Especially here. Everyone has something bad to say about just about everybody, even their friends."

It was true, Spears Corner was a shiny, happy, American flag-flying town on the outside. Pot luck dinners at the local churches every weekend, yard sales by the dozens, and as much school pride as any of the football-loving Texas towns of the South, but beneath it all was an oozing river of deceit, jealousy, and outright hatred between the haves and the have-nots. Hell, even some of the have-nots would stab each other in the back over who the other voted for in the elections. Pat may have been young, but he'd always paid attention. When you're the acting parent in your household, you haven't got a choice. His mom was a whole new person now, for which he had John to thank. God, it was amazing to be able to look to her for comfort and advice, but old habits die hard. The get up and go he accrued in those lean and mean days gone by gifted him with a sense of awareness most teens would run from let alone cherish.

"I don't want you going in that house," she said. The tone was not to be fucked with and her message came across loud and clear.

"I won't, Mom. I just want to see if he's willing to let me do one of the cemeteries. If he acts like a weirdo, I'll tell him I've gotta go and head straight home, okay?"

"Maybe you should bring Danny with you."

He put a hand on her shoulder. "Mom, I've got this, okay? If I get a stranger danger vibe, I'll bolt. Promise."

"I still think you should bring a friend."

He kissed her cheek and opened the front door.

"I'll be fine. Love ya."

★   ★   ★

He rode up to the edge of Fairbanks Cemetery and stopped next to a dented gray mailbox.

Caswe__

It was missing the Ls.

He stared up the dusty, pockmarked driveway. The hammer in his chest began to thrum. He could easily see this being the beginning to a movie on Shudder.

A rusty metal screech called out on cue, sapping a few ounces from his courage.

Jesus, Mom, thanks for getting me freaked the hell out.

He swallowed the tentacles of fear stretching up from his insides as best he could.

He's just a man who takes care of graveyards.

A ghoul.

No, he's a man.

Pat gritted his teeth and shoved off, pedaling up the driveway, doing his best to focus on the bumps and not on the voice in his head telling him to head back the way he came.

The beat-up little farmhouse came into view. Beside the sagging front porch, he saw the swing with the rusty hinges swaying in the gentle breeze coming off the field to the right of the home. The tattered canvas top flapped along to the cringe-inducing springs. A milk crate, faded to an almost pale-peach color, sat beside the swing. A can of Coors Light rested on top. Pat noticed the beads of condensation on the aluminum can as he approached the place. Alvin Caswell had been out here not too long ago.

Was he watching from someplace out of sight?

Pat glanced from window to window expecting to see the ghoul studying him from behind a curtain. Each of the four windows on this side of the house was empty.

No ghouls, no ghosts, no creepy perverts.

"Help you with somethin'?"

The voice startled him, and he felt like a little kid barked at by an adult for doing something out of line.

"Sorry," Pat said. "I was looking for Mr. Caswell."

The man pulled a blue bandana from his back pocket and wiped it across his greasy-looking mustache. "That'd be me. What can I do for ya?"

Pat didn't like the way the guy was looking at him. There was curiosity in the gaze from his beady eyes, but it was simmering with something else. Something darker.

He swallowed hard.

"I have a…a landscaping business. Um, and I…well, I talked with Mr. Fuller – do you know him?"

The man grinned. The look made Pat's skin prickle with goose bumps.

Alvin Caswell nodded and spat a glob of mucus to the dirt before bringing the rag back to his lips. "Yeah, I know him. What's this to do with me?"

Shit. Fuck this. There is something off about this guy. I told Mom I'd bust ass home if something didn't feel right.

"Well, uh," Caswell said, "you come up to my house to tell me somethin'? Or you just come up to see what the old fool on the hill was hidin' up here?"

"I, uh, um…."

The man began to cackle as he made his way to the swing. As he eased down to the worn canvas, Pat was certain the old fabric would give way and drop the man to the ground. It held.

"I was told you took care of the cemeteries around town."

The man's eyes seemed to shrink in his skull. The mustache wiggled as his lip twitched.

"Mm, hmm. I tend to most of 'em. I assume you knew that since you mentioned Fuller." His brows knit together above his pig-like nose. "Did he send you here?"

"No, sir," Pat said. "Like I was saying, I have a small landscaping business of my own, sort of, and I was, uh…wondering—"

The swing let out a drawn-out screech that dug invisible nails up the walls of Pat's stomach.

A grin slithered upon Caswell's face.

"Well, sir," Pat continued, trying not to sound as fucking scared as he was. "Mr. Fuller is letting me take one of his cemeteries." Pat hadn't made an official deal with Fuller yet, but he didn't need to let

Caswell know that. "And well, I was hoping you might consider—"

"Nope."

The words came out like a lightning strike – quick and unmistakable. The ugly smile evaporated.

"I'm sorry," Pat said. "I know that you have most of them, like, a dozen or so—"

"Run along, little boy," Mr. Caswell said.

"Surely, you could use a helper—"

"You deaf *and* fucking dumb, boy?"

Caswell's brow fell above his eyes like an iron beam set to crush Pat and introduce him to real pain.

Pat's mouth went dry; his bladder suddenly weighed as much as a bowling ball.

"Sorry for disturbing you, sir."

"You're goddamn right, boy," the man spat. "Tryin' to screw with my livelihood. Who in the Sam Hill you think you are? Coming up here with that faggot haircut and…wait a minute. You looking at something you like, queer boy?"

Pat gave the indignant man a weak apologetic wave goodbye. Hurrying, he grabbed his bike and hopped on, shoving off without looking back. He felt like someone who'd walked into a bear's cave expecting to skip past its hibernating body only to watch it suddenly rise hungry and raging.

He was pedaling down the gnarly driveway too fast as the man barked something about telling Mr. Fuller to fuck off when his front tire hit a divot in the road and sent his handlebars cockeyed, launching Pat face first to the road.

Pain shot through his cheek and his wrist, but there was no way in hell he was lying here to lick his wounds. Flinching at the hurt in his wrist and face, Pat picked his bike up, glancing back to make sure Caswell wasn't coming (out of his cave) to devour him or finish him off. He wasn't. But the creak and squeal of the swing's hinges called out a rhythmic threat.

He had to smack his handlebars to straighten them back out, something he'd have to tighten later. Limp wristed, sore, and scared as hell, Pat rode his bike to the road and pedaled like each one of his nightmares was real and coming for him.

John's house was on his way home. Pat didn't want his mom to see him like this. He was sure he looked like someone who'd caught a beating. She'd say she'd told him not to go to Caswell's and probably suspect the man had done this to him.

No, he didn't need that.

He headed to John's. He just hoped that his friend was home.

CHAPTER TWENTY-SEVEN

John's car sat alone in the driveway. Pat rolled onto the lawn, ditched his bike in the dooryard and walked straight to the front steps. He knocked on the door and waited. There was a bloody abrasion over the back of his right wrist. He studied it to see if it was swollen or not. It was sore, but he didn't think it was broken.

When no one came to the door, he knocked again. Harder this time.

He heard a thump come from behind the barrier and heard the creak of the floorboards as someone approached.

A few seconds later, John's sleepy face appeared.

"Pat, what the hell happened to you?"

"Can I come in?" Pat asked.

"Of course." John moved aside and gestured for him to enter. "Jesus, man," he said as he closed the door.

Pat paced by the sofa.

"You gonna tell me what the fuck happened or what?"

What had happened? He'd gone to see a creepy guy about a graveyard job, freaked the hell out and then dumped it on his bike like an idiot.

Tears leaked from his eyes.

"Hey, sit down," John said.

Pat did.

"Now, are you okay?"

Pat nodded, wiping his cheeks with the bottom of his shirt. "Yeah," he said. "I just…. I dumped my bike."

"Your wrist is bleeding, and it looks like your shoulder is too."

Pat looked down and saw that John was right. There was a dark wet splotch where the pain pulsed beneath the white fabric. He fingered the collar of his t-shirt and tugged the material back to look at the wound. A glistening sheen of blood covered the ugly scrape.

"Come on," John said, getting to his feet and gesturing toward the hall. "Let's get you cleaned up."

Pat followed John down the short hallway and into the bathroom.

In the mirror, Pat saw a battered kid who would definitely freak his mother out. The right side of his eye was scorched dark red, a patch of scraped flesh exposed and raw.

John handed him a washcloth and a bar of Dial soap.

"Clean the dirt out as best you can. I'll go grab a cold pack for your face…or shoulder, whichever you want to put it on."

"Thanks," Pat said, wincing as he tended to the scuff on his face.

A minute later, John returned. "Here," he said, handing Pat the cold pack.

Pat pressed it against the right side of his eye.

"Take that shirt off. I'll patch that shoulder up first."

Pat did as he asked.

"So," John said as he pressed a warm washcloth to the shoulder wound, "let's hear it."

"I went to Alvin Caswell's place," Pat said. "I went to see if he'd be willing to part with one of the cemeteries he takes care of and—"

John stopped and looked at him. "He did this to you?"

"No, I dumped my bike, like I said, but I was rushing down his driveway and hit a divot or something."

"You'd tell me if something happened, right?"

"Of course," Pat said.

John went back to the wound.

"So, my mom, well, she got me all creeped out about this guy."

"Yeah," John said. "I had an uncomfortable moment with him the other day myself."

"You did?"

"Yeah, I was out there, at the cemetery – it's on my running route – and he sort of appeared out of nowhere and started talking to me. Creepy-ass grin and just weird as hell, if you ask me."

"Yeah," Pat said. "I got that impression, too."

"There's more to your story," John said. "Hold this on here." He handed Pat a piece of gauze to put on his shoulder. "What else happened?"

"I don't know," Pat said. "He was just talking to me one minute, then I asked about helping take one of the graveyards off his hands and he just changed. He got super pissed and acted, I don't know, like some kind of monster. I mean, that's what it felt like."

"Move your hand," John said. Pat did and John placed a couple strips of medical tape to hold the gauze in place. He handed Pat a clean t-shirt. "You can borrow this. I figure the less blood your mom sees the better. Let's get a look at that wrist. Can you bend it, like this?" John made a fist and gesticulated up and down.

Pat copied the move. "Hurts a little," he said.

John took the wrist in his hands and applied slight pressure in a few different spots.

"Not bad," Pat said.

"Good," John said. "It's not broken and I think you're going to be okay." With that, he dabbed at the marked flesh with the washcloth and grabbed some Band-Aids from one of the drawers under the bathroom counter. "Something's not right about that Caswell guy. I'd stay away from him."

"Yeah, I think I've had my fill of him."

"There, almost good as new," John said.

"Thanks. Say, um, where's Sarah?"

John's gaze fell to the floor. Tight-lipped, he leaned back against the bathroom sink and sighed.

"Sorry," Pat said. "I didn't mean to pry."

"No, it's...."

"Really, Johnny, you don't have to say anything."

Pat had never seen John and Sarah upset with each other. The very concept seemed alien to him.

"I...." The pain was clear on John's face. "I fucked up. Major."

Pat didn't know what to think.

"I don't—" Pat began, but John interrupted.

"I got drunk last night. Sarah was upset and left and went to her mom's, and I went out, got wasted and...." He pounded his fist on the counter. Pat saw the tears fill his eyes. Shaking his head, John dropped a bomb. "I got drunk and let someone I shouldn't take me home."

Pat was pretty mature for a fifteen-year-old, but he was still only fifteen. After watching his mother go through all that she'd gone through, he was exposed to more than the average teen, but this – infidelity – was over his head.

"Shit, man," Pat managed.

"Yeah. I don't know what to do about it. And fuck, Pat, I shouldn't be burdening you with this. It's not something for you to have to deal with."

"John, dude," Pat said. "After all you've done for me, don't even think twice, man. You're not perfect. So what?" Pat bit his lip. John looked guilt-ridden.

"I…" John began.

Pat went to him and put an arm around the man. He didn't know all that much about John's life outside of their personal dynamic. Did he have friends? People outside of his wife to confide in? Co-workers? Maybe not.

Pat wasn't about to let him go through this alone. Whatever it was.

"I've never been that guy," John said. "Even when I've had opportunities, it just never crossed my mind. And all this because Sarah wants a baby."

"I thought you said you guys decided not to have kids, didn't you?" Pat said.

"Yeah, well, somewhere between *decided* and *can't* seems to be where the problems come in."

"Oh," Pat said. He'd never been privy to that part of the conversation. "Couldn't you guys, like, adopt? I mean if you wanted to have kids."

"That's the thing, we had wanted to have our own, tried, tried again, and again, and it just breaks her heart every time. I think we talked about possibly adopting once, but it didn't sink in and kind of slipped off the table. That's when we decided to stop trying and decided we're good just the two of us. But I know deep down, she still holds out hope that we can make it happen. I just don't want to see the disappointment and heartbreak anymore." John got up and grabbed a beer from the fridge. "And now I've delivered something worse."

"Do you have to tell her?" Pat asked, walking out to the kitchen. "You're not going to see this girl again, right?"

John shook his head. "That could be a problem – it's someone I work with. But I don't know if I can keep something like this from

Sarah. Even if I thought I could, I can only imagine what it would do to my dreams."

"Your dreams?"

He swigged half the beer and nodded. "Yeah, my shrink tells me guilt sometimes manifests itself in your dreams. And mine have been weird before this."

Pat thought of his own creepy dream the other night. He couldn't remember it, but knew it was something to do with the van he'd seen around town.

"I've been having these recurring dreams," John said. "I'm a kid, a little younger than you, and I'm in these graveyards that never seem to end. There are two other kids my age, I guess, well, there are more kids but they never say anything. It's just me, One Eye and August."

"You remember their names?"

"Yeah, Sarah thought that was something, too," John continued. "There's things...." He started looking around. "Hold on, I've been writing them down."

Pat waited and John returned with the black notebook.

He looked like a mad scientist skimming through the pages.

"Sarah had a book that says the thing with their eyes...One Eye having one eye and August not having any, that maybe there's something I'm trying not to see. Something I blocked out or...." He suddenly looked lost in thought.

"What is it?" Pat asked.

"I just remembered something that Alvin Caswell said to me in the graveyard. He told me a kid from the neighborhood was kidnapped and murdered and that his mother committed suicide shortly after."

Pat pictured Caswell's gross grin upon his face as he spoke of such a tragedy.

"The kid was a friend of mine, well, sort of. He'd only been in Spears Corner for a few months or something. We weren't best friends, but I don't remember when he left and I certainly don't recall him getting murdered."

"Huh, you'd think something like that would stick with you," Pat added.

John's cell phone rang.

He picked it up from the counter.

"It's Sarah," he said. "I've got to take this."

"Yeah, yeah," Pat said. "I gotta get home anyway."

"And Pat," John said.

"Yeah?"

"Just tell your mom what happened. It's better than coming up with a lie."

"I'd tell you the same," Pat said, "but I'm not sure that'd be true. Good luck, Johnny."

"I told you not to call me that," he said.

Pat grinned and made his way out the door.

★　　★　　★

On his way home, Pat couldn't stop thinking about what other creepy things must go through Caswell's head. Talking to a stranger in a graveyard of all places about murders, suicides, and kidnappings, it probably got the weirdo off. He should probably consider himself lucky that he didn't get attacked today and dragged down to the guy's basement.

He shuddered at the thought.

And how come he'd never heard of this local murder? How did John not remember? It had been someone he knew. Being the true crime junkie he was, Pat's need to know more took precedence.

Suddenly he was in no rush to get home and explain his injuries to his mom. Instead he headed downtown. If there was a place that would shed light on this local crime, it would be the Spears Corner Public Library.

CHAPTER TWENTY-EIGHT

Anne Davis, the main librarian, met him at the counter.

"Hi, Patrick," she said.

He was a regular here and all the librarians knew him by name. He loved the smell of old books and dust. The dust sometimes made him sneeze, but like the quiet here, it was part of the ambiance. He could traverse the aisles running his fingers over the old spines and imagining how many adventures, how many mysteries, how many broken hearts and minds lay in wait. Over the last year and a half, since he'd checked out his first true crime, one on the Manson Family he couldn't remember the name of, he and Ms. Davis had become quite close. She shared his love for the true crime genre and they regularly discussed new books and new podcasts – she loved *My Favorite Murder*, he preferred *Murder Squad*.

"What happened to you?" she asked, her brow scrunching over her blue eyes.

"Dumped it pretty hard on my bike earlier, but I'll be fine," Pat said.

She cocked an eye at him, but if she had any further questions about his appearance, she kept them to herself.

"Well, you boys and your bikes." She paused and held up a finger. "Wait, I just got something in that I think you'll like."

She dipped out of sight beneath the counter and came up with a book called *American Predator*.

"Now, this is one I could not put down," she said. "It's about this guy out of Alaska, Israel Keyes—"

"Ms. Davis."

"Oh, sorry, Patrick, I get carried away. What is it?"

"Maybe I'll take that one on my way out. I actually came to do a little local research."

She slid the book to the side of the register. "Oh? What about?"

"Well," Pat said. "My friend John mentioned something today about a kid that got kidnapped around here...I think he said it was in the nineties."

Ms. Davis leaned back against the shelf behind her, crossing one arm over her stomach and bringing her fist up to her chin. "Hmm," she said. "I know something like that happened when I lived in California, I think."

"Does the library have, like, a section of old newspapers, or one of those micro fitch machines?"

"You mean micro*fiche*," she corrected him. She stepped through the little swing door behind the counter and motioned for him to follow her. "While we don't have one of those, I believe we do have *all* the old *Hanson Union Journals*."

She led him out the door and to a set of stairs he'd never been down. The children's section of the library was to the right and up a separate set of stairs; the section she led him to was normally roped off. He'd always assumed it was a basement for storage of discarded shelves, broken book carts, fans...that sort of thing.

She flicked a light switch, and said, "Be careful."

The scent of dust and mildew filled his nose.

"How old is this library?" he asked, swatting at a cobweb beneath the low, dull yellow lights.

"It was built in eighteen eighty-one, designed by Henry Richards. We've had a number of renovations and additions over the years, but it's a classic, for sure."

When they passed through the murky lighting, the path began to shrink as old paintings and random stacks of books crowded in on them.

"Okay, this is what we're looking for," she said, stopping before a shelf of neatly labeled yellow boxes. "The newspaper was a bit bigger in the nineties, so we have a few boxes for each year. Did your friend happen to mention the year the kidnapping took place? I was in Riverside in, oh, I suppose it would have been ninety-two to late ninety-five. I know it falls in there somewhere."

"I think he said it was in nineteen ninety-four."

"Okay then, that's what we'll grab." She reached for the boxes labeled with that year. After sliding them free of their dust-laden crypts, she handed him two of the boxes, which were a bit heftier than he thought they'd be, and she carried the other two.

"Go on," she said, nodding for him to head back the way they'd come in.

He reached the stairs and glanced over his shoulder.

"Go on up," she said. "We'll take them to the James Spears room. You can use the large oak table in there."

He loved everything about the library except for the James Spears wing. It was stuffy and seemed to him like a sort of ghost room. He never went in if he could help it. While the rest of the library and its wings were welcoming and had a calming effect on him, the James Spears Room intimidated him. The rumors he read of Spears, the founder of the town, and his sketchy past – Native slaves, KKK alliance, murders of blacks, and his downright frightening speeches to justify his actions – it was the man's ghostly presence Pat sensed whenever he neared the room.

"Right over there," Ms. Davis said, as she stepped beside him. Together they walked to the large oak table and set the boxes down.

Jefferson Schulz peeked his head in the doorway. "Anne?"

"Yes?" she said.

"Could I get your help on something? Hi, Patrick," he said.

"Hey, Jefferson," Pat called back.

"Well, it's all yours," Ms. Davis said. "Just come find me when you're finished up."

"Thank you. I will."

Pat stared up at the oil painting of General Spears. He wished he could ask to have it covered while he was in here, but instead dug his earbuds out of his pockets, put on some Joe Strummer and the Mescaleros and started with the box marked 'January'. He slowly rifled through each front page and local section, careful not to rip or tear the fragile pages. He saw something about a massacre in Rwanda, a civil war with millions killed, Nelson Mandela became president of South Africa, and the one that stood out for him, the suicide of Nirvana front man/songwriter Kurt Cobain. His punk rock roots had drawn him to the early nineties phenomenon in sixth grade. He'd listened to each of their albums until he felt them soak into his very being. They were soft when Pat needed them to be, and loud and abrasive when he felt like screaming at the world. They were like the next generation's Beatles. The music they created was timeless.

Scouring past the end of winter and through the spring and the first few weeks of summer, Pat found what he was looking for in August.

Missing Spears Corner Youth Believed to Be Kidnapped.

On early Wednesday morning, August 6th, Edna Wilson of Spears Corner reported her son, Ethan, 14, had yet to return home. The youth went out for a bike ride Tuesday morning and never returned. Spears Corner Police are asking anyone with any knowledge of the child or his whereabouts to call the station....

The headline three days later struck like a bullet to the heart.

Body of Missing Youth Found in Litchfield Pond.

According to the report, the victim, Ethan Ripley, was kidnapped, raped, and murdered prior to being discarded in the body of water.

No clues, no suspects, no answers for the boy's mother or the Spears Corner police.

Pat's stomach curdled at the awfulness.

This was in his hometown.

He thought of the green van and suddenly wished he were at home.

CHAPTER TWENTY-NINE

John was sitting on the front steps when Sarah pulled into the driveway and stepped out of the car. He'd asked her to come home to talk to him when she called earlier, but he didn't tell her what it was about. It wasn't something you told someone over the phone. He exhaled the smoke from his lungs, tossed the butt to the ground, and stamped the coffin nail. Being caught smoking was far from the worst thing he had coming his way. Infidelity felt so foreign. He heard it all the time back in the nineties on *Dr. Phil* or *Sally Jesse Raphael*, but it was daytime drama. The act of the deplorable and the inept. Not a sin good-hearted people who'd pulled through years of bullshit and loneliness committed.

Dr. Soctomah may have enlightened him about the weight of something deep and heavy on his mind, but cheating like a no-good son of a bitch made him sick. He'd never be able to live with the sin. As he met her at the car, he bowed his head and couldn't stop the tears that began to fall.

"What is it?" she asked.

He held a trembling smoke-scented hand to his lips. Ripping the Band-Aid off was the only way he'd escape the monster devouring his insides.

"John, please," she said. "You're scaring me."

"Sarah, I...I need to tell you something and you're going to think I'm a fucking asshole."

Her brow scrunched over her watery eyes.

God, this is going to destroy her.

Don't tell her.

But he had to.

"The other night, I went to The Tap Room. I got drunk."

From the look on her face, and the way she stepped back, he knew she already knew what he was telling her.

"I ran into someone, and I was fucked up...."

"John...John, what did you do?"

"I slept with someone else. I don't even remember doing it...." He realized how lame any shitty excuse sounded. He fell silent and let the poisonous ghost between them settle.

She gazed off to her right, arms crossed over her chest, tight-lipped and simmering.

There was nothing he could say. She deserved better, and *sorry* seemed insulting and pathetic. After a few more seconds, he muttered it anyway.

"Sarah, I'm so sorry."

She turned her hurt gaze upon him, and the daggers pierced his heart.

Sarah shook her head and shoved past him.

He stayed in place, his head slung low, on an island designated for bastards. He could save the world from total annihilation right now and it would mean fuck all.

Sarah burst out the door with her Samsonite suitcase. Tossing it in the backseat, she turned to him.

His world stopped.

"I'll be at my mother's. I need...." Her lip quivered. "I need to think...fuck, John." As she started to cry, he stepped to her, but she held him at bay with her hand.

She took a deep, shuddery breath and got behind the wheel.

"I'll call you when I can...when I can talk."

The engine purred to life. He saw more tears slipping down her cheeks as she backed out of the driveway.

His knees weak, John returned to the steps and clutched the porch rail for support. A life preserver in an ocean of starved swells. A warm wind swept across the humidity clinging to his flesh. It should have offered some relief, but he was too damn numb. He wasn't sure if he would ever move again.

A rustling around the corner of the house roused him from his despair.

The sound of someone or something rummaging around out back. He followed the sounds. A tall figure dressed in black slipped out of sight behind his little garbage shed.

"Hey," he said.

August?

Say it. Call out to him.

You look for me.

"August?"

As John circled the shed, a vehicle zoomed past his driveway. He barely gave it a thought as he approached the shed door. What would he do if August was in there?

Listen to yourself. You sound like a fucking crazy person.

He's a dream. There is no August. August is your fucked-up history.

He pulled the door open and was slammed by the scent of spoiled meat and writhing, gluttonous maggots in a hell of heat and detritus.

John gagged and slammed the door closed.

As he stumbled away, the urge and sudden compulsion to flee overtook him. John's trot turned to a jog, and then to a run. His staycation had gone from a much-needed breath to a crumbling pit of a broken man who thought he'd left behind the feelings of abandonment and self-destruction. Yet, it was all still here within him. Every heartbreak, every scar. Each and every living moment of the scared little boy exiled to fend for himself. Too smart to fall into the trappings of corruption that plagued many of the street kids growing up around him in the disillusioned nineties, he marched through another day toward a tomorrow that was never promised to him. Rather than bury his hurt, confusion, and anger in drugs and alcohol or bad relationships, John clung to a few good friends who wouldn't allow him to get completely lost. He worked and focused on surviving. In his dreams back then, he wanted to get out. A tramp ready to run, ready to explode, but real life's vise grip wasn't so free and easy. One girlfriend's lack of ambition led to another and he eventually became the rat in the cage until he was too tired to try. His friend Greg got him his first social worker job at Safeway Care Givers of Central Maine. And in that job, John found something to care about. Helping others was great, but it was the way it made him feel that soon had him pouring every ounce of energy into this new career. He'd found something self-serving that managed to give back. He discovered his purpose and was happy for the first time since his parents' divorce.

By the time he met Sarah, he was content with staying in Spears Corner.

His legs ached from six straight days of running, including a couple hours earlier today, but he didn't want to stop. He couldn't. Not yet. The sun blazed down upon him as John ran faster, pushing toward danger. He could feel it. He hadn't had enough water to be out here in this heat right now, but he wouldn't stop. He thought of the monks or priests who flogged themselves. This was his penance. The pain and exhaustion paled compared to what he'd done.

I told the truth.

Yeah, how's that treating you?

Honesty above all.

Dumb shit, some things are better left unsaid.

He was closing in on Fairbanks Cemetery, his mouth hanging open, his chest tight, his throat sore, when his vision blurred, and he stumbled. Lightheaded, his stomach quickly turning on him, John dropped to the grassy ditch before the graveyard. Crashing here would keep him out of the road, so he wouldn't get run over.

There were no cars on the road, for which he was grateful. He'd rather die of dehydration and ignorance than have people watch him throw his guts up in a ditch in front of the cemetery. He hoped the dead would forgive him this trespass.

When he fished retching, he turned onto his back and closed his eyes.

He wished he hadn't.

128 • GLENN ROLFE

CHAPTER THIRTY

"Tsk, tsk, Johnny," August said.

As Johnny raised his head, he saw the shape of August's skull eclipse the sun. The effect was disorienting.

"Where are we?" Johnny asked, trying to see August's face more clearly.

"Right where we should be."

He didn't like that answer.

"You've had a pretty rough day, huh, Johnny?"

Johnny couldn't recall it ever being this damn bright in Graveyard Land. There was no fog, no crickets, no other kids....

"It's just you and me, Johnny."

"August," he said, trying to sit up, but not feeling well enough to do so without barfing again (again?).

"Yes?" August said.

"Who lives...who is it that lives in that house...over there?" Johnny managed to raise his finger and point toward the old farmhouse.

"No one you want to know, Johnny, but...."

"But what?"

"We all make our acquaintance with the Ghoul. That's just... inevitable."

One Eye appeared from behind August. "Hey."

When the taller kid stepped aside, the sun pierced Johnny's gaze like a laser.

"Leave him alone, August."

Johnny saw the darkness creep over August's features. There was always something sinister hiding beneath the kid's odd exterior; now it was seeping through like oil spilling out under a midnight moon.

And the coldness was aimed at One Eye.

"Go, Johnny. Get up, get outta here and don't look back!" One Eye shouted.

Johnny tried to move but he was so sore. Every muscle felt weak, his head too heavy, his mind floating in mid-air like when he had the flu the day after Thanksgiving. There was something in One Eye's tone that made Johnny rise to his feet anyway. Plus, the look August was giving the kid was like pure, unadulterated nightmare fuel. The blackness in it was *alive*.

Johnny got the sense that something major had changed here. It was no longer just a creepy esthetic – Graveyard Land's true face was surfacing, and he didn't want to be here when it directed its leer his way.

"Run!" One Eye said.

Before he made a break for it, Johnny glanced once more in August's direction. They were pouring out of him, the spiders. His pets. He stood there still as death while hundreds of pitch-black arachnids scrambled over one another, exiting his vacant eye sockets and his open mouth.

Johnny screamed on the inside, his soul grazing the frozen depths of the presence before him. He hurried away, looking over his shoulder to see if August was following him.

"You can run, Johnny," August said as he spat out the last of the spiders. "But you'll be back when you find out she's—"

"Run, Johnny," One Eye cried out again.

Find out she's....

Johnny stopped and turned as One Eye tried to tackle August.

What had he been about to say?

August side-stepped his much shorter attacker and shoved him to the ground.

One Eye screamed as August's spiders moved in a solid wave toward him.

Johnny knew he should go back and help his friend, but he was paralyzed. The grotesque, arachnid smile crawled onto August's face.

"Run, Johnny," August said, his smile falling like a nuclear winter. "Run."

★   ★   ★

John opened his eyes, dazed and blinded by the white-hot sun.

"Sarah…" he muttered, his voice cracked and desiccated.

"Help you up?" the voice said as a shadow eclipsed the daylight.

Wincing, John saw the shape before him.

"Looks like ya passed out. Heat stroke, I reckon. Runnin' in this kind of heat ain't the smartest thing to be doin'. Here," the voice said.

John took the man's hand and let him pull him back to a sitting position. His head swam in the fluid nightmares resonating, clutching for survival in John's reality.

"Upsy-daisy," Caswell said, helping him to his feet.

The odd man's familiar leer was gone, at least for the moment, replaced by a look of genuine concern.

"Thanks," John said. The numbness in his limbs slowly faded as the feeling in them returned to normal.

"Sure, sure," Caswell said, producing the bandana from his back pocket and wiping the sweat from his forehead. "You okay? Not every day I find a live one lying around here."

"Yeah," John said. "I guess I just pushed myself a little too hard."

The man eyed him for a moment.

Something was in his eye, a sort of putrid twinkle.

"Why don't you come on up to the house for a minute, get you a glass of water?"

"Oh, I don't know.... I think—"

Caswell began to walk, gesturing for John to follow. "Nonsense. You need some fluids 'fore ya end up back on your ass. C'mon."

The thought of Pat's experience earlier with this man rushed in. Pat had said Caswell seemed okay at first before flipping his lid and shouting like a madman. Still, he could use some water. He didn't want to end up in the hospital because he was....

What? Afraid?

John reminded himself that he didn't need to go into the guy's house. He'd just wait out front, maybe scope the guy out.

He fell in line behind Caswell and followed him up the dirt driveway.

The farmhouse was a beaten and weathered two-story structure. While the yard was unkempt, it wasn't the nightmare he'd seen in some of the properties around town with their lawns being swallowed up by what could also pass as a junkyard. This place had an order to it. A little schlubby but each thing in its place.

"You can come in if you'd like," Caswell said when he reached the porch steps.

"That's okay. I wouldn't want to impose any more than I already am."

The man gazed back over his shoulder and licked his lips before delivering one of his uncomfortable grins. "Suit yourself."

As soon as Caswell was inside, John glanced around. He saw the swing, half broken but functioning, as Pat had mentioned. An upside-down milk crate held two beer cans. To the right of the house he saw an empty steel clothesline like the one his mom used to have in the backyard of their trailer. He stepped toward the area and saw two push mowers and a wheelbarrow side by side by side, with a selection of shovels and a long-handled axe lined up next to them. Beyond the far edge of the house stood the corrugated metal shed he'd seen from the cemetery. The door stood out like a clown's greasepaint face in a pool of blood. While the rusted shed looked nearly as old as the house, the door looked brand new. The sun glinted off a large padlock guaranteed to keep out any possible thieves.

"I got ya water."

Caswell's voice startled him. John realized he'd ventured nearly to the shed.

"Thanks," John called back, trying to sound far more casual than he felt. He turned, his gaze taking a quick swipe to the other side of the house, and he froze in place.

The vehicle parked behind a garage he hadn't noticed had nearly run him down in his nightmares. The same one that he and Pat had seen around town...the green Dodge van.

"She's vintage," Caswell said.

John started again as Caswell handed him the glass of water.

"It's a 1976 Dodge Street Van. I wish I could get her to run, but I never been much of a mechanic."

John eyed the flattened grass behind the vehicle. Two perfect tire tracks leading right to the van's tires. He saw the license plate.

MIBOYZ

He tried to keep the tremors in his hands still as he held the perspiring glass.

"She's a hand-me-down from my cousin. Hasn't started in over a decade now. I got myself a newer Econoline 'round the other side for work. But she's the real gem 'round here."

John took a few gulps of water. It had a tinny taste, but not poisonous, so far as he could tell. Caswell was lying to him. He thought of Pat's story about how quickly the man shifted from calm and creepy to downright frightening. Unnerved as he was, and smart move or not, John decided to prod the man. "Say, you take care of the cemeteries around town, right?"

"Mmm hmm," he said, "Best co-workers in the world. They don't complain or bitch." The man broke out into a high-pitched cackle at his bad joke.

John gave a half-hearted laugh and finished his drink. He couldn't stop stealing glances at the old Dodge.

"I have a friend, a kid from town that's starting up his own lawn care service. I know he was talking to me about the graveyards here."

Caswell's face dropped slightly. The prideful smile in his eyes darkened.

John pushed on. "Well, I'd kick myself if I didn't ask someone as in the know as yourself, how would he go about getting in on the graveyard game around Spears Corner?"

"He a tall, good-lookin' kid that dresses a little funny?"

"Yeah, he's got sort of a punk rock look to him, but he's really a great kid."

"He was actually up here this mornin'. Asked if I'd let him do one of my jobs."

"Oh?" John said, playing it like he wasn't already privy to their interaction. "What did you tell him? I know he's really serious about this."

"I told him I didn't have anything for him. He seemed nice and all, but I just couldn't stand to part with any of my work." A forced smile appeared. It looked as real on Caswell's mug as the ones you see in kids' school portraits, especially the kids who you know don't have any friends and aren't used to having things to smile about.

"Oh, well, I know he'll keep trying. He's a go-getter."

"I don't think he'll be back."

John was going to ask why not, even though he knew, but Caswell plucked the glass from his hand, and said, "Well, I'm glad to see the water helped ya out. I'd offer you a ride, but I gotta head out of town for a few days. Supposed to leave this mornin' in fact, but I had some unexpected errands to run."

"Oh, that's okay. I think the water did the trick. I really don't live too far."

They started back around to the front of the house. John tried to take one last glimpse of the van.

"Something wrong?"

John looked to Caswell and saw that he was standing next to the axe.

"No, I...I just.... I should get going before my wife wonders where I disappeared to."

"I don't think she's looking for you," Caswell said.

John suddenly found it hard to swallow.

"What's that supposed to mean?"

Caswell turned and walked away.

What the fuck is with this guy?

When John reached the driveway, Caswell stood behind his screen door, partly obscured by the shadows within.

John gave him a wave.

"Better get runnin' home, Johnny."

The door closed before John could reply.

Movement to the left of the porch, the side that led to the garage (and the van) caught his attention.

John edged in that direction, keeping one eye on the front door of the house and the other trained on the shadow dancing on the side of the garage.

A blue Ford Econoline sat parked in front of the left side of the garage, but it was the shadow on the side of the building that sent chills down his spine. Someone was standing out back, just out of sight, but the person's shadow stood tall and stick thin against the light gray of the garage. John halted when the shadow raised a claw-like hand. He watched as it appeared to go to the person's face. A much smaller shadow floated down beside it and dropped to the ground. The shadow repeated the movements; more shapes fluttered to the ground.

He hardly had time to notice when an army of arachnids rounded the corner, standing out like a swarm of black across the dusty dirt drive.

Spiders. Hundreds of them.

John's guts filled with writhing worms at the sight.
They were coming straight for him, too many to count.
He broke into a run and didn't look back.
Run, Johnny.... Run.
And he did.

CHAPTER THIRTY-ONE

August stepped from the shadows as Alvin Caswell turned to him.

"Let's go get the wife," August said.

Caswell smiled. "About fuckin' time."

They pulled onto the road in the Dodge van and headed right.

August knew Sarah was everything to John. If there was one thing that would get through to him, make him come to Graveyard Land with no choice but to pick his grave and complete the circle, it was the woman he loved. There was a weakness there, like a soft spot atop a baby's head, and it was almost too damn easy to dig your thumbs right in.

The Ghoul wanted Sarah *and* Patrick, the pseudo son, but August suspected he knew the Ghoul's perverse reasons for that. Patrick, though a bit older, was the type the Ghoul loved.

August might be reprimanded, but if John was the ultimate prize, the man's wife was the linchpin, not the boy. And he knew just where to find her.

He instructed Alvin to head toward Route 126.

A few minutes later, the van crept up behind the Subaru, closing the distance in a blink of an eye. She was pulled over in the dirt parking lot of a closed roadside market.

They rolled to a stop behind her. Alvin put the hazard lights on and honked the horn. August ducked behind Caswell, watching her eyes in the rearview mirror.

"Call to her," he whispered to Caswell.

★   ★   ★

Sarah's eyes were scratchy and swollen. The tears wouldn't stop. She wanted more than anything to be angry at John. She had every right to want to set flames to every memory, every lie, every selfish thing he'd ever said or done. This topped them all. But it wasn't all his fault. She had been the one pushing him to do the impossible. She'd given him the cold shoulder because he wanted to protect them from the inevitable crushing disappointment and hurt that would certainly linger for weeks if not months to come when their attempts to make a baby inevitably failed again. If anyone was being selfish and thoughtless, it was her. Or maybe it wasn't. Maybe she was just kicking the shit out of herself because it was easier than just admitting she didn't understand what the hell was going on. The tears welled up as a car horn blatted out, scaring the shit out of her.

She clutched her chest with one hand as her gaze darted to the rearview mirror. A van rolled to a stop, its hazard lights blinking. The driver waved a meaty hand out the window to get her attention.

Sarah's hackles rocketed sky high. She was pulled over in a vacant lot on a quiet road. She was vulnerable to anything.

Keep your head on straight. Act tough but stay ready.

She rolled down her window and stuck her head out. "Is everything all right," she asked.

"Sorry, ma'am," the man said. "She just quit on me. Lucky this lot was here and I could just let her coast off the blacktop there. Say, you wouldn't happen to have a phone I could use to call for a tow would ya? I been meanin' to get me one of those space phones, but, well, I just ain't done it yet."

Something about the man's face unnerved her. Something sour in his beady eyes.

Stop it, she chided herself. *You're being ridiculous. Maybe he really needs help. Just call the tow for him and then you can go.*

"I do have a cell," she called back. "Let me get you taken care of." She pulled her head back in the car and snatched her phone off the passenger seat. She searched tow companies near Spears Corner. Several popped up. Just as she clicked on one for Rollins Towing, a strong hand clenched her wrist, spilling her phone to the floor.

She hardly had time to gasp before something that felt like a cement block slammed her in the face and smashed her into oblivion.

★   ★   ★

August watched as Caswell opened the door and hauled the woman out, slung over his shoulder. He passed the van's open driver's side door and went to the waiting arms of the back-cargo area. August's wicked grin welcomed her.

"Take the car," he ordered Caswell. "Get rid of it somewhere where it won't be found for a few days."

The ugly man nodded and closed the doors.

August bound the woman's wrists and ankles behind her back with duct tape. He wrapped one of Caswell's bandanas around her mouth. She didn't rouse.

Caswell and the Subaru were already gone when August climbed behind the wheel, clicking off the hazards. A large, newer truck pulled up behind him. The driver, a burly looking fellow, stepped out and approached his door.

"Hey, saw ya had your hazards on. Is everything okay?" he asked.

August cranked the engine and dropped it in Drive.

He caught a glimpse of the man noticing that the driver of this vehicle most certainly wasn't okay.

August heard the man mutter, "What the fuck?" just before he sent dirt flying from under the Dodge's tires and darted away.

CHAPTER THIRTY-TWO

John dialed Sarah's cell but got the voicemail, which wasn't a surprise. She never answered her phone while she was driving. Next, he tried Janice, Sarah's mother. With each unanswered ring, his hands trembled more and more while he paced a hole in the floor. He needed to know that she was all right. She could be as pissed at him as she wanted, but he couldn't help but think something bad had happened while he was out.

"I don't think she's looking for you."

"Hello?"

Janice's voice.

"Janice, it's John. Can I talk to Sarah?"

"John? No, she's not here. Last I knew she was heading to see you."

His heart hammered.

"John, is everything all right?"

He pictured Sarah crying as she drove down the street, distraught, emotional, not paying attention as she approached a stoplight, a car – a van – t-boning her car—

"John?"

"Sorry," he said. "We just, we had a bit of an argument—"

I confessed to cheating on your beautiful daughter, who has never done a damn thing to hurt me.

"—and I just wanted to make sure she was okay. Can you please have her call me when she gets there?"

"Of course, John."

"Thank you, Janice."

"You two will get by this," she said. "I know you two love each other. We all have bumps in the road. The best couples always fight for their togetherness. It doesn't come easy. Nothing worthwhile ever does."

"Thanks, Janice. I mean it. I appreciate that."

"I'll make sure to have her call when she comes in."

"Thanks. Goodbye."

He hung up and tried Sarah's cell again.

This time it went straight to voicemail.

John put down the phone and walked out the door, down the steps, and fetched his cigarettes from their hiding space.

The spiders crawled back into his mind.

As much as he wanted to convince himself that the illusion was the result of his dumb ass going out in this heat without drinking an ounce of water, leading to the dehydrated state of delusion, he knew better. After the incident here in his yard he thought of the pale face in the shadows that night, or seeing August or someone who looked like him by the fence outside the breakroom window at work and now this... he was either ready to be committed or...something truly horrifying was going on.

CHAPTER THIRTY-THREE

What Pat uncovered about the kidnapping of Ethan Ripley was far worse than he ever could have imagined. And he had to tell John. Maybe the fact that it was suspected that his friend had been abducted by a notorious serial killer would jar his memory.

He waved to Ms. Davis as he flew out the door. He'd placed the newspapers in a neat pile, but hadn't bothered putting them back in order and in their boxes. He hoped she'd forgive him. Stepping out the library doors and hurrying down the stone steps, Pat scanned the street for the ugly green van. If it was lurking near, it was out of sight. The thought did nothing to ease his anxieties, but looking for the danger was half the battle. His eyes were wide open. He picked his bike up from the bush out behind the building where he always dropped it – no one wanted this ugly BMX, it had seen much better days – and started past the nearby police station and city hall. He wondered if Deborah was working today. Did she know anything about Alvin Caswell or his family? She looked old enough to at least have heard something about the family's dark side.

He'd been at the man's house. Stood in his presence, even pissed him off. And he was still here. Pat counted his lucky stars. Although he had no proof the graveyard caretaker was the one following him and harassing him, deep down, the voice that knew was louder than hell.

Had Alvin known about his cousin Llewellyn? Had he seen anything? Had he helped him in any way?

★   ★   ★

Pedaling for all he was worth, Pat made it to John and Sarah's in record time.

He found John smoking on the porch.

"Back already?" John muttered.

Pat dropped his bike and took the proffered cigarette from John's hand.

"You told her, huh?" Pat said, sparking the smoke to life.

John, shoulders slumped, nodded and hung his head, his gaze trained on the cherry at the end of his cigarette.

"Shit, man. I'm sorry."

John waved him off. "It's my own damn fault."

Pat didn't want to dismiss the man's pain or grief or shame, but if he didn't spill what he'd discovered, he'd probably explode.

"Listen," he said. "I came back because I couldn't stop thinking about the van and about what you said Caswell said to you."

John cocked his head up.

"About the kidnapping?" Pat clarified.

"What about it?"

"Have you ever heard of a serial killer called the Ghoul of Wisconsin?" Pat asked.

"I'm not the cult killer guy you are. I know Bundy, Dahmer, Hannibal the Cannibal, that's my extent on those guys, but I'll bite. Who is he?"

Pat thought John had to know one of those was fictional, but he let it slide. "Okay, so check this out," he said, instantly forgetting that he'd been paranoid as hell on the ride over and feeling the thrill that regularly coursed through his body when he talked true crime. "For, like, six years, this creep kidnapped, raped, and murdered dozens of boys in Wisconsin."

John's head lifted at the word 'kidnap'.

"Right," Pat said. "This guy is every Chester the Molester you ever thought of as a kid. He was liked by neighbors and seen as a fairly successful business guy. I can't remember what he did for work, but I guess he made donations to the local church and library, that kind of shit. Behind the scenes though, he truly lived up to his name. He was a ghoul. When the cops finally came down on him, they discovered more than twenty bodies, almost all young boys between, I don't remember exactly, something like twelve and sixteen. In his confession tape he cried. Not for getting caught or for what he did. He said, 'You can't take me away from my boys.'"

"Jesus," John said. He sparked another smoke.

"Wait, you haven't heard the most insane part yet."

"I don't know, that's all plenty fucked up if you ask me."

"His name was Llewellyn Caswell."

Pat took a drag from his own cigarette while John let that sink in.

"Caswell? Like, what? Is he related to our creepy Caswell?"

Pat nodded. "And that's not all. He's from here. That house Alvin lives in, that's Llewellyn's childhood home."

"What are you saying? Are you saying—"

"Wait," Pat said. "It's never been proven, but it's suspected that the kid you said Caswell mentioned, Ethan Ripley, may have been one of the Ghoul's last victims."

"How? You said he lived in Michigan?"

"Wisconsin," Pat corrected him. "But according to an interview with Caswell in August of 1994, Llewellyn's mother died, and he came home for her funeral."

John sat back. "I need a drink."

"One of the articles I read today said it was very possible. The timeline fits. Llewellyn Caswell, the Ghoul of Wisconsin, was home here in Spears Corner when Ethan Ripley was taken and killed."

"He was here with his cousin."

"It doesn't mention Alvin Caswell in anything I saw, but I think we can assume so."

Never in his wildest dreams had Pat ever thought he might have a chance to be involved in any way whatsoever in a huge true crime event.

No sooner had the smile hit his lips than the thought of the van and one of the Caswells here in this town knowing about him crossed his mind and doused the embers of excitement. This was real. There could be glory if they could somehow prove Caswell did it, but there was also the threat of his cousin targeting them. Llewellyn Caswell burned in the electric chair in the late nineties, but his cousin was here and alive and well.

"Wait, when did you find all this out?" John asked.

"I was just at the library."

"So, you haven't been home yet?"

Shit.

"Didn't you say your mom was worried about you going over to Caswell's?"

"Shit, yes."

"Let me get you home," John said, getting up and walking toward the front door.

"It's okay, Johnny, I can ride."

"Don't call me that. It's John. But too bad. I'm not letting you roll these streets with that guy out there."

"Yeah, okay." Truth be told, Pat was grateful for the lift. He wasn't sure how he was going to sleep tonight knowing the Ghoul of Wisconsin's cousin lived in his hometown and that he'd pissed him off, unintentional or otherwise. Alvin Caswell knew who Pat was. Did he know where he lived, too?

★　★　★

When John dropped Pat off, the sun was still burning in the evening sky, the temperature still cooking those without air-conditioning. As Pat pulled his bike from the trunk, John said, "Be sure to tell your mom the truth."

"I will."

"She deserves it, *and* she can handle it."

"For sure," Pat said. "Thanks for the ride."

"No sweat, Pat. Be careful okay?"

"You too."

A thought occurred to him as John walked to the driver's side door. "Johnny, er, I mean, John."

"What is it?"

"Your dreams."

"Yeah? What about them?"

"I don't know, maybe it's stupid, but have you ever seen Caswell or the van in your dreams?"

"I...."

He saw the wheels turning behind John's eyes.

"I got chased by a vehicle," John said. "It could have been the van. I didn't get a good look or if I did, I can't remember. It chased me through Graveyard Land."

Pat shivered at the name of the place. Who named places in their dreams?

"As for Caswell, there is a house. A white farmhouse near the furthest edge of one of the cemeteries. August didn't want us going there. They never said who lived there, or maybe they did, I can't remember at the moment, but it's in my dream journal at the house. One Eye was afraid of the place."

Pat didn't know why John couldn't put it together, but he saw it clear as day. A white farmhouse by the cemetery. Caswell's house sat right beside Fairbanks Cemetery. "Maybe your dreams are trying to tell you something," he said.

"Yeah, that I'm losing my shit."

"No, it's deeper. The kid, Ethan Ripley. You *knew* him, you said something about your dreams and guilt. Maybe it's from when you were kids. Maybe you somehow blame yourself for what happened to him."

"Are you sure you're not the one seeing a shrink?" John said.

"I don't know, man, it all seems to be too much to be coincidence, don't you think?"

The front door to the house opened behind them.

"Patrick?" his mother called.

"Go on," John said. "Hey, Trisha."

"John? Oh, thank goodness," she said.

Ada scooted by her legs and ran to the steps. "Paddy?"

"I'm right here Ada."

"How come you gone so long?" she said. Her pouty face hit him in the heart.

"Sorry," he said. "I fell off my bike and hurt myself a little. I'm okay though."

"You got a boo-boo?"

"A couple," he said.

"I cleaned him up and he hung at my place for a bit," John said. "Nothing a little peroxide and soap couldn't take care of."

"Well," Trisha said, walking over to them, Ada hovering at her knees, "next time, maybe call your mother before she loses her mind thinking all the worst things have happened to you."

"I will, Ma," Pat said. He picked up Ada and put her on his hip.

"Thank you, John," Pat's mom said.

"No problem. I do have to get going, just thought I'd give him a lift back. Talk to you later, Pat."

"See ya," Pat said.

"Tell Sarah I said hello," Trisha said.

Pat watched John's mouth tighten.

"I will."

They waved as he backed out of the driveway.

"Now," his mother said, "let's talk about your punishment for scaring the shit out of your mother."

"Mama, you said a bad word," Ada said. "You said shit."

Shit indeed, Pat thought.

CHAPTER THIRTY-FOUR

John checked his cell at the first stop sign. Still no calls from Sarah. *She'll call when she's ready.*

"Yeah," he answered aloud, "even if it's just to tell me to fuck off."

After pulling up Dr. Soctomah's number, he hit send. The man picked up after two rings.

"Hello?"

"Dr. Soctomah, it's John Colby."

"Hi, John. Is everything okay?"

"No, I'm sorry to be bugging you like this, but I really need to talk to you. Can we meet now?"

"I'm out of the office. Can we set something up for later this week?"

"Please, Dr. Soctomah. I...I cheated on Sarah. I already told her and well, I'm just.... I...."

"Okay, okay, John. I hear you. Now, this isn't something I would normally do, but I just put on a fresh pot of coffee. Why don't you come by my home? It won't be in official capacity, but I can tell you need to talk."

Dr. Soctomah gave him his address. Five minutes later, John pulled up in front of the house.

Dr. Rik Soctomah's house was a cute dark blue cape. A little garden with tomato plant cages sat in the center of the front yard. There was also a beautiful bed of red, purple, and orange flowers lining the front of the home.

Dr. Soctomah opened the door as John reached up to knock.

"Come in," Dr. Soctomah said.

The home's interior was covered in Native American décor, like what he had in his office. Jewelry, decorative baskets, and lots of intricate wood carvings.

"Join me in my reading room."

Bookshelves lined the walls. John thought of Sarah. She would have been in heaven surrounded by so many books. He could see her reading in the red recliner in the far corner, her feet tucked beneath her, a steaming cup of tea at her side, or even writing at the desk near the large window.

They sat next to each other on the futon in the center of the room.

Dr. Soctomah handed John a mug of black coffee and took up a spot next to him.

"Sorry," Dr. Soctomah said. "I ran out of cream this morning."

"Black is fine, thank you."

"So, why do you think it happened?"

"Because I'm a fucking idiot. I was so drunk."

"Forgive me, but was it someone you know?"

John nodded.

"Someone Sarah knows?"

"Indirectly," John said. "It's a co-worker."

"I'm not going to justify or make excuses for you," the doc said. "But under the right circumstances, people are known to falter. Unfortunately, it sounds like you may have found yourself caught up in the perfect storm. Therapy can often act like a net dragged along the bottom of a lake. There are so many things that have settled down there all covered and cozy in the sand deep down below the surface. When we commit to going in for that dive or allowing the net to be dragged, all that stuff down there gets disturbed and floats up. What we get are all these issues that are suddenly out of place and that can initially cause a lot of mixed feelings. It can and it's meant to unleash a lot of locked-away shit, pardon my language. It seems to me, the stress at work, between that of the job itself, combined with the rough relationship with your supervisor and possibly the feelings you may or may not have admitted about this co-worker, certainly could cause the dreams that are keeping you from sleeping well. You take all that with what we were able to disturb from your lake, and how quick it's all been—"

"Doc," John said, "I truly wish that were it."

"Well," Dr. Soctomah said. "Yes, then there's Sarah and the want for a baby."

"There's more."

"More?"

John explained everything he and Pat had witnessed or found out about the green van, Ethan Ripley, Alvin and Llewellyn Caswell, as well as Sarah's dream research.

The doctor's eyes squinted, his gaze someplace else. "Hmmm."

"What is it?" John asked.

"Do you remember the photograph at my office that you asked about?"

"The one at Fairbanks Cemetery? Yes."

"Around the time of that photo, there was a man in the tribe, a bad man. He worked with malevolent spirits. In particular, the Luk, or Wolverine as he's known. The Wolverine is a wicked deity. A monster. This tribesman was excommunicated. He, along with a handful of his followers, moved deeper into the woods. It was believed he cursed the land and promised eternal unrest. When James Spears and his men arrived a few months later, it was thought that this dark shaman's curse had sent them. Many of my ancestors believed the Wolverine had possessed the war hero and coerced him into the slaughter of those who tried to defend their homes."

John didn't know what to say. He'd encountered so much evil in so few hours, it seemed like it was all building to something spectacularly horrible.

"I came back to Spears Corner. I was drawn here. My family, the few who survived James Spears's takeover, wound up in Bear Island only to succumb to the smallpox outbreak there at the time. My mother, my sister and her children now reside at the Pleasant Point Reservation. We are all that remain of my people from the photograph you saw. I chose to return to our original home here in Spears Corner. I felt there was something undone here."

"You think this all has something to do with what? The curse?" John asked.

"If there were sour ground anywhere, it would be here in Spears Corner."

"But what does any of that have to do with my dreams?"

"Dreams are a gateway to the spirit world," the doc said. "The shaman I mentioned, he delved into places beyond our realm. Places we are not meant to tread. Not the way he intended, at least."

"I'm not sure I understand what you're getting at."

"What if this Graveyard Land of your dreams is one of these tainted spirit realms?"

"Is that possible?" John asked.

"Judging from what I know and what you're telling me, I think it's time we stop asking about what is or is not *possible*."

Dr. Soctomah was right.

CHAPTER THIRTY-FIVE

Dr. Soctomah's idea that Graveyard Land could somehow be real was unsettling to say the least. The night was just beginning to fall as John headed home. There was no word yet from Sarah, and the thought of going home where he would just climb the walls or drink himself into a stupor, wasn't enticing. Being there without her would compound his problems and drive him over the edge. Hitting up the bar was out. He imagined running into Kaitlyn again.

No thanks.

He was coming down the Hallowell-Litchfield Road, slowing as he crawled by Crescent Cemetery. This was the coolest, and one of the oldest graveyards in Spears Corner. There were two sections divided by a small pathway that led up a slight hill in the back to the older section. He pulled the car to the shoulder of the road opposite the cemetery, killed the engine and got out.

The sun had begun to dip and lit the sky up in a brilliant crimson that gave way to blood-red orange. It was a gorgeous fiery mix as a backdrop to the graveyard. After crossing the road, he walked through the tall concrete pillars that served as the entrance and walked between the newer graves near the front. Peter N. Dunbar, died August 9th 1977, followed by Helen Peacock, died August 30th 1981. Okay, so they weren't that new, but goddamn it, why did he always have to see August death dates....

Pat's voice echoed in his head. *It's too much to be coincidence.*

John walked to the rear of the front cemetery. The grassy pathway out back slanted before him in a deep shade split by slivers of the amber sunset slashing through the trees.

It would be dark soon. Did he really want to be out here?

Was this one of Caswell's graveyards?

Great, it was either be spooked out of his mind or guilt-ridden and depressed.

Two shitty choices, but at least being out here was a distraction. He didn't know if he'd qualify it as a good distraction, but it served as one, nonetheless.

As he crossed over to the hill that led to the older cemetery, a quick succession of snapping twigs and scuffling feet came from his right. He stopped and squinted into the growing shadows.

He was freaking himself out now. There was no one here but him.

He carried on until he came to a tree that looked familiar. He'd been here before, but…it was in his dream. Staring at the old, towering Oak before him, he recalled August sitting at its base, watching John and One Eye and keeping his creepiness to himself for once, for the most part.

Was that in his journal? He couldn't remember if it was from before or not.

Why am I here?

Avoidance, distraction covered both of those, but was it something else?

This fucked-up supernatural shit was silly. Dreams were just dreams. Sure, they can be rooted in real life, but they don't *show up* in real life.

"What if this Graveyard Land is a tainted spirit realm?"

Movement behind one of the taller monuments caught his eye.

John stepped behind the medium-sized monument closest to him and peeked around the corner.

Could be some dumbshit kids out here fucking around. Or….

Crouched down, he waited. The darkness around him deepened.

He considered calling out but thought it better to conceal his whereabouts. Why give this person the drop on him? He was suddenly taken back to when he and the neighborhood kids would play The Russians Are Coming. Hiding from any headlights that came down the road, pretending it was the Russians like in that movie *Red Dawn*. If they got spotted, they were caught. Had Ethan ever gotten to play?

Why couldn't he remember the kid?

Night had fallen. Here he was alone in the cemetery, creeping around like a weirdo.

John started to rise when the movements came again.

"Looking for me?"

August's voice startled him, making him squeal like a ten-year-old at a monster movie.

John flopped backward, banging his head on the gravestone behind him. A sharp pain burst to life as August's silhouette, standing over him, faded to black.

★　　★　　★

When he opened his eyes, he was surrounded by fog.

Graveyard Land.

He sat up, looking for August and One Eye, but this time, he was all alone.

Johnny climbed to his feet and tried to figure out which way to go. Could he actually explore by himself? An inner voice commanded him to see it all, to take in everything he could. Familiarize himself with every inch of this place, map it out. Without August or One Eye to interfere, he could get the true lay of the land.

As Johnny wandered through the mist, he got the sense that someone was watching him.

Walking on, Johnny didn't notice the growing number of eight-legged critters gathering in his wake.

He was focused on finding out more about this damn place. Besides the Graveyard Land sign, he couldn't recall seeing any others. Back home, every cemetery had a name that was presented on a plaque or rockface – Spears Corner had its own idea of sign making. Crescent, Babbs, Sampson, Spears, Tillersons, Fairbanks...his town had tons of the stone placards. If this were Spears Corner or some catawampus dream equivalent, there would be signs.

The fog swirled and swarmed the grounds, spreading out, growing thicker by the second. As Johnny moved forward, a dim light in the distance beckoned him, a lighthouse guiding him in. Mesmerized, he heard a muffled voice in his mind warning him of the anglerfish and its predatory illusions in the depths. He could be devoured at any moment, but the promise ahead was too enticing. He was ready to go into the light and be swallowed.

John was out here on his own. The shadows threatened to sink poisoned hooks into his soul and spoil him for all eternity. Still, he went forward.

Was he afraid? Yes. Would he falter? Hell no.

The answers were here. He needed to reach the house....

Shapes began to pass through the fog. Johnny stopped. A chorus of whispers came to life, but he couldn't make out what they were saying.

"Hello?" he called out.

More amorphous shapes accompanied more movement. The whispers increased.

One passed close enough for him to see. It was a boy about his size, but he was...naked. They all were. The boys of Graveyard Land were here...all of them...and they were frantic.

And they were coming for him.

Johnny spun and crashed into One Eye. He was naked and crying.

"What's going on? What's happened?" Johnny asked.

One Eye shook his head.

"Are you okay?"

Bruises appeared upon his flesh in deep purple blossoms. Dark, viscous fluid seeped from the boy's ruined eye. His lip split, produced more of the dark fluid.

"I c-can't...I can't..." One Eye stuttered.

"You can't what?"

"Please, don't make me...I don't want to...."

One Eye wasn't speaking to him. His gaze was somewhere else.

The whispers of the other boys swelled around him in the thickening fog.

"Come on, get up!" Johnny shouted at the strange kid. He grabbed the boy's wrist and began trying to pull him to his feet.

"NO!!!!!" One Eye screamed. Johnny let go, startled. "Puh, puh, pleeeeease...."

Hands began to clutch at Johnny's shoulders. He twisted away from them, reaching once more for his friend.

One Eye focused on Johnny. A grotesque smile split across his wounded mouth. "Leave me here, Johnny. Save yourself. It's what you always do."

Johnny let go of One Eye's arm, too stunned to respond.

The others fell upon the boy.

Stumbling backward, Johnny did what he always did.

He ran.

★   ★   ★

John awoke beneath the moonlit sky.

"What are you doin' out here?"

Sitting up, he stared up at Alvin Caswell.

His skin tightened; his head felt fuzzy. It took a minute for John to realize where he was and why he was there.

"I saw your car on the side of the road," Caswell said. "When I seen that you weren't in it, well, I decided to make sure you hadn't found yourself in some trouble. You all right?"

John touched the sticky spot on the back of his head and looked at the blood on his fingers.

"Say, you got a medical condition or somethin'? I find you like this again, I'm gonna start to think you got a thing for lying with the dead." Caswell's gross grin appeared. "You ain't funny like that, are ya?"

"What? No," John said, getting to his feet. He stumbled and had to hold on to the gravestone to steady himself.

Caswell reached for him. "Careful there, fella," he said.

John pulled his arm back. "I'm fine," he said, more forcefully than he'd intended. He didn't want Caswell touching him.

"Sure," Caswell muttered. He touched the front of his pants, rubbing himself. He caught John watching him and smiled.

John averted his eyes. "Thanks for checking on me," he said. "I better get home."

He hurried past Caswell, who was still touching himself.

John started toward the path to the front cemetery. Caswell followed him, humming a tune.

John didn't look back. He didn't like having Caswell this close to him, especially in this back half of the graveyard. How long had the man been standing there before John woke up?

He picked up his pace and was nearly running by the time he crossed the street to his car.

The clock on the radio said it was shortly after midnight.

Jesus.

Hanging his head, he reached back and touched the bloody wound. It hurt like hell, but he didn't think he'd need stitches. He patted his pockets for his car keys but came up empty. The little cup holder he sometimes set them in was empty, as well.

"Shit." He looked toward the cemetery and saw Caswell heading straight for him.

He was about to lock the door when he noticed what the man held in his hands.

"Figured ya might need these?" Caswell said, stepping to the door and handing over the keys.

"Yeah," John said. "Thanks again."

"I figure that's two you owe me," Caswell said.

"What's that?"

"All the rescuin' I'm doin' for ya, I'm startin' to feel like I might be your guardian angel."

"Oh, yeah…." John gave a weak laugh. He just wanted to get away from him. He needed to get the hell home.

He started the car. "Thanks again, have a good night," he said, putting the car in Drive.

"Oh, I will. Got me a little girlfriend waitin' for me at the house."

John didn't know how to respond to that, so he just nodded and pulled away. He didn't believe the creep. He didn't want to imagine the kind of woman who'd be willing to get close to the guy, let alone set foot in that house.

★   ★   ★

When he got home, John checked his voicemail. There was nothing. It was way too late to call his mother-in-law's. He'd have to try in the morning. He poured himself a whiskey and swallowed down a couple Tylenol for his head.

Looking into the bathroom mirror, he tried to see how bad the wound was. The blood was already crusting up around it. He warmed a washcloth with hot water, wrung it out and lightly patted the self-inflicted injury. The thought that Caswell could have been standing in the cemetery the whole time he was knocked out sent his skin crawling with goose bumps. There was someone there who'd startled him to begin with. He'd impossibly thought it was August, but it had to have been Caswell, right? If that were true, he'd left John lying there unconscious for hours.

Another thought occurred to him. He couldn't have dropped his keys. They had been in his pocket. Caswell had touched him. The fucking bastard had gone through his pockets and taken the keys.

"You've got to be fucking kidding me," he said aloud.

He wasn't about to head over there now, not in the dark, not to that house. He'd have to confront the man in the light of day.

After pouring himself another drink, John took to his couch, ready to put this awful day behind him.

PART FOUR:
A MURDER OF ONE
CHAPTER THIRTY-SIX

August opened the door to the shed and slunk in to check on Sarah. Her red, tear-stained eyes went wide as he stepped inside, the light of day shining in behind him. She made quite the fuss behind her gag. August glided over to her. He enjoyed her fear. She turned away, refusing to look at him.

"It's fine," he said. "I know I'm not a handsome devil. I am, however, a devil of sorts. We're going to do something very special tonight, you and I. I hope you're as eager to see Johnny as I am."

At the mention of her husband's name, Sarah looked at him.

"I thought that'd get your attention. Has he figured it out yet?"

She looked confused.

"Probably not. He forgets others so easily, doesn't he? Thinks of himself and what's best for him." August pulled a spider from his mouth and stared at it. "Has he ever mentioned a boy he knew around here back in junior high?"

She shook her head from side to side.

"No? Well, has he ever told you about the time he saw his friend get kidnapped?"

She shook her head again; tears slipped from her eyes.

"I suppose it's not exactly the heroic kind of story you tell your lover. Selfishness is such an ugly thing, wouldn't you agree?" He walked over to her, holding out his arm and watching the black spider crawl onto the back of his hand. After a few seconds, the spider scurried from his arm over his chin, past his nose, and disappeared into one of his black eye sockets.

Sarah squealed and tried to hide her face.

He grabbed her chin and made her look at him. It was cruel, but August leaned in close. "Well, we all have a price to pay for our sins, even the ones we forget."

She tried to recoil but he brought his mouth to her cheek.

He opened up and the spider skittered from his tongue to her flesh. She screeched and jerked, trying to shake it off. Several more quarter-sized arachnids joined the eight-legged dance party.

August got up, shut the door, and left her in the company of fear.

★　★　★

Sarah trembled in the darkness. The horrible, awful boy, it was *him*. It was the kid without eyes from John's dreams. August. What was going on? Impossible horrors from books she'd read – *fiction, those were fiction* – regardless, Sarah and John were somehow dealing with his nightmares come to life.

What had August said? *"Did he tell you about he boy he saw get kidnapped?"*

If that was the case…. God, what else had John not told her?

Defeat settled in around her, like the nuclear fallout from the worst day of her fucking life.

CHAPTER THIRTY-SEVEN

Pat arrived early, waiting on Fuller. He'd tossed and turned all night and felt like a zombie this morning. Despite the golden sunlight trying to warm the cold from his bones at the cemetery gates, he shivered as though a ghost had wandered through him. Pat turned and imagined the van driving down the path between the graves, the Ghoul of Wisconsin behind the wheel, leering at him.

In his head, he heard a voice he'd never heard in his life: *"Feelin' like a hero, huh? Gonna add another body to the count? Be a big man in town that solves a cold case? Pretty big deal. Pretty big target."*

In his years of watching shows like *Criminal Minds, Cold Case,* and *Unsolved Mysteries,* Pat never imagined he'd land in the middle of a story like this. True crime, small town, serial killer....

His phone told him it was after eight already. They'd met up no later than seven-thirty so far. Even then, it was because Fuller stopped off to get them lunch. This felt different. It could be the lack of sleep or all the nightmares he'd uncovered yesterday. He thought the choice of the word 'nightmares' was funny considering John's current battle with his dreams.

Fifteen minutes later, Pat decided to get started. He needed to get to work, even if only to take his mind off Fuller's unexplained absence. Fuller had given him a copy of the key to the storage shed, so he pulled out the mower and decided to start there. As he took off the padlock and opened the door, a shape in the back corner of the shed caused him to let out a whimper, one that would only be more embarrassing if Kelsie Johnson were here to witness it, and stumbled away from the door.

Upon further examination, Pat saw it for what it was – a jacket hung on a shovel.

"Jesus, I gotta fucking relax," Pat said.

★   ★   ★

After finishing cutting the grass and collecting all the dead or dying flowers from graves, Pat took his first smoke break. He couldn't help but smile as Fuller pulled up in his truck.

"Holy shit, Mr. Fuller," he said as the old man stepped from the vehicle. "I thought you'd gone and died on me."

"I ain't ready to join our friends here just yet, junior," he said.

The grin on the old man's face delivered a swell of relief. Pat wasn't sure if he actually thought Caswell had killed the old man, but he certainly couldn't say it wasn't in serious consideration.

"Take a seat," Fuller said.

Pat set down the giant black trash bag full of dead flowers and hopped his rump up on Fuller's tailgate.

"What," Pat said, "no lunch this time?"

The old man laughed and patted him on the back. "Remind me when we wrap up, and we can swing by the A1 Diner on our way out."

"I was just messing with you—"

Fuller waved him off and scrubbed at the salt and pepper whiskers covering his weak chin.

Pat fell silent awaiting his forthcoming declaration. You didn't have to be Sherlock to see the man had something he wanted to say.

"You surprised me," Fuller said.

"Yeah, I tend to do that to a lot of people."

"I bet," he said. "You're dedicated, hard-workin', motivated. That ain't what you see in the kids these days."

Pat wondered how many *kids* Fuller actually took the time to get to know. He thought about posing the question but held his tongue instead, preferring to hear what the man had to say.

"I mean it," Fuller said. "I thought for sure you was gonna whine and mope and do a half-ass job. But you—"

"Surprised you?"

"Yeah, and don't interrupt me. I got something I mean to say and I think if you can shut your yap for a second and stop crackin' wise you might like what I'm tryin' to tell ya."

"Sorry, Mr. Fuller."

"Seein' what you done today, what you done this past week, I think you deserve a real shot. How's about you take over my daily duties – I'll swing over for the burials, of course. You not being old enough to run the backhoe or knowing how to handle the machine... yet. Think that's something you can do?"

Pat didn't know what to say.

"I...yes, I won't let you down."

"Don't go makin' promises, just say yes, sir, and we'll get at it."

Pat shook Fuller's outstretched hand. "Yes, sir."

★   ★   ★

They were finished within the hour and made the diner shortly after one. Mr. Fuller agreed to subcontract not only the Helen Cemetery but also Babbs. Pat had his foot firmly in the door. Caswell was another story, but at the moment, Pat felt more accomplished than he could remember ever feeling in his entire life.

"One other thing I gotta tell ya," Mr. Fuller said between bites of his burger.

"What's that?" Pat asked, sipping his lemonade.

"You ever wonder why it is we got so many graveyards in this town?"

"No, but I mean...I guess, no, I never really thought about it."

Fuller scratched his chin and gazed out the window. "This area was tribal land. Passamaquoddy. Hell, there was a time half the population here had Injun blood in 'em. Some out of love, some from somethin' worse. Anyway, when James Spears and what was left of the 34th regiment came home to Maine, they wanted to stick together and build their own community. Spears decided to take this land as his own and start his family and this town...let's just say he didn't have the etiquette to do so properly. No, he barged in with his men, told the natives to clear out. When they didn't, he and his men, heroes in the war but now twisted from it, went on and slaughtered those too proud to leave and any man, woman or child that dared defy them.

Pat's throat felt like a dust catcher.

"Long story short," Fuller said, now gazing into his coffee cup, "the natives, what was left of 'em, fled but not before one of them cursed this land."

"Why are you telling me this?"

"I do the work in the daytime. Earlier the better. Ain't no way I want to be out there after dark or anywhere near it."

"Why?"

Pat thought of his strange encounter in the back half of Crescent Cemetery. The shadow, the voice...the damned spiders.

"Trust me," Fuller said. "The dead are dead, but that don't mean they're gone."

"Have you...have you seen ghosts?" Pat asked.

Fuller fell quiet, drawing into himself. He fidgeted with his spoon, tapping it with his finger.

"Mr. Fuller?"

"Ain't what I seen, but what I heard. Voices, whispers, little things."

Pat thought of his own experience.

"What about shadows?" Pat asked.

From Fuller's pale expression, Pat thought the old man was seeing one right now.

"I've seen shapes in the dark, moving between the graves or just beyond, but that's it and that's enough. Ain't worked near sunset since. You'd be best to do the same. Hope I ain't scared you off from the job."

"No." It wasn't a lie, not exactly; he wanted this gig, but he couldn't hide the goose bumps. Rubbing at his arms, Pat said, "I'm good."

"Good. That's real good."

CHAPTER THIRTY-EIGHT

"I think we need to call the police," John told Janice over the phone. "It's been twenty-four hours since either of us has seen or heard from her."

"But her car's gone," the woman said. "She had to have gone off. Maybe she just needs to clear her head without you or me trying to give her our opinions. She's always been hard-headed."

She was certainly that. Still, it felt off.

"Why wouldn't she at least let one of us know that she was leaving?"

"Because she knows we'd try to talk her out of it. Listen, Johnny—"

John cringed at hearing Janice call him that, but said nothing.

"When she was oh, I don't know, nineteen or so, Sarah got mad at her boyfriend at the time. A nice fella named Aaron, I loved him – not that I don't love you, you know I adore you. When she broke it off with the boy, I was so sure that she was throwing her future away. She just up and took off on all of us. It was only for a couple nights, but it's what she needed. Scared the death out of me, but she was an adult and she made a choice. I told her yesterday morning to go home. You don't work things out from afar. She's probably just as irritated with me as she is with you."

It made sense. John remembered Sarah telling him that story. Isolating herself allowed her the space to think and see things more clearly. She said it was a way of resetting her perspective. After hearing that her mom told her to come home it seemed even more possible. Now, if they found her car abandoned somewhere – no, he stopped this train of thought before it could gain more steam. He'd always had a thing for what Dr. Soctomah called 'catastrophic thinking'. It was part of his anxiety issues. Always preparing for the worst possible outcome.

"Well," John said, "if we don't hear from her by tomorrow, I'm going to the police."

"I'll go right along with you. But let's give her one more day. If I hear from her, or you do—"

"I'll call you, for sure," he said.

"Thanks, Johnny. Take care."

"You, too, Janice."

He hung up the phone and tried Sarah once more, but it went right to voicemail.

He was pacing again. There was no way he could sit around; he'd never be able to concentrate on a damned thing. And it was too early to start drinking. Besides, he was getting tired of drowning his sorrows.

*   *   *

The pavement felt good under his sneakers. The heat of recent weeks had dwindled to a much more tolerable seventy-five degrees with a bit of overcast delivering a nice breeze. It was a welcom change. John decided to take a slightly different route, heading left at Gilly Street and cutting over to 126 before heading back toward Spears Corner Road.

Never in a million years could he have imagined cheating on Sarah. Yet, it had happened and nothing short of a time machine would erase that fact. John thought of kids, teenagers caught in a robbery, just trying to score some cash to maybe feed themselves or their mamas and the shop owner goes for a gun, the next thing you know the shop owner's got a hole in his skull and the kid's in prison, locked up for a knee-jerk reaction to a shitty situation.

A situation he got himself into, John's head reminded him.

You can't argue your way out of this one, Johnny boy.

Not you, too, he chided himself.

Maybe he did deserve what he had coming. Sarah leaving him, his dreams working on him from the inside out, whatever the hell was going on with Caswell and the green van.

John stopped.

Caswell and that damn van.

When he realized just where he was, John's gaze turned toward the tree line dividing Fairbanks Cemetery from the Caswell property.

What if that sick bastard grabbed her? What if she's trapped in there right now?

He remembered the brand-new door on that shitty old shed.

He was contemplating his next move when something wet dripped from the trees and smacked his forearm.

There was nothing there. More drops thudded against him from above.

Webworm caterpillars.

They writhed on the ground.

He looked up and saw a web over his head was coming undone, dropping the insects down upon him. Moving out of the way, he backed toward the road. More larvae rained down from overhead. He looked up and saw another deteriorating web and another. The number of caterpillars falling was impossible. Thousands of them, landing in his hair, wiggling down the back and front of his t-shirt. He yelped and one landed on his teeth. John spat and gagged as they continued to fall, now pelting him like hail. Using his arm to shield his face, he saw someone in the trees watching him. A tall, lanky shape, black as the night but hiding in the light of day.

"No," he muttered.

Honk!

The sound of the car horn blaring less than two feet from him scared the shit out of him. John dropped to the blacktop and stared up at the grille of Burt Marsden's Silverado.

"John!" Burt shouted. "Jesus, what the hell are you doing? Are you trying to get yourself run over?"

John's whole body trembled. He swatted at the invisible bugs he was certain were crawling all over his flesh.

"John?" Burt was at his side. "Are you okay?"

"They're all over me," he said, searching in vain for the caterpillars. They were gone.

He gazed back toward the graveyard, scanning the path and the trees above. The webs were there, a few anyway, but they were fully intact; he couldn't see anything moving on the ground below.

Burt grabbed him under the arms and hefted him to his feet. "You on something, man?" he asked.

"No...it's just...no...I...."

"Get in, let me give you a ride home."

John let Burt walk him to the passenger seat and help him in.

As they were driving away, Burt went on about how he'd seen John back into the road swatting at his arms and head, but the rest trailed away.

John couldn't remember ever feeling so untethered from reality.

What if he was becoming schizophrenic?

Did it run in his family?

It wasn't until Burt led him through the door of his house that he remembered what he was thinking before whatever the hell it was that just happened.

He needed to know that Sarah was not in that house.

Something tickled his elbow. John twitched, ready to swat at anything dancing across his skin. Nothing was there.

Maybe he'd go back after dark. Right now, he needed to take a hot shower.

CHAPTER THIRTY-NINE

The pounding on his front door woke John from a dreamless slumber. He must have dozed off on the couch. It was already dark out.

The thumping increased.

"Hold on," he shouted, trying to shake off the grogginess.

When he opened the door, Pat stood there holding a bunch of papers.

"You have to see this," he said.

Thunder growled. A summer storm was brewing, and it looked like it was going to be mean. Black clouds had turned the day to night and the wind was whipping the trees in his yard like they'd tried to steal from the gods.

"Come on then, get in here," John said.

Pat walked straight into the kitchen and began spreading out the papers over the table.

"What's all this?" John asked, going for a beer.

"Do you know the history of Spears Corner?"

"You mean James Spears slaying the Natives, evil shaman curses, the ghosts of the Spears House, that sort of thing?"

Pat stopped. "Yeah, how did you know?"

"I had a very enlightening conversation last night with my therapist. He's from the Passamaquoddy tribe and he told me some pretty horrendous shit."

"Whoa," Pat said. "What are the chances?" He shook it off and searched through the photocopies on the table.

"Yeah, pretty eerie," John said.

"James Spears was a piece of work," Pat said.

"And we have statues of this fucking asshole in town to this day," John said.

"Money, man," Pat said, and shrugged. "Care if I smoke in here?"

"You know what, go for it."

Pat lit a smoke and took a drag before carrying on. "The Spearses *still* own this town, from the churches to the jails."

"All is quiet in the world tonight..." John muttered.

"What?"

"Nothing," he said. "Just a song. Where does your research lead us to the Caswells?" He was interested to hear just how much of what Soctomah thought lined up.

"Get this," Pat said, the odd excitement exuding in his every movement. "The Passamaquoddy had a split with the ones that wanted to stay and fight and the ones that wanted to carry on someplace else. They knew the white man was not to be trusted, like, ever, so one of the fiercer ones, a shaman, was said to have put a curse upon the town and the land, like what you said."

John nodded.

"Well," Pat continued, "according to this book I found by a former local, a Native American writer, an Eden Silko, her book says the Passamaquoddy that stayed close were of a darker set of beliefs. A small tribe that practiced black magic."

John thought of Dr. Soctomah's devil shaman and his ambitions.

"Okay," Pat said. "So you know what I told you about the Ghoul of Wisconsin, right?"

"Sure, local creep. Moved away, came home to kidnap and murder Ethan Ripley and went...what? Home to get caught and executed?"

"Right, that's the CliffsNotes version, but I found a book by Emily Gibson, a true crime author, that dove deep into Caswell's story. According to her book, the Ghoul never made it to the electric chair. He slit his own throat in his cell."

"Fuck," John said.

"He had notebooks filled with rituals and stories of spirit worlds. Like every Native belief in the spirit world, from what you see in the movies to stuff that would make Bundy and Dahmer look like Boy Scouts. According to Gibson's book, one of the rituals that stood out above all the others was one by a Passamaquoddy shaman disliked by his people here in Maine. It talked about manipulating the spirit world. It involved sacrifice and blood and a clear, focused vision of the world you'd like to create. In the same chapter Gibson mentions passage upon passage in Caswell's notebook about a place called Graveyard Land."

Pat saw the air leave John's body. "Just like in your dreams," he said.

"Motherfucker," John managed. Soctomah was right.

"What if he succeeded?" Pat asked. "What if he made his own grotesque spirit world, and that's what this Graveyard Land is? That's what he wanted. In the interrogation room, he referred to his yard at his home in Wisconsin as Graveyard Land. Where his boys were. Where he could keep them with him forever."

"What the fuck does this have to do with me?" John asked.

"Dude," Pat says. "Are you kidding?"

"What?"

"Shit, Johnny, maybe you are oblivious."

"Don't fucking talk to me like that," John said.

"August," Pat spat.

"What about him?" John felt the rage boiling up inside.

"Fuck, man. August, your dream kid, he represents Ethan Ripley. You can't remember the kid. You blocked him out of your memory. You said August has blacked-out eyes and that it could mean you can't see something or you're trying not to see something, right? Your dreams are screaming at you to remember."

"I...." John felt a wave of nausea roll through him.

He closed his eyes and turned away.

Run, do what you do best.

"No," John whispered. "He would have killed me, too."

"Holy shit," Pat said. "You *were* there. You were with him. Did you see it happen? Think."

John clenched his fist. Pat stepped back, giving John some space, but not backing down completely.

"I mean," Pat continued. "It would explain why you choose not to remember him...the guilt, the tie-in with the Ghoul of—"

"Stop fucking calling him that!"

Pat took another step toward the door.

"He's a fucking man!" John shouted. "A fucking sick perverted piece of shit. Do not glorify this animal with some catchy fucking nickname because you get off on these fucks."

"Did you see it happen?" Pat dared him.

"Get the fuck out of here, Pat. Go home. Now."

"Johnny—"

"And stop fucking calling me that!" John launched the beer bottle across the room. It smashed against a wall several feet from Pat's head and scattered glass and beer to the floor.

"Sarah was right to leave. You're a selfish fucking prick," Pat said, tears welling up in his eyes.

He ran from the house.

"Pat," John yelled. "Fuck. Pat, wait!"

His front door slammed shut. John rushed after his friend.

Pat was already pedaling like a bat out of hell from his driveway.

God, John thought, *I really am a piece of shit.*

CHAPTER FORTY

Pat was barely two streets away from John's place when the green Dodge darted across the street and clipped his bike. Pat flew over the handlebars and crashed to the tar in a mad tumble of pain, shock, and dancing stars.

He couldn't move his left arm, and realized he was lying on it. Rolling to his back, he tried to get his blurred vision into focus. Someone was rushing over to him.

"Gosh, I'm so sorry," the man said.

Pat smelled him before he saw who it was.

"Say, let me help you up," Alvin Caswell said.

Only he didn't try to help Pat to his feet; instead, the man snatched him by the hair and dragged him to the back of the van. Pat tried to push him away, but every part of him seemed to scream in refusal. He'd definitely fucked up his right leg and he thought his left arm might be broken.

Caswell picked him up and roughly dropped him in the back of the van. Then he climbed in behind him and closed the doors.

"Wait...no..." Pat whimpered.

Caswell had rope and a roll of duct tape. Pat tried to kick him with his good leg, but the man easily deflected the weak shot and punched Pat in the stomach.

"Ugghh," Pat cried out. What little fight he had in him wheezed out with the air in his lungs.

Caswell bound Pat's wrists and quickly repeated the move, cinching his ankles together.

"Puh, puh, please...let me go...."

"Sorry, buddy boy," Caswell said. "You've been invited to the party. We need to make sure Johnny shows up."

He turned away before returning with a dark-stained rag and the roll of tape.

"I can't have you yelling for the cops. Now, open wide."

"No, no," Pat said, jerking his face away.

Caswell hauled off and backhanded him. More stars came out to waltz their way to this two-man show.

A truck rolled up behind them.

Caswell opened the door and stepped down.

Pat saw who it was.

"Mr. Fuller!"

"Hey, Caswell," Fuller said, stepping from the vehicle. "You fat bastard, what the hell are you doing?"

Caswell forced the rag past Pat's teeth. Pat gagged at the taste of oil and gasoline as Caswell taped the rag in place.

"Wait here, boy," he said.

When Caswell turned to face Mr. Fuller, Pat saw the knife Caswell had hidden behind his back.

Wide-eyed, Pat yelled behind the gag, flipping out and flopping like a dead fish.

Caswell marched forward, meeting Fuller in two steps. His arm swung out.

"Get that boy out of your van or I swear to God I will – ugh—" Fuller stopped.

Pat watched Caswell pull the knife free and plunge it back in three more times.

NO!!!

Fuller collapsed into Caswell's arms, drooling blood from his mouth.

"Come on, Fuller," Caswell said, dragging him to the van and shoving him in beside Pat. "What's the matter, boy? Never seen someone kill a man before?"

Caswell smirked and slammed the doors closed.

Pat watched Fuller's eyes zone out and that was it. He was gone. Tears fell as Pat heard Fuller's truck rev to life and rumble forward.

A minute later, the truck fell silent, and the driver's side door of the van opened. Alvin Caswell slipped in and started the vehicle. "Sorry about that, boy. I had to ditch the nosey bastard's truck. We're good to go now. Hold still back there, yeah?" The creep cackled as they began moving down the road a little way before pulling over and stopping again. Caswell got up, came to the backseat and stared down at Pat.

"He'll come for you won't he, boy?"

Pat couldn't believe this sick fuck had just killed Mr. Fuller.

"Are you gonna cry or do you maybe want to kick my ass?"

Caswell reached for his face. Pat squirmed out of his reach.

"You play nice and you might get your chance."

Caswell moved his large rump to the front of the vehicle, and they drove off, bound for the impossible.

Pat's worst fear had come true. He was inside the van and was now a victim in the tangled web that only a few hours ago he thought was so cool to be a part of.

Welling up at his own ignorance and his inability to see this coming, he remembered what had happened.

Alvin Caswell had been waiting for him.

I'm so sorry, John.

CHAPTER FORTY-ONE

The phone blared to life. John stumbled from the bathroom, hurrying across the room, nearly tripping over the coffee table on his way to answer it.

"Hello, Sarah?"

"No, John, it's Trisha."

"Trisha? Is everything all right? Is Pat okay?"

"Well, I'm probably being a paranoid helicopter mom, but Pat went to work early this morning – he's doing some work for Edward Fuller at the cemetery – and I was expecting him home by now. He isn't with you by any chance, is he?"

Shit. He never should have let him leave alone. Not after all the stuff they'd uncovered.

"Ah, no, he's not. He was, here I mean. Just a few minutes ago. You just missed him."

"Oh? Oh, good. Shoo," she said. "I've just been worried. My anxieties are a little out of whack lately."

John could sympathize.

"Listen," he said. "Do you want me to go see if I can catch up to him? Give him a ride home?"

"Oh, no, you don't need to do that. I'm sure he'll walk through the door any minute. Thanks though."

"Are you sure, it's really no problem."

"No," she said. "You're fine. Say, how's Sarah? Is she home? I'd love to say hi."

"Ah, no, she's at the store. Grocery shopping. I'll let her know you said hello."

"Oh, okay," she said. "Thanks, John."

"No problem, Trisha. Oh…can you have Pat give me a ring when he gets home? I needed to ask him something."

"Sure thing. Take care."

"You, too."

John had his keys and was out the door the second he hung up.

He wasn't sure why he'd lied to Trisha. Maybe to ease her worries? Or to cover his own assholish ways? Sarah was not grocery shopping and Pat had left nearly half an hour ago. He definitely should have made it home by now.

John owed him an apology. He'd track him down and deliver it in person. Then he'd make sure he got home safe.

What if August got him?

He pushed the thought away. He wasn't ready to give in to this macabre fantasy of Graveyard Land. Not yet.

Pat thinks it's possible.

He's a naive teenager desperate for this true crime angle to be legit. This shit was pretty coincidental, John would give him that, but rogue shamans, fucked-up death rituals, and a sicko's version of a spirit world. No fucking way. He'd believe in Jesus walking across the Hanson Union River before giving credence to that nonsense.

Cruising down the road, he saw the old outlet road that led to the Ropes. It was an old swimming hole that he and his friends used to frequent. Hell, all the neighborhood kids went there at some point.

An old memory played in his head.

He'd been down there only once that summer.

And he'd brought Ethan Ripley to show him.

It took him forever to get Ethan to swing out on the rope over the water. The kid was scared of everything. Once he got in though, they had a blast. Ethan had told him he used to not be such a chickenshit. That he used to ride dirt bikes with his Uncle...Peter or Paul, one of those biblical names. An accident had injured the tendons in his... hand. Which is why it was so curled up and gnarly looking.

Dirt bikes...something about dirt bikes....

There was something important just beyond his reach.

The sandpits.

He told John he still had a Honda CR-80 dirt bike, and they could ride it sometime if they had a place to go. Said he couldn't do jumps or ride like a daredevil anymore with his hand like it was, but that he still liked to putt around on it when he could.

That's why they went to the pits....

And that's when they saw the green Dodge....

A horn blared, startling him from his daydream.

John drove on and found himself following a familiar path.

He cruised downtown, past The Tap Room. He thought he'd seen August driving the van here last week. Continuing to Water Street, he stared at the kids milling about on the sidewalks in front of mostly vacant storefronts. There had been so much more here when he was young. The place always seemed to be buzzing with business and life. The card shop, the pool hall, Weigand's Martial Arts studio, Greatest Hits record store, Spears Corner Fruit, which sold magazines and comic books along with other convenience store junk. He'd got his Jolt cola and Slim Jim rations there regularly before they went out of business. Had he ever been there with Ethan or was that after they closed?

Pulling up in front of the Spears Corner Public Library, he gazed across the road. A new brewery had taken up the space long ago vacated by the record store. Breweries seemed to be one of the only flourishing businesses around this part of the state.

John went inside the library, instantly hit with the smell of the place. Sarah was the one who came here all the time. He couldn't recall the last time he'd actually set foot inside.

"Can I help you?"

A skinny guy with a bad mustache and glasses set down the pile of books in his hands and stepped to the counter to meet John.

"Ah, maybe. I'm looking for a friend of mine. His name's Pat. He's got a Mo—"

"Patrick Harrison?"

"Yes. Have you seen him?"

"Sure, he was here earlier. Is everything all right?"

"But he's not here now?"

"I haven't seen him come back. He's not in trouble, is he?"

"No, I just needed to ask him something. Can you do me a favor and ask him to call his mom if you see him?"

"Of course," the man said.

"Thanks," John said.

He made a quick check of the library to be certain Pat wasn't hunkered down unnoticed in a corner somewhere. Coming up empty, he stepped outdoors and stared across the street. Two burly guys with thick beards and beer bellies were talking at the door to the brewery.

John could close his eyes and still see the Greatest Hits logo on the window. It was that store where he spent the majority of his time down here as a kid. He could still hear Soul Asylum, Hole, Counting Crows, and Billy Corgan's strange but beautiful voice croaking out an acoustic song about how he used to be a little boy.

The van crawled through his reverie.

Caswell.

Pat was right.

That day he and Ethan were biking around, he'd seen the van. He'd seen it more than once driving past them.

John got in his car and drove up Winter Street and took a left around the outskirts of the Spears Corner Common. Two large Catholic churches cornered the place. Next to the St. James Church sat a small cemetery. This one always gave John the creeps as a kid. He wasn't sure if it was because it was across from the park or because it was next to the church. Maybe it was his irrational fear of churches given to him by seeing the movie *The Exorcist* when he was way too young. Whatever it was it seemed silly now.

Patrick wasn't at the park, not that John had expected to see him here, but as he came around to Brunswick Avenue, John headed out toward the old sandpits.

The pits were about two miles up the avenue. He pulled onto the dirt road, stopped and stepped out of his car. The wind had picked up, and the storm was almost here. The clouds gathered like hands around a throat, growing darker to the west, closing in to suffocate the light from the sky.

He walked past the cheap metal pole that, according to the slanted sign, was supposed to keep out unauthorized vehicles. There was no one else here as far as he could tell, so he strolled through and walked to the edge of one of the larger sand piles. Instantly, he felt like he'd been punched in the guts.

The woods to his right...that's where—

You ran.

You left him.

That day…John had been here. He and Ethan had come to scope it out, and when they were getting ready to leave the green van was here…and a man seemed hurt.

CHAPTER FORTY-TWO

1994 (2)

Llewellyn crept down Water Street in his trusty Dodge, making his third pass on the heavily foot-trafficked stretch that served as the epicenter of downtown Spears Corner. There were all kinds of boys and girls shouting and fussing, screeching joyous howls and cussing each other out, but there was only one boy he was hoping to see. Would he be out here today? If Llewellyn had to guess from the brief moment he'd seen him, the kid had the look of a loner. He was probably glued to a nine-inch television set in a back bedroom somewhere playing Nintendo. If he did have friends, Llewellyn pictured them to be the Dungeons & Dragons type, holed up in a basement rolling dice and swallowing buckets of Mountain Dew.

Kids these days. When he was growing up, you watched prime-time TV shows with your family, *All in the Family, M.A.S.H., The Mary Tyler Moore Show.* You ate meals at the supper table at the same time every evening. There were no video games, no cable TV channels, no VCRs or video rental stores. You were outside keeping yourself occupied, using your imagination and playing with your friends until you were called back in.

Parents were different then, too. If your kid acted up or sassed you, you hit him with the belt. If you needed something at the corner store even near dark, you sent them out to fetch it. Thoughts of abductions and random killers lurking in the shadows waiting to feed off your poor children was barely a consideration if one at all.

Llewellyn didn't dare dream of how much fun he would have had if times were the same today. What kind of wide-open playground would he have to roam and watch and take whatever he wanted whenever he liked.

He'd seen a few that interested him, the boy with the acoustic guitar out front of the library for one, but his stomach was rumbling.

There would be plenty of time still. First he would feast. Not here though. The less people saw his face in town the better. There was a great little truck stop diner on Brunswick Avenue called Ricky's Place. He could order to-go and sit in the dirt lot scarfing down a sub while he gave the next wave of kids time to show up to strut their stuff downtown.

★   ★   ★

The diner was busy, but it was mostly old fuckers and big rig drivers come in off the I-95 exit just up the road. He grabbed a roast beef Italian and a Coke and took his lunch in the van.

As Llewellyn munched on his delicious sub, a native man stepping from the wood-paneled station wagon caught his attention.

There were a few reasons he'd returned to Spears Corner, Maine. His mother's funeral, of course, but there was something much more important. Eden Silko. Eden was the author of a novel on the Passamaquoddy tribe in Maine. Llewellyn had placed a call to Eden this morning to set up an interview. Her book held a possible key for Llewellyn's dream. There was tell of a shaman in this very area back in the mid-eighteen hundreds, and right around the time James Spears showed up to plant his big flag in the center of an already established town.

Llewellyn could give a flying fuck about the utter slaughter of innocents. What caught his eye was the shaman lost in this tale. A man who stood for something more. A man with not only charisma and a sense of direction but also an admirable ambition. A vision beyond what was expected and what was possible.

But that was for tomorrow.

Llewellyn had set up the interview with Eden Silko under the guise that he was a writer for a Midwest magazine visiting the East Coast in search of the most strange and amazing tales.

Finished with lunch, he headed back downtown in hopes of catching his fly.

He spotted the boy and a friend on his first sweep of the Shop 'n' Save parking lot.

Fate was on his side.

Llewellyn gasped when a red Escort nearly clipped the boy's friend. After a quick exchange with the driver and some checking the friend over, the boys rode out of the parking lot and headed toward Jefferson Stream. Llewellyn and his cousin had fished striped bass out of that waterway all through their childhood. He crawled through the lot, eased onto Maine Avenue and pulled around to Arcade Street, where he parked behind the new bottle redemption and liquor store, Tiger Town. He had a clear view of the boys as they stood skimming rocks into the sparkling stream.

It was a gorgeous summer day. The humidity still made Llewellyn sweat like mad, but the sun felt good on his forearm as he hung it out the window. He sipped his Coke and practiced patience. If it took all day for the opportunity to present itself, Llewellyn would wait. Since setting eyes on the lanky boy again, he already decided he wasn't leaving town until the boy was his.

★   ★   ★

He was starting to fall asleep behind the wheel when the boys climbed up the embankment and biked past Tiger Town. Llewellyn started the van and decided to drive down Arcade Street and loop back around to the start of Water Street. He was betting they'd check out some of the stores. There was a sports card shop, a music store, Reny's Department Store, Gerrard's Pizza, and a new pool hall, as well.

He spotted their bikes outside the entrance to the sports card shop.

Cruising by, he saw them through the window. The friend stared him down. Llewellyn turned his gaze to the road. Had the friend noticed him following them? It was possible, but nothing that worried him. Still, it was always better to stay back and watch from afar. It was hard knowing the boy was so close. The impulse to be near him was hindering Llewellyn's better judgment. It had been happening more and more lately, like his need for them, his hunger and desire was growing. He didn't want to get sloppy now.

He pulled around and waited outside the post office at the corner of Water and Bridge. When they came out, he noticed the friend was definitely scanning the street before they began riding in the opposite direction. Llewellyn let them cross at the traffic light down the block before pulling out and venturing in their direction.

It was another hour before the boys headed up Church Street toward the Spears Corner Common.

They were climbing around the gazebo at the center of the park drinking sodas and taking turns jumping over the railings of the structure. Llewellyn imagined the boy working up a sweat. He licked his lips as the pressure built in his pants.

The friend climbed the steps and stopped, his head craned in the van's direction.

Fuck.

Llewellyn pulled away. He shouldn't have parked so close.

Sloppy, man, he thought. *You're getting too fucking sloppy.*

As he pulled up to the Stop sign near the Catholic Church, he saw the boys mount their BMX steeds and book ass toward Brunswick Avenue.

He didn't want the friend to spot him again, but he also couldn't lose them. Not now. He wanted to make his move sooner than later.

Staying under the speed limit, he ducked behind a U-Haul truck. He had to make a few stops to keep his distance. Eventually, they pulled off the avenue and rode out of sight. As he rolled to the driveway, a smile cracked his face.

The Authorized Vehicles Only sign on the gate welcomed him.

The Gardiner Gravel Pits.

This was his moment.

He slowly drove beyond the gate. He and Alvin had been here plenty growing up. There was only one main way in and out of the pits, and he parked near the first pile of gravel, right before it.

He stepped from the van and heard their voices as one of them hooted for the other.

Llewellyn hurried to his knees and leaned against his back tire.

The friend was already trying to warn the boy from checking on him, but the boy came anyway.

When he tried to help Llewellyn to his feet, the Ghoul of Wisconsin snatched the kid by the back of the head and rammed his face into the side of the van again and again. When he let go, his heart pumping blood like the thunder of Ragnarok, Llewellyn watched the boy collapse into a pile.

He could see the front of the friend's yellow shorts darken as he pissed himself.

Scooping up his prize, Llewellyn shoveled the unconscious boy into the back of the van and shut the doors.

He set into a full sprint after the friend.

★   ★   ★

He had to give up after the kid booked it out a small trail that let out to another road. Would he go straight to the cops? There was no time to wait and see.

Llewellyn raced home, grabbed his belongings and told his cousin he was leaving for a couple nights. He needed the van and would return it before heading back to Wisconsin.

That night, in a cheap roadside motel in Winthrop, Llewellyn Caswell introduced the boy, Ethan Ripley, to his dark side. And it was every bit as wonderful as he'd hoped.

★   ★   ★

The following day, the boy was reported missing, but no word came out about any suspects or vehicles. Either the police were holding back important details for some reason or the friend hadn't told anyone. Fear could hold so many things in check.

Still, Llewellyn couldn't take any more chances. That morning, he strangled the life from Ethan Ripley's beautiful brown eyes. Watching the boy's lights go out, Llewellyn felt an odd sadness he'd never encountered before. Back home, he still had his boys. They were all over his property. There was no way he could take this one with him, but gazing into those brown eyes, an idea occurred to him. He needed to take a part of Ethan with him.

When he finished collecting his keepsakes from Ethan Ripley, he promptly disposed of the body in Litchfield Pond, where he could rot with the bones of Steve Norton.

Llewellyn rented a Ford Escort from a Hertz in Augusta and met with Eden Silko about the Passamaquoddy shaman. After getting the keys to the proverbial golden gates from the woman's in-depth knowledge of not only the medicine man's intent but also the precise rituals he used or planned to use, Llewellyn strangled the writer with his belt and left her to spoil behind a dust-covered organ in her basement.

★   ★   ★

He returned home ready for the next exciting and glorious chapter of his life.

CHAPTER FORTY-THREE

John stood in the spot where he'd seen the boy get attacked all those years ago. Closing his eyes, he saw it again.

Oh God, the man snatched Ethan and John had abandoned him.

And he'd been so scared that he'd get in trouble or that if he ratted on the man, the kidnapper would find him and take him, too, John never told anyone what he saw.

Crumpling to his knees, he sobbed.

He'd seen Ethan Ripley's kidnapper and kept it to himself.

Tears ran down his cheeks while the wind fluttered his hair.

"I'm sorry," John cried. "I'm so fucking sorry."

"But are you really, Johnny?"

John spun around on bended knee.

"No, no, you're not real," he said.

August stood twenty yards away.

"I don't think denial is working so well for you anymore, Johnny. And I don't think it's going to help your friends."

"What are you talking about?"

John stood as August took a wide arc around him and stepped to the tree line. August snatched a leaf from one of the one of the maples and twirled it between his fingers.

"How are you gonna save them if you keep trying to hide from the truth?"

"Save who—"

And it hit him. He had them. Some fucking how, August had Sarah and Pat.

"Ah," August said, "now you get it."

"Where are they? What have you done to them?"

"Oh, Johnny, it's not me you really have to worry about."

"Where are they?"

"Ah, ah...first things first."

"I'll go to the police."

August turned to him, those two black eye holes calling him forward, sucking him in, and devouring his will. "You, Johnny? Go to the police? If I could still laugh I would."

"I'll…I'll do it."

"No, you won't."

"I will," John said. The words fell impotently past his lips. Staring into August's eyes, John felt himself shrinking, withering inside. He was suddenly very much the scared twelve-year-old who pissed his pants and left his friend with a killer.

"What you *will* do is join us in Graveyard Land one last time," August said, stepping into the forest. "We'll be waiting for you, Johnny. Don't let us down…or else."

He was gone.

Raindrops, light at first and then thick and striking like a relentless swarm of hornets, began to fall.

Thunder rolled to life overhead as John stood in disbelief.

Drenched in failure, failure to save Ethan, failure to keep Sarah safe, to keep Pat safe, and swallowed by the sins of his past, John walked back to his car like a zombie, dead on the inside, rotten to the core, and filled with maggots ready to finish him off.

He was soaked when he climbed behind the wheel and started his car.

Passing the Town Hall and the police station, John knew August was right. He wasn't going to tell anyone. Who the hell would believe him?

He was out of options. He knew where he had to go, and there was only one way to get there.

★   ★   ★

John drove straight home and ran into the house and to the medicine cabinet in the bathroom.

He snatched the bottle of sleeping pills he'd purchased earlier this summer when he was having trouble sleeping from dealing with all the bullshit at work.

He'd stopped taking them once the boys of Graveyard Land started waiting for him.

After grabbing a beer from the fridge, he swallowed down two of the pills. He didn't know if that'd be enough, so he took two more. He didn't want to overdose on the damn things.

An urge to leave a note struck him. He was going to Graveyard Land intent on facing the full evil that awaited him there. He knew he might not make it out. He grabbed a pen from the counter and scratched out a note on the yellow lined pad sitting by the house phone.

Taking his beer with him, John walked to his bedroom and picked up the dream journal from his nightstand. Maybe there was something in here that could help him. Something he could use against August.

He flipped the cover open and gasped.

His head already starting to feel heavy, he stared at the blank pages. All his notes were gone. He fanned through the entire book.

"No," he said.

He flipped back to the front and saw two black, inky scratches for eyes staring back.

Tiny black dots began to appear around the sketched black holes. The dots began crawling and multiplying, taking shape...spiders. Dozens of them moved out from the ink-black eyes to the edge of the notebook. John felt one tickle his hand.

He dropped the dream journal and swatted the spider from his skin. The book had landed flat, August's eyes still staring up at him. The spiders poured from the ink and crawled to life across his floor.

They were everywhere.

Despite his fear, John felt too damn tired to run. He stumbled to his bed and slid back toward the headboard as they began to climb over the comforter. He kicked his legs at them, but there were too many.

They swarmed him in a blanket of thousands of tiny black legs.

He tried to cry for help when one skittered over his lip and funneled into his open mouth.

★　　★　　★

It was One Eye who shook him awake. Johnny sat up, coughing and trying to spit the spiders from his mouth. But they weren't there.

"Johnny," One Eye said. "Come with me now. There's not much time."

Johnny couldn't shake the feeling of creepy crawlies tracing the topography of his flesh. He jittered and twitched like a kid with some kind of bad physical tic as he followed One Eye through the graves.

The boy waved him over to a tall gravestone set before a bush.

"Down here," One Eye said. "Quick, I don't know when they'll come but I have to tell you before they get here."

"What is it?" Johnny asked, crouched below the outstretched bush and tucking in beside the boy under the natural bower it created.

"I'm sorry I couldn't say anything before. August would've killed me. Or worse."

Johnny couldn't figure anything worse, but he shut up and listened.

"It's about August."

"What about him?" Johnny asked.

"That's not his real name."

Johnny knew before One Eye said it.

"His name is or, I mean, it was—"

"Ethan. Ethan Ripley."

"Yeah, you figured it out?"

"I…I remembered."

"Well, he's after you, but it's not just him. It's the Ghoul."

"The Ghoul?"

"This is his place. His place for us. All of us."

"All of you?"

"He calls us his boys."

The Ghoul and his boys….

"The Ghoul is Llewellyn Caswell," Johnny said.

One Eye dropped his chin and nodded.

"And if you're his boys…oh my God," Johnny whispered. "You're all his, his…."

"We survive here. He leaves us alone, mostly. He likes to know we're here with him."

"Is this place, Graveyard Land, real?"

"It's a spirit world," One Eye said. "We're always here with him, but he told us it wasn't complete. That one of his boys was still out there."

"Me?"

One Eye nodded.

"Can we stop him?"

"Oh, I don't know about that," One Eye said, suddenly tucking his knees up to his chin and hugging his legs.

"If he...if he created this place, then there must be a way to destroy it."

"But what does that mean for me? For all of us?"

"Are you happy here?" Johnny asked.

One Eye looked away, a tear rolling over his plump cheek.

"Listen," Johnny said, placing a hand on his shoulder. "I need to find August, er, Ethan. Where is he?"

CHAPTER FORTY-FOUR

Sarah awoke in the blackness to the sound of rain stinging the shed's metal roof and someone fiddling with the door lock. Her insides clenched anticipating the horrible boy who'd brought her here. The door swung open and a large man dragged another body inside and placed it opposite her.

"Hey there, girly," the man said.

Gray light invaded enough of the shadows to illuminate his face. She didn't know his name, but she recognized him from town. She'd seen him somewhere before.

"I brought you a little company."

She looked down at the unmoving body. It was a man. He was older, also familiar, and badly beaten. His face was a collage of deep purple bruises. His ruined nose aimed the wrong way. Dried blood was cemented to the side of his face.

Sarah swallowed hard.

Oh God, she wanted to scream for John. To tell him they could work out all this bullshit. That he was the most important person in her life, that—

"And one more," the big man said, carrying someone in over his shoulder and tossing them next to her like a sack of potatoes.

Sarah sucked the air between her teeth.

Pat.

His face was bruised, one of his eyes swollen, his lip cracked and caked with a little blood.

Bastards.

"You kids behave, or I'll have to come back and punish ya." The kidnapping piece of shit chuckled at himself and closed the door, leaving them bound and blind. The sound of the pounding rain was maddening enough to make her tremble.

*   *   *

The rain was a blessing. Alvin didn't mind getting wet while he worked. And he had two graves to dig. Llewellyn's little spooky boy hadn't come back yet, and that was probably for the best. Llewellyn had assured Alvin if the boy interfered in any way, he would be reprimanded and reintroduced to the old ways. Alvin didn't know the depths of his cousin's depravity, but he'd heard enough to know the unpleasantness would be far from simply getting the belt or a backhand.

He grabbed a small aluminum ladder along with his best shovel and walked across the yard and through the trees over to the cemetery. The job would be so much quicker with the backhoe, but the less attention he drew to himself from any lookie-loo passing by the better. The rain would make the ground softer. Digging the grave by hand would be a lot of work, but nothing worthwhile ever came easy. That's what Aunt Loretta used to say.

He stopped before the graves, set side by side, and stared at the markers of Loretta and Llewellyn Caswell.

He dropped the ladder, broke the earth with his favorite spade, then with the rain pelting down and the wind swirling around him, Alvin began the arduous task.

*   *   *

By the time he'd dug down to Llewellyn's coffin, the night had fallen around him. The rain continued but at a softer pitter-patter. He set up the ladder and climbed from the hole, a member of the undead lurching out from the grave like in them old Romero flicks. The thought brought a grin to his face.

Night had come down hard, and he needed light. Alvin also wanted to call the police station and let them know he was working out here. They knew his job entailed some night digs and he liked to give them a head's up when he worked in the later hours so that they didn't stop by and bother him, thinking he was some sort of modern-day grave robber.

In the house, sopping wet and dripping all the way across the living room, he placed the call, telling them it was a last-minute service requested by an out-of-town family with old ties to Spears Corner. With the police taken care of, Alvin gobbled down a sandwich and finished a Coors Light, grabbed his Coleman lantern, and headed back out to the cemetery to unbury his aunt.

CHAPTER FORTY-FIVE

"Come with me," Johnny pleaded.

One Eye averted his eye and shook his head.

"Okay, but I understand." Johnny got up to leave, but turned back. "I never got your name."

"Henry," he said. "Henry Bixby."

Johnny reached out a hand and the boys shook. Henry cracked a smile.

"Good to know you, Henry."

"You too."

⋆　⋆　⋆

It didn't take Johnny long before he found just who he was looking for.

Standing against the wrought-iron fence, staring over toward the lit-up farmhouse, August waited.

"You actually showed up," he said.

"So, what should I call you?" Johnny asked. "August or Ethan?"

"That one's easy, Johnny," he said, his wicked eyes locking on to Johnny's. "Ethan died the day you left him with that monster."

"I know." Johnny dipped his head and kicked at the ground.

"Oh, you know?" August said, his voice quiet yet brimming with venom. "You *know*?"

Johnny raised his chin to see August approaching him, his dark shadow crawling with insects. He took a step back, unsure of what August was capable of.

"You *left* me…with *him*!" August pointed toward the farmhouse.

"I'm sorry," John said.

"Oh yeah, I see that. I see how sorry you are. Out here with the rest of us now, aren't you? Well, you've finally showed some real courage, Johnny. Bravo."

"I didn't know what to do. I freaked out."

"You let it happen. This is *all. Your. Fault.*"

"I know."

"Stop saying that!" August said.

Johnny bit his lip.

"Because you have no idea what I went through."

Johnny stayed quiet. August was right. After all this time, the boy deserved to let him have it.

"Do you want to know?" August said, coming within feet of him, his insect-filled shadow trailing close behind. "You want to hear about what he did to the boy you left behind?"

Johnny couldn't speak. He didn't know what Ethan had been through and he didn't want to know.

"He took me…he took me to a motel. He took me there and he made me take my clothes off. He watched me. He tied my hands to his bedpost…."

Johnny didn't need to know this. He clenched his eyes shut tight, grinding his teeth.

"Oh, I'm sorry," August said. "Is this too hard for you? Is this too much for you to take?"

"Please, Ethan," John said. "I said I was sorry."

"Shut up!" August said as he rushed forward and shoved Johnny to the ground. "Ethan's dead. *He's dead!*"

Johnny broke. Crying from the bottom of his wounded soul. It was true. All of it. He'd abandoned Ethan with a child-molesting serial killer rapist. Caswell did all those awful things to him because Johnny left him. And he kept it to himself all these years. If he had just told someone, anyone, maybe he could have saved the boy.

"He raped me that night. Over and over again." August's voice came out in a cracked whisper. "Then he choked me until I thought I was going to die. And when I was able to breathe, and thought that I'd made it through…. Then, then he did it all over again."

John couldn't speak.

"The next day, when he wrapped his hands around my throat for the last time, I wanted it. I wanted…to die."

August lowered himself to the ground, curling up in his shadow of writhing critters. They surrounded him, enfolded him, like an army of bite-sized guardians.

"Why did you leave me?"

The voice was no longer that of the spine-tingling malevolent thing from Graveyard Land – it was Ethan's. The way he sounded before.

"I don't know.... I was just a stupid, scared-shitless kid," Johnny said.

"So was I," he said.

The silence grew arms and legs adorned with wounds and scars, holding both imminent doom and salvation. It fell upon them like the fog of Graveyard Land.

"You have to give yourself to him," August said.

The bugs had covered every inch of August's flesh, and as they began to disperse, sliding away in one flawlessly fluid motion, like melting snow, they revealed the kid Johnny once knew. No longer the macabre character he'd seen in his dreams all these weeks. It was Ethan Ripley sitting beside him.

"The only way to save your wife and your friend is to surrender to the Ghoul."

"Please, I can't," Johnny pleaded. "I can't do that."

"He sent me after you, because you're the last one – the one that got away."

"No, there's got to be something else we can do."

Ethan shook his head and said, "He says this is the only way."

"What if...." Johnny wanted to argue, but it wasn't up to him. He didn't make the rules here, but.... "What if you and I go together?"

"What?" Ethan looked wounded.

"No, hear me out. We go and take him on—"

Ethan scooted away from him, shaking his head. "No, he's too strong."

"There's got to be a way to stop..." Johnny looked around, gesticulating at the dream world surrounding them. "...all of this. This isn't a good place."

"But it's his. You don't know what he can do."

All this time and Caswell still scared them to death. Even Ethan, who had seemed so in control and so intimidating as August, but it was just a façade. Underneath it all, he was still the frightened, awkward kid Johnny took pity on back in 1994.

"You've been here much longer than I have," Johnny said,

tempering his tone, trying to get through to him. "If *he* created this place, then there has to be a way to destroy it. One Eye, I mean Henry, didn't think it was possible. What about you? Honestly, in your heart and soul, what do you think?"

Ethan tucked his knees to his chin.

"You must have at least considered the idea before, right?" Johnny asked.

"I..." Ethan tried. "If we knew how he made it, then...maybe we could undo it, but I don't know what he did or how he did it."

"What if I think *I* do?" Johnny asked.

CHAPTER FORTY-SIX

Sarah couldn't let these motherfuckers win, even if one of them wasn't quite normal. She thought of his eyes...the empty holes. There was no denying that it was the creepy kid from John's dreams. *How* didn't matter right now. The strange boy and the big goon stood between them and escape. She'd read about monsters far worse. Last fall, she picked up a book by Jack Ketchum that made it impossible to go to sleep or be home alone at night for weeks after she finished it. A woman in a cabin in Maine got taken by savages that lived in a nearby cave. They eviscerated all her friends. It was hands down the scariest thing she ever read.

Now, it was her and Pat's asses on the line and there was no way she was surrendering to whatever sick plans their kidnappers had plotted out.

She began working her wrists and hands, trying to get out of the duct tape. She needed to find something in this shed to help cut it. She'd caught glimpses of the interior when the boy without eyes was here. There was a high workbench behind her and to her left. She thought she'd seen tool handles lined up over that way too. There was no telling when either of their captors would be back, so she would have to work fast. They may only get one shot.

She sat up, blind in the complete darkness, and put her weight on her knuckles, raising her rump and scooting toward where the bench and handles had been, tracing her fingers over anything she found. There was dirt and debris, cobwebs – which reminded her of the creepy kid kissing the spider onto her cheek. There had been so many, where had they gone? Or were they ever really here? She shivered and kept searching. Her legs bumped against the man she didn't know. She hadn't heard a thing from him – no movement, no breathing. Sarah was certain he was dead – an unsettling thought, but a motivator if ever there was one.

Her back found the corner of the bench, then her elbow smacked into something that clattered to the floor.

She felt a surge of hope as she wrapped her fingers around the wooden handle and pulled it through her hands, only to find it was a fucking broom.

"Fuck," she muttered.

Stay positive. Stay focused.

The next end she found caused her heartbeat to quicken. Her hands clutched onto the blade of an ax. With her hands bound, it took a little more concentration and effort to get the ax into position so she could use it. After standing its handle up so that she could get a good angle to rub the tape against it, Sarah managed three strokes before the tool fell again. She took two slow, deep breaths through her nose, remembering her lessons from her virtual yoga guru, Adrienne, and got the tool set up again. This time she managed almost ten strokes before it fell over. A sudden scuffle in the room startled her. Coming from her right – *Pat*. She couldn't communicate yet with her mouth still taped, so she didn't waste time trying, she just went back to working her bindings against the blade.

She was sweating up a storm; the muscles in her shoulders, triceps, forearms, and wrists burned with every move. Finally, Sarah felt the tape give way.

Adrenaline surged. Reaching up, she clawed the tape from her mouth until she was able to pull it away and cast it aside.

"Pat?" she asked, moving toward him.

Feeling around, she found him and picked at the tape covering his mouth.

As it came free, she heard him mumbling and trying to spit.

"What is it?" she asked.

She touched his lips and felt the cloth. She pulled the fabric free and listened to him take in some deep breaths of his own.

"Pat," she whispered. "Are you okay?"

"Yeah," he finally said. "Well, my arm is really freaking sore and my leg is messed up, but I'm still here, so that's good, right?"

"Yes, who's with you?"

"Mr. Fuller," he said. After a moment of quiet, he said, "That fucker killed him."

"Hold on," she said. On her hands and knees, she found the ax and used it to saw at the tape around her ankles. Once she was completely free, she moved to get Pat out of his bindings.

"Are *you* all right?" Pat asked.

"I'll survive," she said.

"They took us to get to John," he said.

"Why? What do they want?"

"I don't know if you'd believe me if I told you. It's kind of weird."

She thought of John's dream creep who spat spiders. Gliding into the shed and getting close enough to prove he was fucking real.

"Trust me, I've already been introduced to weird. What do you know?"

A light sparked to life between them.

"I knew there was something good about being a smoker," Pat said, holding up a lighter.

She could have kissed the smile on his face. She went to work freeing his ankles instead.

"I can get that," he said.

"I'm sorry," she said. "About Mr. Fuller."

"I didn't know him that well, or for that long really, but he didn't deserve this."

Sarah placed a hand on his shoulder. "We need to be ready when they come back."

"They?" he asked.

"Yeah, the guy that brought you in here and the…I don't know the *other* one."

"I didn't see anyone else," Pat said.

"You were going to say something about things being weird, well, I saw a tall kid with…without eyes…I don't how or what or—"

"August," Pat said.

"Wait, what? How do you know about him?"

"John told me about his dreams." He let the lighter's flame die. "Sorry," he said. "It was burning my thumb."

"It's okay," she said.

"Sarah, I think John's dreams have everything to do with this."

"How is that even possible?"

"I don't think we can worry about that. Whatever it is, some kind of old magic or whatever, you've seen it. You've seen August. I've been seeing him for the last week or two."

"Don't tell me you and John are sharing dreams. What is this, like Freddy Krueger or something?"

"No, August isn't the boogeyman," Pat said, "but I think he's working for one. These guys are involved with a dead serial killer named Llewellyn Caswell."

"Caswell," she said. "That's the guy that did this to you."

"He's Llewellyn's cousin."

Pat told her about killer Caswell's taste in victims, his trip home to Maine, the kidnapping in Spears Corner, and his arrest upon his return to Wisconsin.

"So, John saw this Llewellyn guy take Ethan Ripley?"

"He didn't say it, but, yeah, I think so."

"That's the secret," she said. "That's what the dreams have all been about. Oh my God. How did he not tell me?"

"Honestly," Pat said, "I don't think John remembered."

Pat brought the lighter to life.

"We've got to be ready when that guy comes back." She picked up the ax. "We have to hit whoever comes through that door with everything we've got."

Pat nodded.

"And then we find John and figure out a way to put an end to this."

"I hope he's okay," Pat said. "We kind of said some shitty things to each other before I left."

"Yeah." Sarah remembered her own parting words with John, his admission of infidelity. She wiped a tear trying to squeeze its way out. "Our last conversation wasn't so sweet, either."

CHAPTER FORTY-SEVEN

A vehicle crawled past the cemetery gates as he climbed from the hole. Relieved that it wasn't a cop, Alvin was nonetheless ready to meet whoever it was closer to the entrance should they stop. Telling people you were digging a hole for a fresh one was a lot easier if they didn't look down and catch you with a coffin, let alone two.

The car moved along. He watched the red taillights get devoured by the night.

He'd yet to pry either coffin open; he wanted to leave some of the fun for when the pretty lady arrived. Most people had never seen a dead body and even fewer got to see the desiccated bones and decades of rot and ruin delivered upon the deceased.

He grabbed the lantern and headed back to the shed.

A wild electricity surged through his veins. Before today, it had been more than twenty-five years since Alvin had instilled the kind of fear in another person that he saw in the boy's eyes. Sure, he'd made people uncomfortable his entire life, but there truly was something that cranked things up another level when the person across from you thought their life was in your hands. The desperation, the pleading, the slow collapse of hope. There was nothing like it. And his cousin Llewellyn had pushed that intimidation and power play beyond anything Alvin had ever fantasized.

Approaching the shed, salivating at the promise of things to come, Alvin stopped cold. In the pitch black, a light was coming from inside the shed. The dull glow extinguished as quickly as it had appeared.

The wind and storm had withered an hour ago. He could now clearly hear the buzzing of mosquitoes and the croaks and pips of cicadas, frogs, and other nocturnal critters. Closing his eyes, Alvin listened for *other* sounds. The ones people didn't want you to hear. Whispers, secrets, schemes. Alvin wasn't born a fool.

As stealthily as he could, he crept away from the shed and toward the house. He eased open the front door and stepped inside. Was it possible they'd busted loose from their bindings? Sure, but even so, they couldn't get out. They'd find plenty of makeshift weapons to attack him with, but they had already fucked up.

Edward Fuller was dead as fuck. Stabbing the tough guy/would-be hero had been a treat in and of itself, so that left the kid and the woman. Alvin liked his odds.

After picking up his Ruger from the coffee table, Alvin headed out to see exactly what kind of surprise was waiting for him.

Still soaked and muddy from digging holes in the rain, he approached the door to the shed without the guidance of the lantern and with the heightened senses of a cougar stalking its prey.

Slowly, he slid the key to the padlock from his pocket. Alvin tucked the pistol under his arm, caressed the lock, and with the steady hands of one that took great care of the dead, he eased the key into the hole, careful to push it in one notch at a time.

When it was fully inserted, he took a slow breath and turned the key.

★   ★   ★

Pat covered Mr. Fuller with a blue tarp they'd found in the corner of the shed. It was the least he could do. He really hadn't known the man long at all, but beneath the fear and uncertainty of their current situation, it still hurt.

Holding a ball-peen hammer he'd found among other rusted tools, he felt a bit of comfort having Sarah with him. He would do his best to protect her for John. In the time Pat had known her and John, Sarah had never seemed to be the needy-princess type and she sure as hell wasn't fucking around or backing down now. Standing with her back to the wall beside the shed door, she clung to an ax. Pat thought she looked like she had been ripped right off the screen from *Mad Max: Fury Road*. She'd make a nice lieutenant in Furiosa's rebel force. If anything, for Pat, Sarah represented a much-needed sense of hope.

He took his burning thumb from the lighter and they fell back into darkness. "How much longer do you think he's going to be?" he whispered.

"I don't know, but it feels like soon, right?"

"Yeah," he said. He wasn't just pacifying her. There was an energy present, a raw nerve that felt ready to tear wide open at any second. Pat imagined it was probably what the victims of the murderers he'd ever read or watched documentaries about felt at some point. He always thought learning about so many awful cases would somehow prepare him for one should it ever happen to him. Being in the thick of it now, he realized he was simply scared shitless. It had been a long time since he'd felt like a kid, and right now that's all he was. He wasn't even close to being calm and as far removed from being methodical about any of this as a person could get. He just wanted to see his mom and Ada again.

"Sarah," he said, fighting the urge to cry here now in front of her. "I just want you to know, I mean, whatever happens, you and John have meant the world to me."

She found his arm in the dark. "Hey, we're getting out of here, you hear me? Both of us."

"Yeah."

He heard the click of the padlock, and then all hell broke loose.

CHAPTER FORTY-EIGHT

Dr. Soctomah's story about the evil shaman, the curse of Spears Corner, it all made sense to him now. This reckoning was inevitable. How John wound up in the center of it all was irrelevant. He, Ethan, Sarah, and Pat were all part of it, regardless. He wasn't about to let the people he cared about pay the price for his sins. Llewellyn Caswell and his reign of intimidation and horrors had to end.

"Do you really think we can stop him?" Ethan asked. His bony shoulders slumped, but there was something tucked in the corner of his voice, the smallest glimmer of hope.

"I won't bullshit you, Ethan," Johnny said. "I have no idea how powerful any of this is."

He looked around the lingering fog and graves. Were there even bodies buried here? Was it all for aesthetic?

"What I can do is make you a promise," Johnny said.

Ethan met his gaze.

"I am going to go after Caswell with everything I've got."

"But you're…" Ethan raised his crippled hand toward Johnny, "…you're no bigger than any of us here."

Johnny hadn't thought about that. He was twelve here, physically, but he was still the adult him *now* mentally. An advantage he'd have to make work for all of them.

"That's why your part is the most important," he said. "You gather the other boys. You have to make sure they have confidence in the plan, though. You have to show them that you believe it will work."

"But I…I don't know—"

Johnny placed a hand on his friend's shoulder. "You can do this. This is our only chance to put an end to him. To this place. We have to confront him, all of us, together."

"But what if he—"

"No buts."

"What if he kills you?" Ethan asked.

Johnny knew the outcome was just as likely as any other. He had every shot of failing them all, but he'd failed them already, hadn't he? Johnny had left Ethan in the hands of this sick fuck. He'd screwed up so many things with Sarah, and God, if anything happened to Pat....

"I owe it to a lot of people to stand up and try."

A slight uptick of Ethan lips warmed his soul.

"I'll get them to the house," Ethan said. "But why don't you come with me? We should all do this together."

Johnny shook his head. "No, I'll need to keep him distracted. You said he sees all here, he's always looming over everything. If I go to him, maybe it'll provide a chance for you guys to come funneling in and we can catch him off guard."

"You're right."

Johnny stood up, offering a hand to Ethan. "Go on."

"Be careful," Ethan said.

"You, too."

He watched Ethan disappear into the fog, then Johnny turned toward the dim light glowing in the darkness. Caswell's house.

He was ready to give his life for theirs.

Whatever it takes, he told himself.

CHAPTER FORTY-NINE

The door smashed inward, and Sarah swung the ax as hard as she could at the shape blocking their escape.

The blade caught part of him but skipped through too easily. She'd overswung and was off balance as the sharp edge bit into the door frame.

Pat rushed to her side to catch her as Caswell cried out.

"Oh, you fucked up now, girly," Caswell said.

All the air in her lungs escaped when Caswell punched her in the solar plexus.

"Sarah!" Pat cried.

She doubled over and couldn't do a thing as she watched Caswell's fist fly forward and knock Pat to the ground behind her.

A light burst to life above them.

Caswell stood leering at them, his clothes dripping wet and covered in filth. He was enjoying the hell out of this.

"You two are something all right," he said. He reached back, yanked the ax from the wood frame and tossed it to the ground outside before closing the door and returning his attention to them.

Sarah saw the gun in his hand and turned to see if Pat was okay.

He was on his hands and knees; blood dripped from his chin, his lip busted wide open from Caswell's punch. She saw the anger in the boy's eyes and watched him clutching the hammer in his hands. She caught his gaze and shook her head, trying to convince him not to do it.

He began to rise.

"Did I tell you to stand up?" Caswell said.

"Fuck you," Pat growled, holding the hammer at his side and out of Caswell's sight.

"Oh, now you're a big man, huh? Where was this bad boy when you came to my doorstep the other day? I seem to recall a scared little shit, running for his life, crashing his bike in my driveway. That *was* you, wasn't it?"

Pat saw the gun in his hand.

Caswell turned it sideways.

"Oh, you think I need this?" He set the gun atop a milk crate to his right and held his meaty paws out, beckoning Pat to bring it on. "You think you got the sack now, boy? Come on. Come on, I said!"

Everything happened in a heartbeat.

Sarah darted forward for a low blow, but Caswell's knee met her chin. Pat swung the ball-peen hammer, but Caswell easily ducked the swing and used Pat's momentum to grab hold of him and slam him against the wall. Caswell pulled Pat into a chokehold. The hammer fell.

Sarah's hands trembled. The coppery taste of blood filled her mouth. Searching with her tongue, she found that Caswell had knocked out one of her front teeth.

She spat blood as she backed away.

"Sorry for messin' up that pretty face, girly, but it ain't really gonna matter where you're goin'."

"Let him go," she pleaded.

Instead, Caswell tightened his hold on Pat's throat. Pat's feet kicked outward, his eyes bulging, his hands clawing at Caswell's forearm.

After a few seconds, Caswell let up, but still held on to him.

"I don't need a gun to end this pathetic piece of shit," he said.

"Let him go and take me," she said.

"Oh, ain't that sweet, huh, boy?" Caswell said in Pat's ear. "She's willing to trade herself for you."

Pat's head flew backward into Caswell's face.

"Ugh," the bastard moaned.

Pat shrugged free of his arm and made a play for the pistol.

Caswell caught him by the limp Mohawk and roared as he pulled Pat around and slammed him face first into the unforgiving door. He did it twice before Sarah broke free of the shock and rushed forward to save him.

She unloaded her bony fists upon Alvin Caswell's face, smashing him in the eye, the cheek, and the nose, swinging as hard and fast as she could.

He opened the door, raised an arm to defend himself from her fierce blows, and tossed Pat out into the night. Hopping out of her range and onto the back lawn, he started to laugh.

Sarah stumbled past the door and into the misty rain outside.

"Pat," she said, "are you okay?"

He lay on the ground not moving.

"You fucking monster!" she yelled at Caswell.

He had the gun trained on her. At some point he'd grabbed it again. Blood streamed past his grin from where Pat's headbutt had busted his nose.

"Go ahead," Sarah said. "Just fucking do it already!"

"Oh, I like you," he said.

"If he dies I swear I'll find a way to make you fucking pay," she said.

"Oh, he *is* going to die, but not until I have a little fun with him first."

"Please," she said, kneeling next to Pat and reaching for him. "Pat, can you hear me?"

He was still breathing, but Caswell had knocked him out.

She screamed when Caswell clutched her hair and dragged her away from Pat.

He bent down and punched her in the face so hard it spun her around and dropped her to the mud.

Caswell kicked Pat back inside the shed and put the padlock back in place.

Sarah tried to get back to her feet.

Caswell spun, his awful laugh filling the space between them as he rushed at her.

The butt of the gun slammed into the side of her head again and again.

She tried to stay conscious, but the blows kept coming.

Sarah fell into the black.

★   ★   ★

Alvin hadn't killed the boy yet, but in all the excitement, he'd almost gotten carried away. Luckily, his closest neighbors were mostly six feet under, and the rest were half a mile down the road. No one would think anything of the woman's screams even if they heard them. Probably just think it was the storm.

He'd come back and take care of the boy after he finished Llewellyn's bidding.

"Come on, girly," he said as he hefted her up and slung her over his shoulder like a bag of sod.

He considered the lantern but decided he could finish this in the dark.

After setting her down beside the grave, he slid the ladder into the muddy hole and climbed down. The coffin lay open. It was wet from the light rain, but he didn't think it mattered. He reached up and dragged the unconscious woman down with him. He couldn't imagine she'd wake up, not after the beating he'd just given her, but he was gentle just the same. He lowered her into the empty casket, her purpled and bloody face that of a bruised angel.

"Sweet dreams, girly," he whispered as he maneuvered around so he could close the lid. He climbed the ladder, pulled it from the hole, and on his knees, began scooping armfuls of wet dirt on top of the casket. Once the lid was covered, he got to his feet, grabbed his shovel and worked as fast as he could to fill the hole.

*   *   *

By the time he'd finished, he was exhausted and ready for a good stiff drink. He needed to fill in Llewellyn's grave, too, but he'd come back before daylight to do that. He'd earned a quick break before going back to deal with the little punk prick.

Alvin crossed through the line of trees separating his property from the cemetery and hoped Llewellyn and his spooky little friend would be satisfied with his work.

CHAPTER FIFTY

Johnny walked across the yard. A foul wind accompanied the ever-present fog as he stepped before the red door and knocked. The house was exactly like the real one where he'd had his uncomfortable interaction with Alvin Caswell, the Ghoul's cousin.

"Shit," Johnny muttered.

He looked over his shoulder at the land of graves stretching out into the ground fog beyond. He remembered yelling at Pat for using the moniker for this monster. Well, if the murderous prick had ever earned the nickname, this macabre spectacle probably counted for something.

As he turned back to the house, the door creaked open. The sound wrapped bony fingers around his spinal column.

"Well," Llewellyn Caswell said in a raspy voice, "look who finally showed. The one that got away."

Johnny was face-to-face with the Ghoul of Wisconsin.

"You and your little one-eyed buddy the ones that threw that rock through my window?"

Johnny barely remembered that trip here. But he recalled thinking it would get this monster's attention.

Johnny nodded, unable to find his voice just yet.

"Get your ass in here."

Stepping over the threshold, Johnny closed his eyes and took a deep breath and hoped Ethan would do what *he* never could. Johnny opened his eyes in a room set up like some sort of sick pervert's torture porn hideaway. There were whips hanging from hooks by the window to his right, a rust-stained, soiled mattress on the floor near the far wall, and gay porn on the giant television across the room. There was no traditional living room furniture in sight, but a giant bed at the center of the room instead.

The moment had arrived, and Johnny swallowed hard, sick to his stomach. After what he'd allowed Ethan to go through, he deserved whatever this monster wanted to do to him.

Tears filled his eyes as he turned to face his past.

Ethan owed him nothing. If he decided to leave Johnny at the hands of this beast, Johnny knew he had it coming. All of it.

"We've never got the pleasure of being introduced," the Ghoul's voice slithered in his ear. Johnny smelled the scent of rot and decay. This was not a place of the living in any manner.

"I saw you," the Ghoul said.

"And...and I saw y-you," Johnny managed.

"Yes, and you never, ever told anyone. What a *pathetic* excuse for a friend."

The guilt and shame boiled over, threatening to swallow Johnny where he stood.

"I'm curious," the Ghoul said. "You could have told anyone. Your mom, the police, some idiot kid from school, but instead you just swallowed..." The Ghoul licked the back of Johnny's neck. "...it all."

"I was too afraid...."

"Yes?" the Ghoul said, circling him.

"I was afraid you'd...you'd come for me next."

"You thought I'd find out where you lived and what? You'd wake up one night to find my face in your window? My hand on your thigh...."

The Ghoul clutched the back of Johnny's neck and forced him over to the bed in the center of the room.

"Oh, Johnny, we're going to have eternity to play out each and every one of your fantasies."

He tossed Johnny down.

Johnny scurried back on his rump, placing his back to the headboard.

He needed to try and stall as long as he could.

"Why did you do it?" Johnny asked.

"Do what? Take your friend?"

"Why did you take any of them?"

"Is this where you try to psychoanalyze me? Really? It's a bit late for that, don't you think?"

"I bet you were raped by a priest or something," Johnny said.

"Would that make it easier for you?" The Ghoul licked his lips and rubbed himself. "If I told you I took my boys and forced them into acts they didn't want to do. When I'd force them to suck on me, and to take me inside...."

Johnny covered his ears. God, he didn't want to hear any of this.

"Oh, I'm sorry, did you think you could just come to my home? That you could just waltz into Graveyard Land and what? You'd get to run around playing patty cake all day and night? Is that what you think goes on here?" The Ghoul unbuttoned his shirt and shed it to the floor. "Did they not tell you the truth? One Eye and August?"

"Henry...and E-Ethan," Johnny whispered.

"What's that?"

"Their names."

The monster of a man clutched Johnny by the jaw.

"They're called whatever I tell you they're called. I'm the god here. You hear me?"

Johnny whimpered.

"Mm," the Ghoul moaned in his ear. "That's the sound of ecstasy around here."

He leaned in and forced their lips together.

Johnny thrashed at him, swinging his twelve-year-old fists in a flurry of rage and fear. One shot caught the Ghoul in the ear, knocking him to the side. Johnny tried to flee but a powerful hand clamped his ankle.

"You want some pain first, huh?" the Ghoul said.

Johnny's wrist snapped under his tightening grip. He cried out when the Ghoul twisted his arm until Johnny felt something crack in his elbow. A heat accompanied a sudden deep ache within. He fell to the floor, holding his broken arm.

"Did they tell you how I hurt them?" the Ghoul asked. "How I'd choke them inches from death before pulling them back from the precipice?" He planted his boot into Johnny's kidney. "How I'd throttle them and fuck them, and do it all over again?"

He undid his leather belt and pulled it from the loops of his slacks. "This was one of my favorite things to do," he said.

The belt whizzed through the air and slapped across Johnny's back.

"I used to love them, you know."

Another sting accompanied the next lashing.

"It wasn't only pain and sexual pleasure. You're each so fragile and beautiful to me." The Ghoul crouched down next to him and tried to look him in the eye. "Do you believe me, Johnny?"

"You're just a child-molesting piece of shit!" Johnny cried.

The belt whipped through the air again and again and again. The Ghoul hauled off and kicked him in the stomach, stomped his knee, and then thrashed the belt against his back and shoulders again.

Breathing heavy, he tossed the belt aside.

Johnny rolled in agony on the floor.

Where are you, Ethan? Please....

"I'll give you a bit of credit. You've got more fight in you than I thought you would," the Ghoul said. "But we've got plenty of time to work that out of you."

"You're w-weak...and sad," Johnny cried.

The Ghoul dropped to his knees beside him.

"You want to see power, boy? Hmm?"

He backhanded Johnny, knocking him into a ring of stars and blurry vision.

"I created this place for us. *I* made this all happen."

Please, Ethan. Johnny thought. *Please, I know you don't owe me shit. I left you for dead, but please...help me stop him.*

"How?" Johnny asked, hoping the son of a bitch would take the bait.

"How did I do it? Well, that's not anything that really concerns you. Let's just say you wouldn't understand."

"It was the shaman...the evil one," Johnny managed, daring a glance at the front door.

"Huh," the Ghoul said. "Well, look at that, maybe you're smarter than I thought, too. Ain't you just full of surprises?"

"If you made this place, it can be destroyed," Johnny said. He tried to sit up but the pain in his elbow made him too lightheaded.

"That, Mr. Big Brain, is where you're wrong. This place is eternal, but like I said, none of that matters."

The Ghoul caught him looking at the door.

"Oh, what? Do you think you can make a run for it? Tsk, tsk, tsk, Johnny."

He circled Johnny, licking his lips and running his fingers through his gray chest hair. Johnny got a bad, bad feeling.

"You've felt the whip and my boot. Now," the Ghoul said, reaching for the button on his pants. "Now, I've got something else for you, hmm?"

"Please, Ethan…. I'm so fucking sorry," Johnny cried.

"Yes," the Ghoul whispered, dropping to one knee and leaning into Johnny's ear. "Let's beg for forgiveness. We can beg together."

Johnny felt the man grinding against his hip.

Tears streaked Johnny's face.

If Ethan chickened out, or if August had returned, Johnny was on his own. If he didn't fight now, they would all die.

The Ghoul reached for Johnny's sweatpants and yanked them down. "Now let's flip you over, boy." He practically drooled.

Johnny gritted his teeth and brought his knee up into the Ghoul's groin as hard as he could.

The monster grunted, but the weak attack only served to piss him off.

Johnny tried to shove him but caught a punch to the face instead. Bright stars danced in his sight as he felt the Ghoul's hands upon his hips.

The front door burst open accompanied by a roar of children like something out of *Lord of the Flies*.

No sound had ever been sweeter.

Ethan led the charge, rushing through with a thick stick held over his head. Henry and the others funneled in behind him with wooden weapons of their own.

"What the hell is this?" the Ghoul asked, climbing from Johnny and trying to get to his feet. "Get out of here, all of you, or you can all take your turns next. You hear me?"

"Get off him!" Henry shouted.

"What are you going to do? Any of you? You think you've got a say in any of this?"

"We're putting an end to this. To you," Ethan said.

The Ghoul stood. "Well, well, well, look at you," he said. "What? You think because you look like you used to that you're not under my spell? That you're not dead?"

"We're done. We're all going home."

"You're not going anywhere!"

Johnny watched, his entire body sore and shrieking out. The boys didn't falter. They closed in like a pack of wolves.

"I said get out!" the Ghoul barked, but his bite was gone, a glimmer of fear in his eyes.

"*Nooo!*" Ethan yelled.

All at once, they unleashed every ounce of pain and humiliation the Ghoul had ever introduced to them.

He thrashed out, trying to fend them off, but it was too little in the swarm of sticks and knuckles raining down upon him.

Johnny sat up and slid away, holding his broken arm.

He saw one stick smash in the Ghoul's teeth – blood exploding like an erupting volcano. Another shot cracked the monster's jaw, sending it into an awful angle, and yet another caved in his eye socket.

Johnny tucked his bare legs to his chest, closed his eyes, and cried, but couldn't block out the sickening sounds as they beat the Ghoul into a bloody pulp.

He didn't look again until a hand shook him.

"You have to go," Ethan said. Henry joined him, as the boys continued to destroy Llewellyn Caswell once and for all.

"We'll finish this, but you need to get to Sarah before it's too late," Ethan said.

"Where?" Johnny asked.

"You picked a grave, remember?" Henry said. The boy had black-rimmed glasses with a patch over one lens. "She doesn't have much time. Go, quick before it's too late." He helped Johnny to his feet and shoved him toward the door.

He went outside and looked back one last time.

Ethan stood in the doorway.

"I'm sorry," Johnny said.

"I know." The boy nodded. "Go. Save Sarah and Pat."

Ethan backed into the house and closed the door.

★   ★   ★

The fog swirled over everything. It was so thick Johnny could barely see where he was going. Somewhere here, he'd chosen a grave. He needed to find it and find it fast.

Stumbling through the trees, past the gravestones, he saw the names appear.

Howie Goodwin... David Greeley... Bryce Wakefield... Carlton Cole....

There were so many.

Edward Willis Jr....Nathan Meyers....

Ethan Ripley.

Johnny dropped to a knee and placed a hand on the gravestone.

His turned his attention to the grave next to Ethan's....

Johnny Colby.

...*the one that got away.*

The stone cracked. A hole in the ground opened before him.

"Goodbye, Ethan. Goodbye, Henry."

He rolled into the grave and closed his eyes.

CHAPTER FIFTY-ONE

John awoke in his bed.

Gasping for air and reaching for his broken elbow, he opened his eyes and sat bolt upright.

The room was dark save for the red LED light of his alarm clock. It read: three forty-six.

Sarah.

He rushed into the living room, turned on the lights and looked for his keys. He couldn't remember where the hell he'd dropped them.

"Come on, John, you fucking asshole. What'd you do with them? Think!"

He checked the cushions, tossing them to the floor, but found nothing but crumbs and lost pens. He ran into the kitchen and cleared the table and the counter.

There was no time for this bullshit.

He grabbed his cell phone and headed out the door. He dialed Dr. Soctomah's number and sprinted down the wet blacktop.

The doctor picked up after several rings.

"Hello?"

"Dr. Soctomah, it's John. Meet me at Fairbanks Cemetery."

"John? Is everything all right?"

"I think they buried Sarah alive. I need your help, please."

"I'm…I'm on my way."

John clutched the phone and ran as hard as he could. His knee called out, more from the dampness than the physical exertion.

The cemetery wasn't far, but he knew every second counted.

★   ★   ★

Sarah opened her eyes to a complete blanket of darkness. She could hardly breathe. The smell of death enfolded her. She tried to get up and found herself trapped.

"Oh God," she whispered.

She sucked in one short breath after another.

She reached up and felt the silk lining.

A vision of her grandmother's wake flashed across her mind.

She was in a coffin.

Sheer terror barreled through her.

Was she buried? Is that why it was so hard to breathe?

"John," she wheezed. "Please help me...."

★　　★　　★

John heard a cry of pain as soon as the graveyard came into sight.

Pat.

He ran into the graveyard and heard Pat cry out again off to his right.

It was coming from Caswell's property.

John burst through the trees and saw a light within the shed.

He sprinted to the door, scanning the ground for anything he could use as a weapon.

There was nothing. He turned and saw the van sitting by the garage. Hurrying over, he grabbed the first thing he found, a tire iron.

As he gripped the tire iron, he heard Caswell howl, and Pat roar.

Pulling the shed door open, John saw Pat swinging a hammer at a shirtless Alvin Caswell. Caswell's man-boobs glistened with blood.

Caswell crumpled between them, blood gushing from multiple wounds on his face and head.

Pat was in his underwear, covered in crimson.

"Oh my God, Pat," John said. "Come here."

Pat stood, his hand trembling as he clutched the ball-peen hammer.

Caswell's chest continued to rise and fall, but the man did not move. Stepping past him, John saw Pat's shirt on the floor. He picked it up and handed it to the boy.

"Let me have it," John said, reaching for the hammer. Pat gave it over. His crying eyes met John's.

"Pat," John said. "Where is Sarah?"

Pat blinked, and his eyes regained a bit of their normal energy. "He...he took her...."

"Where? Do you know where?"

Pat shook his head.

A voice called, "John?"

John turned and yelled, "Dr. Soctomah! We're over here in the shed." He turned back to Pat. "Pat, I think he buried her. I have to go look. Come on."

★   ★   ★

Pat pulled on his shirt and was reaching for his pants when Caswell moved. He had the gun in his hand.

"John!" Pat shouted. "Gun!"

The barrel of the pistol rose, aimed right at Pat's face.

John grabbed Caswell's arm as the weapon fired.

Pat felt the bullet whiz past his ear as he stumbled backward and tripped onto his ass.

"Pat," John yelled. "Go! Find Sarah."

Another man, one Pat didn't recognize, appeared in the doorway.

John swung at Caswell, still trying to pry the gun from him. Before Pat could move, the gun went off two more times.

John moaned and fell on top of Caswell.

The man from the doorway hurried in and threw two huge punches into Caswell's already bloody face. The gun fell at Pat's feet as John slid down and lay on his back. Pat saw two entry wounds. Blood blossomed, spreading across the holes in his chest.

"Johhhnnnnn!" Pat cried, dropping beside him. "No!"

Pat saw the gun and picked it up.

"No, don't!" the man said, grabbing the gun before Pat could squeeze off a shot. "It's not worth it, son. What's your name?"

"Pat."

"Pat, I'm Rik. John called me."

"Sarah," Pat said. "She's out there...in the cemetery."

"Where?" Rik asked.

Pat got to his feet, hurried past him and ran to the graveyard.

As he rushed through the trees he spotted the ladder and the pile of fresh soil.

"Over here!" he shouted.

He ran toward the mound and saw the aluminum ladder lying in the grass.

The sky was lighting up around him.

He read the gravestones.

The open grave belonged to Llewellyn Caswell.

Pat slid the ladder next to it and hurried down. He managed to raise the casket lid and gagged. Pulling his shirt over his nose and mouth, he saw not one, but two sets of bones. He stood and looked at the neighboring grave.

Loretta Caswell.

Save her, he heard a voice say.

"Sarah!" Pat shouted. He snagged the ladder and climbed out of the grave.

"What are you doing?" Rik asked.

Pat found the shovel leaning against the gravestone. "He buried her alive."

"Who?"

"That murdering bastard. That son of a bitch buried Sarah. Help me!"

Rik looked unsure at first but dropped to his knees and began clawing handfuls of dirt from the grave.

"Sarah!" Pat called out. "Hold on!"

It was taking too long.

He had to keep shoving away visions of her lying there dead.

Pushing past the pain and exhaustion, past the possible horror awaiting him, Pat dug and dug, deeper and deeper.

Without a word between them, both men worked nonstop.

Pat didn't know how long it had taken them, but the sun was up, the first rays of dawn following them into the ground.

Birds chirped encouragement for them to keep going.

"Please, please, please, Sarah…."

★   ★   ★

She could hear someone digging above her. Someone was coming.

She tried to call out, but her voice was barely audible. The air within the casket was too thin.

She was getting sleepy.

She closed her eyes, and heard no more.

★   ★   ★

The shovel thunked against something hard.

"Sarah!" Pat shouted.

They worked double-time, uncovering the brown casket.

"Sarah, if you're in there, hold on!" Pat said. "Hold on, we're coming."

They cleared the top of the casket and made divots in the dirt just above the coffin.

Rik helped him as they reached down, clawed for the lip of the casket and pulled it open.

"Sarah!"

"Oh my God," Rik said.

She lay there, eyes shut, unmoving, her arms limply resting on her chest.

"No!" Pat said. He dropped down and tried to lift her out of the coffin. "Hold on, Sarah!"

Together he and Rik got her out of the ground.

Rik cupped his hands together and made a step for Pat to climb up and out.

Once Pat was up, he slid the ladder down in the hole.

"She's not breathing," Pat said.

Rik hurried out and moved Pat aside. Kneeling next to Sarah, he started compressions.

"Come on, Sarah," he cried. "Come back to us."

Rik counted sixty compressions, breathed into Sarah's mouth and repeated the process again.

"Please, God, please," Pat cried.

Rik looked Pat in the eyes. "Hey, what's your name?"

"Pat."

"Pat, my cell is in my back pocket. Grab it and call the police. After that, go stay with John until they get here."

"But he's with…with…."

"I pulled John out and locked the guy in the shed."

"Oh," Pat said. "Yeah, then yeah. Can you save her?"

"I'm trying."

Pat didn't want to leave Sarah's side, but if John was still alive, he didn't want him to be alone either. He slid the phone from Rik's back pocket and dialed nine-one-one.

Suddenly, Sarah gasped.

Tears spilled down Pat's cheeks as he told the nine-one-one operator where they were and that several people were in need of medical assistance.

They wanted him to stay on the line, but he hung up and handed the phone back to Rik.

"Yes, oh God, Sarah," Pat said.

Her eyes fluttered open.

"She's okay," Rik said. "Sarah, can you hear me?"

She looked Rik in the eyes and nodded. "Dr. Soctomah? Where's John?" she asked.

She was trying to get up.

"Sarah," Rik said. "Let us go – Sarah."

"He's by the shed," Pat said.

She was up and stumbling beside Pat as they hurried to John's side.

"There he is," Pat said.

John lay in the mud, the door to the shed locked beside him.

"What happened?" Sarah cried.

"He saved my life," Pat said. "But...but Caswell had that gun."

Sarah dropped next to John and reached for his face.

"John, can you hear me?"

His eyes twitched open.

Blood dribbled down his chin as he gasped for air.

"S-s-s-s-sorry," he sputtered.

"Oh, John," she said. "So am I."

"L-love you," he said.

Sirens echoed down the back road.

His breaths grew shorter fast.

"I love you, too."

And just like that, he stopped.

"John? John!" Sarah cried.

Her head dropped to his chest as she bawled.

Rik placed a hand on Pat's shoulder.

Pat met his gaze and shook his head.

Dr. Rik Soctomah walked over to Pat and opened his arms.

Pat hugged the man and cried against his shoulder.

CHAPTER FIFTY-TWO

Alvin Caswell spent a week at Maine General Hospital before he was transferred to a cell at the Hanson Union County Sheriff's Department. He was found guilty of two counts of kidnapping, two counts of attempted murder, and two counts of murder in the first degree for the killings of Edward Fuller and John Colby. Caswell was eventually sentenced to life in prison. Shortly after his conviction, he confided to detectives that his cousin Llewellyn Caswell had confessed to him that he had murdered Steve Norton, Ethan Ripley, and Eden Silko.

John Colby gave his life saving his friends. And that's what was carved on his headstone. He was laid to rest on August 21st in Fairbanks Cemetery in accordance with the note Sarah found in his dream journal:

Hi, guys.

I'm not sure who is reading this, but I wanted to write it as I'm not sure I'll make it back this time.

I have been a selfish asshole. I have been caught up in my own worries and troubles and concerns my whole life. I haven't been fair to myself or to the ones I care about.

To Dr. Soctomah: Thank you. Thank you for dragging the lake with me. I needed to see what I refused to see. You gave me that ability and that strength.

To Pat: You are the coolest, most amazing and inspiring young man I've ever had the pleasure of meeting and I am happy to call you my friend. I hope your company is a great success. I know it will be. You're too ambitious for it not to be. Take care of your mom and that baby sister of yours. I love you, kiddo.

To Sarah: I have hurt you so bad. Just know that nothing you did caused me to make the mistakes I made. You deserve the world and if I get back and you are willing to let me try, I will work to give you just that. Keep the magic in your eyes and love in your heart and please write that damn book!

I love you now and for always.

If I don't make it back, I do have one request. I would like to be buried next to Ethan Ripley in the Fairbanks Cemetery. I promised myself that I would never leave him alone again. I know it might be a hard thing to do, but I have to keep that promise for a friend.

-Love, John

★   ★   ★

Counting Crows played from the boombox behind them. Johnny stared at the door to the farmhouse that for so long had instilled such fear in them all. He was thinking of their own August and everything after.

"He's gone for good," Ethan said.

Johnny smiled.

"I thought this place would, I don't know, disappear," he said. "That you guys would be free, ya know?"

"Hey, you guys want to ride?" Henry asked. The kid still wore thick glasses with one eye painted black, but that didn't stop him from wanting to cruise around on the dirt bikes they had found.

"Last one out of the cemetery has to sleep in their old grave," Henry yelled as he started for one of the bikes.

"Shouldn't we be running?" Johnny asked.

"He needs the head start," Ethan said. "Listen, thanks for everything you did."

"Oh, I don't think I did that much, man. You wouldn't have even been here if not for me."

"Yeah, but they all would have. You saved them all."

Johnny gave his friend a slight grin.

"About what you were saying," Ethan said. "About destroying this place. I'm glad we didn't. We have Graveyard Land all to ourselves," Ethan said. "We have each other. And now that it's ours, we can make it whatever we want it to be. *That's* freedom. *You* helped us do that."

"Well, you guys did it too, you know. I would have been gobbled up by him if you hadn't shown up when you did."

"Yeah, you know, you're right," Ethan said.

He punched Johnny in the thigh, giving him a gnarly Charlie horse before bolting off toward the dirt bikes.

"That's dirty," Johnny said, limping after him.

"I don't want to sleep in the dirt tonight. Been there, done that," Ethan said just before kick-starting the bike. "Come on, Johnny," he yelled.

And this time he did, happy to be with his friends.

EPILOGUE

Sarah tried to keep her breathing under control. Pat and his mom were gathering the bags for the hospital as Sarah's mom tried to keep Ada at bay.

"How are you doing, hon?" Trisha asked.

"Oh, you know, never better." Sarah clenched her teeth as another contraction hit, and howled behind her teeth.

"Oh, that baby is coming," Trisha said. "Let's get you up. Pat, bring the car around."

He smiled at Sarah before flying out the door.

"I wish John was here to see this," Sarah said, taking Trisha's hand and letting her pull her to her feet.

"He is," Trisha said. "Come on, you don't want to have that baby in the back of a car. Trust me, it's no fun, and it's a freaking mess."

"Mom," Sarah said, her cheeks burning with embarrassment.

"Go now," Janice said. "I'll bring this little jumping bean. We'll meet you guys over there."

"Did anyone call Dr. Soctomah?" Sarah asked.

Pat appeared at the porch steps. "I did. He's meeting us there, now come on."

★   ★   ★

That May afternoon, Sarah gave birth to a healthy baby boy.

Holding him to her chest, she looked up from his precious face, and glanced around the room. Her mother stood with Trisha and Dr. Soctomah had a hand on Pat's shoulder as Pat held Ada up so she could see the baby.

It suddenly occurred to her that she and John had a family all along.

Her heart felt so big it could burst.

"Can I hold that baby?" Ada asked.

"Not yet," Sarah chuckled. "Do you want to say hello to him?"

"Okay," she answered.

Pat carried her over and leaned close enough for his little sister to see the baby.

"What's your name?" Ada said to the baby.

"His name is John Patrick Colby."

"Hey," Ada said, "like my Paddy?"

Sarah met Pat's gaze. Tears streaked his face.

"Yep," Sarah said, crying too, "just like your Paddy."

Pat reached over with his free hand and squeezed Sarah's.

"Hi, Johnny Paddy," Ada said.

John Patrick cooed at her, and Sarah couldn't think of any better proof that there was indeed magic in this world.

ACKNOWLEDGEMENTS

I wanted to say a thank you to my wife and kiddos for putting up with a struggling writer. This one was written during the Covid-19 pandemic, so finding the right headspace was a constant challenge. Late nights, early mornings, and trying to figure out how to deal with whatever crazy news each day would bring had my anxiety at an all-time high. I wouldn't have been able to finish this book if not for the love, the space, and the understanding of my family. I love you!

Thanks again to my fantastic editor. Don D'Auria is the best in the business. I have believed it since the days of the Leisure Horror Book Club, and having worked with him on my own books since 2014, that notion has only been confirmed time and time again. Thank you, Don.

The idea for this book came to me in 2014. My family moved to a new place a town over from where I grew up. One of the things I started to notice was the amount of cemeteries around this fairly small town. I remember thinking it should be called Graveyard Land. And that was all it took. I wrote the first three chapters and set it aside. I never ended up going back into the manuscript until it came time to write my next book for Flame Tree Press.

My wife has been a social worker for most of our marriage. I've heard plenty of real-life horror stories (minus the names, of course). We're both fans of true crime documentaries and podcasts (*My Favorite Murder* being my personal favorite), and we both grew up on a steady diet of *Unsolved Mysteries*. I'd never written about serial killers, but I knew it was just a matter of time. My antagonist here certainly represents many of the real-life monsters that have made headlines over the years. I do not condone such heinous behavior, and my heart goes out to anyone that has ever had these nightmares come true.

Lastly, it wouldn't be a Glenn Rolfe book without the music...

While I am a child of the 80s, it was the 90s that broke my teenage heart over and over again. From my parents' divorce and getting lost in that broken home shuffle, years of fear and confusion sandwiched between the death of a rock icon and my own father's passing, it wasn't until I was among my friends that I found a place to belong. And it was the music, always the music, the soundtrack to many nights of leaning on one another and laughing with one another, and sometimes, crying with one another that shaped my journey into adulthood. Albums such as Soul Asylum's *Grave Dancers Union*, Gin Blossoms' *New Miserable Experience*, and Counting Crows' *August and Everything After* spoke to me. We were all struggling, but we were all doing it together. Music has that power. Long before the internet came along, it was songs and artists that connected us. As long as we had our records, we were never truly alone.

To anyone reading this book, you are never alone or forgotten.

FLAME TREE PRESS
FICTION WITHOUT FRONTIERS
Award-Winning Authors & Original Voices

Flame Tree Press is the trade fiction imprint of Flame Tree Publishing, focusing on excellent writing in horror and the supernatural, crime and mystery, science fiction and fantasy. Our aim is to explore beyond the boundaries of the everyday, with tales from both award-winning authors and original voices.

•

Other titles by Glenn Rolfe:
Until Summer Comes Around

Other horror and suspense titles available include:
Snowball by Gregory Bastianelli
Thirteen Days by Sunset Beach by Ramsey Campbell
Think Yourself Lucky by Ramsey Campbell
The Hungry Moon by Ramsey Campbell
The Influence by Ramsey Campbell
The Searching Dead by Ramsey Campbell
The Queen of the Cicadas by V. Castro
The Haunting of Henderson Close by Catherine Cavendish
The Garden of Bewitchment by Catherine Cavendish
The House by the Cemetery by John Everson
The Devil's Equinox by John Everson
Hellrider by JG Faherty
The Toy Thief by D.W. Gillespie
One By One by D.W. Gillespie
Black Wings by Megan Hart
The Playing Card Killer by Russell James
The Sorrows by Jonathan Janz
The Dark Game by Jonathan Janz
House of Skin by Jonathan Janz
Hearthstone Cottage by Frazer Lee
Those Who Came Before by J.H. Moncrieff
Stoker's Wilde by Steven Hopstaken & Melissa Prusi
Creature by Hunter Shea
Ghost Mine by Hunter Shea
Slash by Hunter Shea
The Mouth of the Dark by Tim Waggoner
They Kill by Tim Waggoner

•

Join our mailing list for free short stories, new release details, news about our authors and special promotions:

flametreepress.com